Praise for Jess Vandermire, Vampire Hunter series...

"Reading a Lina Gardiner book is like riding an out-of-this-world roller coaster with your favorite people in the world."
—Joyce Lamb, *USA Today* bestselling author

"Lina drops crumbs of information like Gretel dropping crumbs to find her way home; instead of home, though, we are led to the startling denouement so smoothly, we are left gasping."
—*BittenbyBooks.com*

"Gardiner just crushed all the genre competition... The best book I've read all year!"
—*Dark Angel Reviews* on *Grave Illusions*

"*Beyond the Grave*, the second book in Lina Gardiner's Jess Vandermire, Vampire Hunter series, features all the elements that made *Grave Illusions* such a wonderful read—including great character development. I can't wait to read the next book in the series.
—Keri Arthur, *New York Times* bestselling author

"I would highly recommend this latest edition of the Jess Vandermire, Vampire Hunter series to anyone who enjoys a good, detailed paranormal series and almost non-stop action."
—*Keeper Bookshelf* on *Grave Expectations*

Books by Lina Gardiner

Jess Vandermire, Vampire Hunter

Grave Illusions

Beyond the Grave

Grave New Day

Grave Expectations

Graves of Wrath

Sons of Horus

Black Moon Awakening

Graves of Wrath

Vampire Hunter, Book 5
City of Bones, Book 1

by

Lina Gardiner

*To: Mary Frances
Best Wishes
Lina Gardiner*

ImaJinn Books

This is a work of fiction. Names, characters, places and incidents are either the products of the author's imagination or are used fictitiously. Any resemblance to actual persons (living or dead), events or locations is entirely coincidental.

ImaJinn Books
PO BOX 300921
Memphis, TN 38130
Print ISBN: 978-1-61194-876-9

ImaJinn Books is an Imprint of BelleBooks, Inc.

Copyright © 2018 by Lina Gardiner

Published in the United States of America.

All rights reserved. No part of this book may be reproduced in any form or by any electronic or mechanical means, including information storage and retrieval systems, without permission in writing from the publisher, except by a reviewer, who may quote brief passages in a review.

ImaJinn Books was founded by Linda Kichline.

We at ImaJinn Books enjoy hearing from readers. Visit our websites
ImaJinnBooks.com
BelleBooks.com
BellBridgeBooks.com

10 9 8 7 6 5 4 3 2 1

Cover design: Debra Dixon
Interior design: Hank Smith
Photo/Art credits:
Woman (manipulated) © Fifoprod | Dreamstime.com
Bones (manipulated) © Leeloomultipass | Dreamstime.com
Hallway (manipulated)© Unholyvault | Dreamstime.com

:Lwgt:01:

Dedication

Special thanks and much love to my mother, Marie Young, Who always supported me in every one of my varied artistic endeavors, especially writing. She was so proud.

Love you Mom, RIP—2017.

Chapter One

LESS THAN A MONTH ago, Jess Vandermire, Captain of an NYPD Vampire Hunting Team, would have said her job was one of the most significant things in her life. It gave her a reason to rise from her death-state each evening and face her dark existence. She lived and breathed hunting the undead.

Strike that. For all intents and purposes, she didn't exactly live or breathe, which made the fact that she had a wonderful, warm-blooded soulmate in John Brittain even more crazy.

How'd she get so lucky?

Still, a part of her would always be a vampire hunter, regardless of how much she loved being with Britt. It was in her blood . . .

But, her beloved brother, Regent, had been sent to a church in Paris for a three-month assignment. Although he knew the timeframe, he hadn't been given any details about the job. Even though Regent didn't appear to be overly concerned, she chewed on her lip as she stared, unseeing, out the window. The pieces didn't fit . . . and her cop's gut didn't like it.

Suddenly, Jess felt Britt's radiating warmth behind her before soft lips caressed the back of her neck. "Britt, not in the office," she said weakly.

"I shut the door." He spun her around and kissed her until she started to feel actual warmth.

When she sighed, he released her. "Still worrying about Regent?"

She reluctantly stepped back from his embrace. "None of it makes sense, Britt. Why are they being so vague about his duties in Paris?" She didn't mention her fears to him, but then again, she didn't have to. Both of them knew that the church had been using Regent's talents with ancient vampires. They'd all just barely survived their last encounter with an olde one. Now they were sending Regent to France, alone. Jess was afraid for her brother.

"There's always the chance that they don't actually need his expertise with vampires. Maybe they simply need a priest?" Britt said.

"Is that what your gut is telling you?"

He cleared his throat. "Not really."

"At least the church doesn't know the full extent of Regent's abilities," she said.

"After last year's encounter with Cardinal Vasilli and Uriel, the church probably has a good idea," Britt reminded her softly. "I don't trust Vasilli one bit. Think about it. He turned Uriel, an angel, into a voracious vampire. What kind of man of the cloth would do that? Here's hoping he doesn't have a hand in Regent's new assignment."

She remained silent for a few moments. Then she squared her shoulders. "That settles it, then. We're going to Paris, Britt. Regent is going to need us."

"Just like that?" Britt said, less surprised than she'd expected. "What about the vampire-hunting team?"

"I have a lot of time off coming. And so do you. You haven't taken any leave since you started with my team four years ago." She should have noticed that. Humans needed vacations for their health. She looked him up and down. The question being—was he still human, or had he become more angel?

"Oh, I'm coming, doll. Besides, you'll need someone to help get you through the airport and to the hotel, just in case things go sideways."

"To be honest, I hoped you'd say that," she said. "Let's go talk to the chief."

"Poor man isn't going to know what hit him," Britt said, pulling her office door shut behind them.

"Let's not tell Regent we're going to follow him to Paris. He'll think we're babysitting him and try to make us stay here. So we'll sneak over a few days after he leaves."

THAT EVENING, WHILE Regent got ready to board the red-eye flight to Paris, Jess put on her best tough vampire persona. She hated the thought of him going to Europe without her as backup. Something wasn't right about this whole thing.

Regent toyed with the handle of his carry-on bag, barely making eye contact with Jess. "I know you'd prefer I stay here, dear, but the church has only given me two choices," he said. "Either I go, or I retire."

Retire? He'd never mentioned that part to her before, and it made her even more suspicious. Why was it so important that Regent be in Paris? Who had initiated this trip and what were they up to?

"Holy hell, Regent. I didn't realize they'd blackmailed you into going. Are you sure you want to do this?"

He stared into nothingness. "I'm doing it. And don't worry, dearest. I've always been able to hold my own, and we've been through a lot, Jess. So don't worry about me. I'll be fine."

She'd never dream of shaking his faith in his abilities. But due to the fact that Regent now looked decades younger than his seventy-three years, Jess knew that everyone forgot that her brother was indeed, a senior citizen. Including Regent, himself.

"Of course you will be fine," she said forcing herself to sound like she meant it. Thank God she'd be in Paris in the next couple of days, and would be able to keep an eye on him.

Meanwhile, Britt wrapped an arm around Jess's tense shoulders. She leaned into him. "And, I'll keep an eye on Jess. You don't have to worry about her."

Regent didn't exactly look appeased. "I know you will, my son, but what if there's an outbreak of—you know what. . . . Don't forget, Jess literally died when she tried to save Uriel from vampirism," he said under his breath then looked over his shoulder in case someone was listening. "I'll be worrying about both of you."

"In case you haven't noticed, I'm already dead," she whispered back. "And, with Britt's angelic DNA, we'll both be fine."

"Don't joke, dearest. You nearly didn't come back to us last year," Regent said.

"But I did come back. I'm hard to kill." She tried to joke again, but it was obvious Regent wasn't having any of it. "Besides, the team is fully trained now. And truth be told, they don't need me as much, now that Jane's on board. I'd probably be stuck behind a desk more often than trolling the streets."

"I doubt that," Regent said, rolling his eyes.

Jess ignored his comment. "Jane's like a ninja when she's hunting vampires. And she's got a whole team of highly trained people behind her. She's been taking her team out without us for a few months now. Britt and I don't get to see as much action as we used to."

Most of what she'd just said was true. Jane had been a weak, tiny vampire on the brink of self-annihilation when Jess had found her and had given her a reason to go on. But she had taken on the mantle of vampire hunter with a gusto no one had expected. Jess's little prodigy had done very well, and Jess had no worries about her taking over while she and Britt were in Paris.

"If this new lieutenant is as good as you say, maybe you could come and visit me for a couple of days?" Regent said.

Jess slipped out from under Britt's shoulder and wrapped her arms around her baby brother, giving him a rare hug. Regent blinked back tears and she pulled away quickly. "You never know," she said, trying to hide her concern for him.

Jess didn't know how she'd manage, even for a short time. She'd always been able to see Regent whenever she needed to. His prayers had saved her partial soul, over and over again. He'd been strong for her his whole life, but now, with the changes in his physiology after being kidnapped and secretly regressed from being a seventy-three-year-old senior to a man in his mid-forties, they were all left wondering about his physical health. She feared that his youth might merely be superficial.

If he was being sent to Paris because they had a vampire problem, he'd need backup. And they'd always worked as a team.

But she couldn't go yet. They still had a snag to get past. In order for her to follow her brother to Paris, they had to figure out a way to get her through security without anyone realizing she had no pulse. That meant her amazing forensic vampirologist, Sampson Case, only had a few days to finish up the tiny machine that mimicked a pulse rate without setting off any alarm bells when she went through the metal detectors.

And if they managed to get past that hurdle, she could only hope that Britt's prayers would be strong enough to let her survive the sunlight long enough to reach her hotel. Because it would be morning when they arrived.

Being able to withstand sunlight for a short time made her unique amongst vampires, a residual effect from Regent partially saving her soul through prayer and baptism when she'd first been turned. Because of him, she'd managed to maintain a tiny shred of her humanity. But it was a shred that constantly teetered on a precipice, ready to tumble over into the darkness at any moment.

A FEW DAYS LATER, Jess leaned forward and stared out the window of their jet. In the darkness below, tiny pinpoints of light dotted the ground. Before she knew it, they were over the ocean and the plane had risen above the clouds until there was nothing to see. Who knew flying would be so liberating?

Would she come face-to-face with vampires in France? No doubt, they'd be sophisticated, compared to the vampires she'd come across in North America. And much older. But that didn't matter. She wasn't there to fight them.

In fact, she wanted to stay beneath the radar. No fighting on this trip, unless she was forced to defend herself. At home in New York, her ability to withstand sunlight had made her a target by vampires who wanted to usurp her ability to walk in daylight—improbable at best. And there were others who wanted her dead, simply because she killed vampires for a living. Now *that*, she could understand.

Hopefully, the European vampires would be unaware of her abilities, as well as her job. She could use a break.

She settled back in her chair. For the first time, she fully embraced the word *vacation*. That is, if embraced meant admitting she was scared as hell. What would she do with her time?

Hours felt like days before they'd landed and grabbed a taxi to their apartment, which was tucked into a hidden recessed courtyard in the old part of the city. She'd found the apartment online. It had boasted a darkroom for photography—which meant no windows. She'd immediately found construction workers in the city and paid them a bundle to put in a heavy door with locks, turning it into a bedroom, before she arrived. She'd miss her specially designed window on the city in New York, but at least she'd have a safe room.

Britt had been saying extra prayers during their flight. The poor man had to be exhausted, but she'd needed the added protection. Praying for herself had little to no effect.

As added security from the sun, she'd worn a heavy, hooded jacket, a scarf, dark sunglasses, and gloves. She stood out on the summery Paris morning, but she had no choice.

The taxi driver had been instantly weirded out by her attire. He spoke in French at first, then switched to English when he realized they were American. "What is wrong with your girlfriend?" he said to Britt.

"She has porphyria," Britt said. "She gets burned if she goes outside without protection. It's an autoimmune disorder."

"Man, that sucks," he said, then turned his radio up in order to avoid any further discussion. Twenty minutes later, he'd dropped them off, handling the cash they'd paid him carefully, as if one of them had something contagious.

"If he thought porphyria was bad, imagine if he knew the truth," she joked, standing in the middle of the sidewalk directly in front the building that housed her apartment. Having never been in another city, let alone another country, she didn't realize a place could *smell* older than New York.

Britt slid an arm around her shoulder. "Let's get you inside. You've already been out here too long."

That's when she realized his gaze had focused on her wrist, which had started to steam. She adjusted her hood, then pulled her hands under her sleeves for cover and climbed the stairs to the front door.

Their apartment was on the third floor, and took up the whole level. Knowing apartments in Paris were notoriously small, she hoped it would be as big as it had seemed online—the benefit being that they allowed renovations. And, she'd be near her brother, and make sure he was safe. That was what was important.

BRITT BIT BACK a yawn and followed her into the apartment. During their flight and the drive to their new digs, he'd been silently reciting the required prayers for her soul. Now that he could stop praying, he guessed this so-called vacation would test their togetherness to the full extent.

He wasn't sure Jess was ready to be unemployed. She had too much energy to be content sitting around and doing nothing. He'd have to find ways to keep her occupied, physically and mentally. A few ideas immediately came to mind.

"How did Regent sound when you talked to him before we left New York?" he asked, following her as she checked the rooms. Her safe room had been completed on time and her fridge had already been installed and filled with blood. She'd given the contractor a medical reason for the blood, and the man had bought it.

"He sounded a little lonely," she said. "But I'm sure he'll be happily surprised when we show up at his place tonight."

"It'll definitely be a surprise." Britt took her hand in his, stalling her for a moment. "Has he started working at his new church yet? Does he know why he was sent here?"

"He was a little vague about that. I'm pretty sure he's still unaware of the role the church wants him to play in Paris."

Britt frowned. "That's a little odd, given that they threatened to make him retire if he didn't come."

"I thought so, too. I'm glad we'll soon be able to talk to him in person. Then we'll find out what's going on."

"It'll be nice to see Regent," Britt said. "And I've heard that, like New York, Paris is a city that never sleeps. You and I will have fun seeing the sights at night." He searched her face for signs of how she was feeling.

She actually grinned at him. "You already sound like a tourist.

Where should we go first? The Eiffel tower?"

"But, of course!" he said with a fake French accent.

It was only when they found her medium-sized darkroom that he cringed. It was nothing like her palatial bedroom in New York. The Parisian contractors had replaced the door with heavy-grade steel and a coded lock, but the inside of the room was brutally dark and more crypt-like than anything he'd seen in a cemetery. Even a bed and a table with a lamp couldn't change that. He didn't have to ask if she liked it. He already knew the answer.

Even though his prayers had allowed her to stay awake during the day, she looked as if the heaviness of death encroached. She'd have no recourse but to let it happen, and it would have to happen in that mausoleum of a room. Even though it was the safest place for her, he hated to see her go inside.

"I'm going to try out my room, Britt," she said, her voice giving nothing away. He was sure she must hate it, too.

And, if he knew Jess—and he did—she'd find another solution to that dark, windowless so-called bedroom, and soon.

He smiled into her eyes and brushed a few locks of silky brown hair behind her ear. "I think I'll take a nap, too. I'm sure we'll have lots of exploring to do when you wake up."

His lips brushed hers and he wanted to wrap her in his arms and protect her from the realities of her existence. That's what really bothered him. He couldn't help her, even though he had some angelic abilities. But they were still foreign to him, and for the most part, consciously inaccessible.

Somehow Britt had been able to save Jess's friends, James, Terry, and baby Sephina, from vampirism, but he'd failed the woman he loved. How many times had he despised himself for that?

Jess shut the door and clicked the lock. He turned away. He wasn't tired, but he wouldn't leave her alone, even though she was locked in her safe room. So, instead, he decided to set up his Wi-Fi and do some virtual sightseeing, looking for places for them to visit whenever she was ready.

The Realtor had arranged to have things set up when they arrived, and the man had left the Wi-Fi password on the dining table. All Britt had to do was set up his laptop and sign on. Before he started surfing, his stomach rumbled, and he looked in the cupboards. Too bad they hadn't thought about arranging to have the place stocked ahead of time. Luckily, he had some snacks left in his carry-on bag. He munched on a granola bar then went back to the computer.

Out of curiosity, he checked for an English news broadcast in Paris and found several. He started scrolling, looking for anything that might relate to the reason Regent had been sent to Paris. He noted that a few tourists had their wallets stolen by pickpockets near the Eiffel Tower. It was tourist season, so that wasn't a surprise. And a bank had been robbed. But again, that was fairly run-of-the-mill and nothing that required a priest's special abilities.

He scanned almost the whole paper before he spotted something on the last page. The article was so small, he almost missed it. Two citizens had been attacked by an unknown assailant, and were now in the hospital. One man said he'd been attacked by a shadow figure. The article went on to discredit the victim, saying that he'd been partying for three hours at a nightclub and his memory of the incident had likely been blurred by drinking.

Shadow figures? Now, that might require a priest with special abilities. But if there were shadows attacking people in France, what were they? Or had the guy just had way too much to drink? Rubbing his tired eyes, Britt turned off the laptop and found a comfy spot for a nap in the living room. He wasn't interested in climbing into bed right now, maybe because his room was at the opposite end of the apartment, quite a distance from Jess's safe room.

He stared at the ceiling for a while, his thoughts running rampant. Eventually, he felt himself drifting off and he let himself go. He was close enough to hear if anyone tried to get in Jess's room.

SECONDS AFTER THE sun had set, Jess awoke. Disoriented for a moment, she considered that she might have been buried alive. Well, not technically alive. At home in New York, there were huge windows that opened onto the panorama of the city, something that never ceased to impress her.

But this was France. And she was locked in a sealed box.

She'd been excited about the opportunity to see another country. But she wasn't impressed with waking in this dark, tiny room, even if it was in Paris. The room reminded her that she was an ungodly creature that deserved this kind of life. She dragged herself off the bed, even stiffer than usual.

She popped in the code, and the door opened easily. Good thing, because she was feeling a little claustrophobic. She didn't think Britt would be awake yet. Jetlag had probably left him tired. So instead of bothering him, she made her way to the fridge and poured some blood into a glass. Gross! It wasn't possible to have her little pre-made packets here—yet. She'd have to work on that.

She heard the shower running. It seemed Britt wasn't as tired as she thought he'd be. He came out ten minutes later, freshly showered with wet hair and looking pretty fabulous in his jeans and T-shirt.

"Evening, handsome," she said.

His gaze licked over her, setting her ice-cold skin afire. How'd he always do that? Maybe it was the angelic presence in him. Too bad she'd been told by the angel Uriel that Britt could never help her become human again—and she could never let him know that it was impossible to save her. Uriel had warned her that Britt needed to believe in that possibility. Telling him the truth could break his spirit, making him give up on learning what he could do with his special abilities.

"Are you hungry?" she asked. Britt must be starved.

"Always, doll," he said, eyeing her again with a ferocious need that made her cold-dead heart vibrate with instant desire.

As much as she wanted to accept his tantalizing offer, she glanced at her watch. It'd been a week since she'd seen Regent, and she really wanted to go straight to his place and surprise him.

Britt instantly reined back his sexy vibe. "We should see Regent first. I'll grab a sandwich on the way."

She could have kissed him—and much more than that. But she'd save those thoughts for later. Right now, her baby brother needed to know they were here for him. She was sure she'd heard desolation in his voice on the phone yesterday.

The taxi driver delivered them to Notre Dame, where Regent worked, by what they figured to be the most circuitous route. She had the feeling the trip might have been shorter if they hadn't been tourists. Unfortunately, once they got there, the huge gothic church made her whole body react—violently. Of course it would have a formidable effect on vampires. And even though she'd been blessed with a partial soul, she wasn't immune.

She stumbled and nearly reeled backward the moment they got out of the taxi. Britt caught her, concern etched onto his features. She held up a hand to indicate she was okay, even though she could barely take a step forward.

"Can you manage?" he asked.

"Of course. I'm fine," she said in a clipped voice.

He frowned. "If you say so, doll."

She let out a long shaky breath. "I do, but even so, I think I'll stay here. No sense tempting fate by entering the building."

"Not a problem. Shall I go inside and get Regent?" His expression appeared pained.

She'd thought she'd be able to go inside, but now she realized how painful it would be. Why go through that if she didn't have to? "Thanks, I think that'd be best."

He squeezed her shoulder. "It's strange. I know this church is giving off bad vibes for you. But I have to tell you, the whole city is giving me *bad* vibes. I can't explain it."

"Really? How so?"

"It's a deep feeling in my gut," he said. "Something's not right about this place."

He looked to the other side of the street and his mouth thinned. "Maybe we won't be bored here, after all."

"Oh, geez, Britt, bite your tongue. Let's hope we don't catch sight of even a single vampire. I want to spend our time here as civilians, not as cops who hunt vampires. I think it will be like a breath of fresh air."

He chewed on his lip. "Maybe."

Her gut swooped. She'd never heard him talk like that before. Truth be told, it wasn't only the church giving her pained vibes. They'd passed a few other buildings on their way into the city that made the hair stand up on the back of her neck. She'd put her off-kilter feelings down to the fact that Paris was a centuries-old city. It had seen its fair share of battles and death, and the city seemed to resonate with the shadows of those dark times in history.

She watched while Britt made his way inside the church, her eyes never leaving his form. How she could feel so much for this man? Vampires didn't find love—they didn't deserve love. But somehow Britt was the positive to her negative, and in her universe, defying the odds seemed to work for them.

Despite the discomfort, she sat on the ledge of an enclosure encased by shrubbery, and waited. And waited. She glanced at her watch and frowned. Shouldn't Britt have found her brother by now?

She knew Regent would be shocked to see Britt. But because she couldn't enter the church, she'd miss out on that first reaction, damn her black soul. Now, she was really feeling sorry for herself, and she needed to shake it off. She knew Britt would share every nuance of Regent's reaction with her when they got home.

Across the street, dark shadows seemed to pool in the strangest places. Shadows that seemed somehow out of sync. Is that what Britt had sensed? She stared hard at the other side of the street, searching with her enhanced vision until somehow, she saw one of the shadows move without warning. Had it been a trick of the light?

Dread clawed at her gut while an icy sensation crawled up her spine and wrapped around the base of her skull. Someone must be watching her—a tourist perhaps, or someone strolling past taking in the beautiful sights—nothing more sinister than that, surely. She'd imagined the shadow.

She ran her hands up and down her bare arms, though it made no sense. She could never feel the cold because her skin was almost always icy, unless Britt had his hands on her. Only he could send a flash of heat through her, only he could set her on fire. But tonight, something chilled her to the bone.

Even worse, that cloying sensation of being watched became more pervasive.

She considered Paris's vampire contingent again. She imagined there were a lot of them in the city, since vampires originated in Europe. But, whatever was watching her wasn't a vampire, she'd bet her life on it.

She jumped when footsteps stopped next to her. No one ever caught her off guard. Luckily, Britt didn't comment on her reaction.

"Regent's not here," he said. "I found someone inside who gave me the address of his apartment, though, as well as directions as to how to get there. Apparently, it's not far from here."

"I already had his address, but the directions will help. Let's go," she said to Britt, flicking another quick look at the other side of the street. How many of those shadows were wrong? Too many? Jetlag might have made her delusional, because when she looked again, she could see nothing there. Still, the feeling persisted.

She stalled Britt for a second by touching his arm. "Do you feel like something's wrong here? It's not the church, but there's something off. A pervasive presence that's almost palpable to me."

Britt halted and rubbed the back of his neck. "You feel it too, huh?"

She gritted her slightly elongated teeth. "Damn it. This can't be happening. We are supposed to be on vacation. Why do I feel like we'll have to battle this out before long?"

A car passed them, its lights blinding them for a moment. In that moment, she could have sworn she saw the outline of something grotesque growing out of those inhuman shadows. "Over there! See that?"

BRITT DIDN'T HAVE to follow her finger since he'd already been looking in the direction of the out-of-sync shadows. He'd noticed that spot as soon as they exited the taxi. The ground was in full shadow where an overhead streetlight should completely illuminate the sidewalk. After reading the article in the newspaper earlier, he had the feeling he knew why Regent was here. But what were those shadow figures? Why did the church think Regent could help? Sure, Jess's brother had fought vampires in his youth and he understood the underbelly of New York City, but this was different. He decided not to tell Jess about the article. He'd keep his supposition to himself for now. She needed to see Regent first.

"Jess, I think we should move on before it gets too late. We want to see Regent before he goes to bed." And before they had to deal with whatever that dark, emanating menace was. Perhaps something evil drawn to the old church?

Fear lingered in the depth of her gaze, making his blood run cold. Jess Vandermire wasn't afraid of anything, no matter how evil. Whatever the hell that mass had been, it had scared her as much, or more than, it had scared him.

"It's this way to Regent's place," Britt said, immediately aware that they'd have to head toward the shadows.

"Let's cross to the other side of the street for a while," she said.

He agreed. He wasn't ready to come face-to-face with whatever the shadows were. At least, not yet. Maybe they were just overtired and their imaginations were trying to come up with something to keep their instincts finely honed. Yeah, that was it. They were looking for trouble where there was none.

He cleared his throat and looked back at the shadows, to make sure nothing was following them.

He'd taken several surreptitious glances back as they strolled along the street until his mind and his inner alarm system finally relaxed. Whatever had been on the street was gone.

"Did you say his apartment is on the second floor?" Jess asked, looking up at the tall building.

"Yes."

"Good. I see lights. It looks like he's still up."

Britt glanced up at the second floor apartment. She sounded pretty excited for a tough, unfeeling vampire. He'd let her have her uber-bad-girl delusions for now.

She rang the buzzer. "It feels okay here, doesn't it?" she said unexpectedly.

He nodded and pulled the entry door shut behind them. "That aura of danger was pretty strong back there though, wasn't it?"

"At least it didn't follow us," she said. "I would have been ticked if it held us up from seeing Regent."

"Hello? Who's there?" Regent's voice crackled through the intercom.

"Oh, just a surprise guest or two," Jess said with a laugh.

"Jess? Is that you? What in heaven?" The buzzer rang for the door to open, and they stepped inside and headed for the stairs.

He was in the hall when they made the landing. "Jess! How'd you ever manage to get here? Is something wrong?"

"Nothing's wrong, dear," she said, giving him a quick hug. "We just couldn't stay in New York without you."

Regent shook his head back and forth in obvious disbelief. "What about the police force? How did you get away?"

"We took a leave of absence," she said.

"No! You didn't. How?"

"I almost blew it at the airport when I was telling you about Jane and her team. She's taking over for me. I feel quite safe leaving the city in her capable hands."

"How long are you staying?"

"Three months, same as you," she said matter-of-factly. "That is, unless your term here changes."

Tears flooded his eyes and he blinked them back. "My first instinct is to tell you that you shouldn't have come. . . . But I'm so glad you're here." He sniffed. "What will you do, though? You'll be so bored." The fact that he hadn't balked at them staying for the duration of his time in Paris told Jess that her brother felt out of his depth. Her decision to come had been the right one.

Britt scanned Regent's meager apartment from the kitchen. The church superiors hadn't put themselves out in their efforts to make him comfortable. This place left a lot to be desired. And, Regent himself looked pale, and not quite himself.

No wonder coming here felt so right. They *were* needed. Still, it shocked him to see Regent appearing so ill after only a week. Jess's brother had been extremely healthy, especially since he'd been physically altered back to middle age last year. No one knew what the side effects would be or how long his artificial youth might last. It was another reason Jess wouldn't leave him alone for long.

Britt held out a hand to Regent in greeting.

"My son," Regent said, shaking his hand vigorously. "I'm so glad you're here."

Again, Britt's gut twisted. Regent knew something. He looked tired, but there was more to it. And Britt had a feeling it was bad. Because Regent had never been afraid of vampires. So what was going on here, had to be something worse.

Great.

Chapter Two

THE NEXT EVENING, Regent was back at work, deep in the bowels of Notre Dame, secretly trying to track down a lost script for the Vatican. He'd been told the script was the key to dealing with the outbreak of shadows terrorizing Paris. He'd been sworn to secrecy about them, and he regularly met with a group of priests who were also involved in the search.

He wanted desperately to warn Jess and Britt about what was going on but was torn. As long as these shadows weren't threatening the city, he'd keep his word. But if he thought for a second Jess would be at risk, he'd tell her and Britt everything.

It was a miracle Jess had been able to fly to France. Even with extended prayers, it was a risky endeavor for her. What if they'd scanned her in one of those machines? They might have realized she was, for all intents and purposes, dead.

He leaned against the door casing. He'd been feeling weird ever since he'd arrived. He'd put it down to missing Jess, but deep down, he knew there was more to it. Ever since the cardinal had told him about the shadows—and then he'd witnessed his first one—he'd been feeling uneasy, as if waiting for . . . something.

Worse, soon after his arrival, he'd learned he wouldn't be given a church. He'd always had a church, and wasn't sure how he'd manage, until he'd been told about the church's desperate need to find an ancient script that had been lost centuries ago.

Unfortunately, he hadn't found anything today. It was the end of the day, and he packed up his things to leave, then headed out of Notre Dame using the main entrance. The sun had set, and Jess would likely be awake by now. Would he see her again tonight?

A wave of dizziness forced him to sit on a bench a block away from the church. He inhaled deeply several times and leaned back against the wooden back and closed his eyes. He said a few prayers until the dizziness passed.

It wasn't a bad place to sit. The scenery in Paris had to be one of the highlights of his work here, along with the people and the food. He drew in a satisfying breath and gazed down the street where the lights of the Eiffel Tower sparkled in the distance. It was an almost magical sight. He often watched young couples with small children on the streets. Seeing them enjoying the city of lights was life-affirming for him. Tonight, the only person walking past him was a solitary young woman with a stride that reminded him of someone—Jess? Happiness filled him when he realized she'd come to see him again.

"Jess," he shouted, fearing she hadn't noticed him, sitting there on the bench. "Where's Britt?"

She strode past him without even turning her head.

"Jess?" He pushed himself to his feet, wobbling for a moment before calling out to her again. She walked quickly down the sidewalk and was nearly out of range. "Jess!"

She didn't offer the slightest sign she'd heard him. With Jess's hearing, he could have whispered her name and she'd have heard it.

He raced after her, but she was moving too fast. So he changed his mind and headed for the sidewalk café that had become his nightly indulgence. He'd have a cup of tea and a croissant with cheese for dinner before he made his way home. Then he'd try to figure out why Jess had ignored him.

To his surprise, half an hour later, Jess crossed the street and walked toward him on the sidewalk near the café where he was finishing up his dinner. She was still alone. Again no Britt?

"Jess?" This time he stood and managed to make eye contact with her, waving her over. "Jess, I'm here."

She frowned at him and pointed at herself. "*Moi?*" she asked.

He nodded. A weird feeling crept up his spine. It *was* Jess—but it wasn't Jess.

"I'm sorry, *monsieur*," she said. "I am obviously not who you think I am."

At the sound of the woman's French accent, Regent's legs gave out, and he dropped back onto his chair. He could feel the blood draining from his face.

She must've noticed his reaction because she faltered.

It was Jess, wasn't it? But when had she cut her hair? "Jess, don't fool around, get over here, now."

She approached him finally and he stared hard at her. She was playing a joke on him surely, because her hair was different. A wig? "Jess, what is this? It isn't like you to play games."

"*Excusez-moi?*"

"You're really not Jess, are you?" he said finally. The woman's voice was a little different and there was a definite French accent. Jess couldn't fake that. "I don't understand any of this. *Je regret* . . ." he started to say in broken French, then switched to English again when he remembered she'd answered him that way. "I honestly thought you were my sister. You look so much like her."

"I look like your sister, you say? And you couldn't tell the difference?" she asked, a little haughtily. "I very much doubt your sister looks like me, *monsieur*."

"A doppelganger if I've ever seen one," he said with a weak smile. The similarities were amazing . . . right down to the fact that this woman looked like she, too, might be dead. What was wrong with him?

She stared at him for a few moments, then turned and strode away without another word.

"Odd," Regent said to himself. That woman had looked exactly like his sister. And he'd have sworn she was a vampire, too. Then again, maybe it was just his addled brain playing tricks on him. He'd been off lately. Fatigued and forgetful. But now he was seeing things. And that scared him more than he cared to think about. He pressed a hand on his forehead. No. No way. She was real. He'd swear it.

ON THEIR SECOND evening in Paris, Jess waited for Britt's alarm to go off. Since he didn't need much sleep these days, she was surprised he was still in bed. She walked to his room and knocked lightly on the door.

No response.

She knocked again and waited. When he didn't even mutter back, she pushed his door open. "Britt?" The bed was made and he was gone.

In New York, he wandered the streets a lot while she slept. He must be doing the same thing here.

She'd barely made it back to the kitchen when she heard the key in the lock. She strode to the door to greet him.

"Look who I ran into," Britt said, stepping aside so she could see Regent.

"My two favorite men." That was about as emotional as she could manage. After all, she'd gone overboard and hugged him when they arrived. If she kept that up, he'd think she'd gone soft. Her exterior vampire demeanor was both a blessing and a barrier from feelings she couldn't allow. Any crack in her exterior, and she might shatter to bits, or turn to the dark.

"I'll put the coffee on," Britt said. Then he went to the kitchen and opened an upper cupboard. To her surprise, the shelves were fully stocked.

"You've been busy," she said.

He smiled at her and patted his waistline. "I can't eat croissants every day."

Not long after that, the disgusting smell of brewed coffee filled the place. It was all she could do not to cover her nose with her hand, but she'd never say that to either of the men. She didn't want to do anything that would make them stop drinking their favorite brew whenever she was around.

Regent took a sip of his coffee and set it down. He seemed distracted. Either something was wrong with him, or he had something on his mind. "Everything okay, Regent?" she asked.

"Actually, I have a very strange story to tell you," he said. "Earlier tonight, I saw a woman who looked exactly like you, Jess. I mean exactly. Well, except for the French accent. And, I think she was a vampire."

Jess frowned. "You're sure she was a vampire?"

"Of course I am. I'm not delusional, yet." He'd made his statement a little too strenuously, and he looked a little uncomfortable.

"Exactly like me? She must have had something different about her. Longer face, taller in stature, shorter, heavier—something?"

"Not as far as I could see," he said vehemently. "Oh wait. She had a different haircut."

"Two gorgeous women in one city. I'll have hit the double-my-pleasure jackpot," Britt said.

"Not funny, Brittain," Jess said. "Besides, you know what they say—everyone has a double somewhere. I guess mine is in France."

Regent leaned his arms on the island in the kitchen. He had dark circles under his eyes again tonight.

"Regent, you look tired. Are you getting enough sleep?" she asked.

"I think so, dear. In fact, I seem to be sleeping more than usual, given that I have too much spare time these days," he said.

"Have you found out why the Vatican brought you here yet?" Jess asked.

Regent paused. He obviously wanted to tell them something, but couldn't. "Just paperwork, as far as I can tell," he said. "Maybe they just want to keep a closer eye on me. After all, I failed to help the vampire they'd sent to me in New York."

"That can't be right. We saved Uriel from vampirism together. How could anyone be angry about that? Without you, it wouldn't have happened."

Who would have believed that a fallen angel as powerful as Uriel could have been turned into a voracious vampire? But it had happened, most likely deliberately to see what the consequences would be. Cardinal Vasilli had been involved in turning Uriel, she'd bet her eyeteeth on it. Although they'd saved Uriel in the end, it had been touch and go for a while. Jess had even died in the process. But her sacrifice had given Uriel the final spark he needed to fight off the horrors of vampirism. As a vampire, Uriel's thirst had known no bounds. North America could have been lost to his hunger, but as an angel, his abilities were also boundless. He brought Jess back, though still as a vampire even when he could have restored her humanity. According to him, she was important in the fight against her brethren. Her vampirism was a gift, and she'd remain undead because it was her destiny and her duty.

"Maybe I'm wrong." Regent slumped back in his chair. "After all my years with the church, I should never have been demoted to a paper shuffler, even if it is in France." Again, he sounded as if he was holding back something important. Regent wasn't a good liar.

Jess caught Britt's irritated expression. That made her feel a little better because it meant they were thinking the same thing—Regent wasn't telling everything. She considered mentioning the shadows but held back. Regent looked too tired and too feeble to have to face something else otherworldly tonight.

"I think you need to watch your back, Regent. I'm getting vibes about this place that I've never had before, and I haven't seen many vamps out and about," Jess said. "Which is odd since vampires should be more prevalent here."

"Maybe this area isn't the local vampires' favorite haunt? You said Notre Dame was painful for you. Perhaps it bothers them, too?" Regent said. "Though, I'm positive the woman I saw was one." He rubbed the back of his neck.

"She really looked that much like me?"

"Dead ringer," he said deliberately, biting back a grin while Jess groaned at his pun.

"Well, I'm going to keep an eye out for her," Jess said.

Regent made no attempt to hide his now weary expression. "It's a big city, dear. Most likely, we'll never come across this person again."

"Maybe." She shrugged her shoulders. "At any rate, you're tired. Want us to walk you home?"

"Thanks, I'd appreciate that. It'll give me a little more time with you." Regent linked his arm with hers on the sidewalk. Other than Britt, he was the only person who'd dare.

"You sure you don't want to take a taxi, Reej?"

"Now Jess, I'm not that feeble. Besides, I like to see the city at night—the lights, the excitement. It's all so different here."

"Yes, that it is," she said, getting an odd knot in the pit of her stomach. It was the kind of *different* that scared the bejesus out of her.

A few minutes later, once she saw Regent inside, Jess rejoined Britt on the sidewalk. The idea that she had a lookalike running into Regent didn't sit well with her. She turned to Britt. "Why don't we scope out this neighborhood tonight? It's strange we haven't spotted any vampires at all."

"Didn't you tell me they'd be more sophisticated here?" Britt said. "Maybe they don't hunt the streets at night. Maybe they have better places."

"Such as?"

"I don't know. Private parties? Clubs? Vampires are supposedly older here. Wiser. They likely have more funding, at least the smarter ones do." He paused. "Remember Constantine."

"It's hard to forget Constantine, given that he killed you and initiated your angelic DNA."

Britt cleared his throat and cringed. "You had to remind me. Still, it was Constantine who served the more sophisticated vampires in New York by providing higher-class people as their fodder. European vampires might get their blood supply that way too."

They crossed Pont Neuf, the oldest and most beautiful bridge in Paris. She stood in the center, admiring the architecture and the Seine River flowing through the city—street lights illuminated colorful jewels on the river creating beautiful, undulating art. Even this late at night, the streets were occupied with citizens, revelers, and sightseers. It seemed Paris really was a city that didn't sleep.

Britt took her hand and slowly pulled her toward him. "I don't know about you, but I think we should at least do a little kissing on this romantic bridge. Maybe there's some kind of magic here for lovers. Let's try it."

"You don't believe in magic, Britt," she said with a laugh. The rare sound tinkled on the air and disappeared.

His lips crushed against hers with a fiery passion. Not waiting for her to meet him halfway, he took the kiss with a desperation that made her bones feel weak.

One of his hands slid up her back and wrapped around her neck. His other hand felt warm against her waist. There was sense of ownership in that hold that thrilled her in a way she'd never imagined possible for a vampire like her.

The promise in his kisses spread like wildfire through her veins, heating her blood and making her heart pump.

"Maybe we should go home?" she said, unusually breathless.

"I thought you'd never ask," he said, taking her hand.

They'd only gone a short distance when that uneasy sensation started building inside her again. What the hell?

"You sense it, too, don't you?" Britt said in a low voice, meant only for her.

"I do. What is it?"

"I'm not sure," he said. "But I think we're about to find out."

Jess followed the direction of his gaze. Shadows thickened on the sidewalk ahead of them. Even stranger, it appeared there were three shadows moving toward them, merging and moving apart again. They were darker than the night, but she could make out nothing else.

She knew one thing for certain, though. Her instincts about coming to Paris had been dead-on.

Her throat went dry. "For Regent's sake, we need to find out what is going on here. Surely other people have seen these shadows? Someone must be talking about it?"

Disappointment flared in Britt's expression. "I meant to tell you . . . I read about people claiming to be attacked at night, though they didn't know exactly who, or what, their assailant was. One witness said he'd only seen a shadow. Needless to say, the cops thought he'd had a bit too much to drink."

"So much for going back to the apartment," Jess said.

"Raincheck, babe?"

She planted her hands on her hips and eyed the approaching darkness. "I just wish I didn't have this impending feeling of disaster. I don't think we should turn our backs on these things, either."

"Agreed. Maybe we should back away slowly. "

"This is the second time we've seen them. What if they're following us?" she said.

She and Britt began backing away as they would with any predatory wild animal, while not breaking focus on the shadows.

"We sure as hell need to find out. I wonder if holy water would scare them off?"

She shivered involuntarily. She'd been burned by holy water once, when Britt had used it against an attacking vampire. It wasn't something she wanted to experience again anytime soon. But these shadows were definitely menacing. Who knew what would stop them, or if they were even actually dangerous?

"Maybe they're drawn to me because I'm so dark? They might be attracted to evil of any kind," she said. "Maybe that's why we've both seen the shadows. I'm the catalyst."

"You're not evil, my darling. How many times do I have to tell you that?" he said, his eyes still glued to the shadows.

"You see me through rose-colored glasses. The rest of the world sees something completely different. Even members of the black ops team. Some of them are almost more afraid of me than they are the vampires we combat."

"That's because of your kick-ass reputation and your abilities, doll." They took two more steps back. The shadows moved closer again. "Some of the team members are like wild dogs. Somebody's got to be alpha or they'll go off at the wrong time."

"Did you just call me alpha?" she said, not taking her eyes off the encroaching shadows, either.

"That's why I respect the hell out of you," he said. "You're such a bad-ass, and not just on the streets." When they backed onto the bridge, the shadows' momentum halted, then they faded away.

"It seems they're not interested in crossing this bridge with us. Maybe they have an issue with water?"

"Maybe. That's something we'll have to remember if we ever run into them again."

"Home?"

"Definitely. Via the other side of the bridge. Not that we're running from them. We just need to be more prepared for next time we run into them."

"And we'll be packing holy water," Britt said.

Chapter Three

THE NEXT NIGHT, Regent sat, waiting at the same café in hope of seeing Jess's lookalike again. Maybe she regularly took this route? This time, he'd convince her to meet Jess. He'd even tucked a picture into his wallet to prove that his sister looked exactly like her. He also considered calling his law firm in New York. He and Jess had been adopted. If the firm could find their adoption papers, they might be able to learn if there had been another child. He intended to do that, right away. But not until he learned a little more from this woman first.

He waited so long, his tea had gone cold. Even though his back was cramped from sitting here so long, he stayed until the wee hours, waiting, hoping. But Jess's twin never appeared.

Reluctantly, he paid the tab, threw his napkin on the table, and stood, ready to return home.

He missed New York sometimes. He loved the people, the melting pot of accents and lifestyles, and the sense of homecoming the city offered. People here were friendly enough, but too often, he couldn't communicate with co-workers who didn't speak English. Again, he questioned the reasons he'd been sent here. He didn't seem to be qualified at all for the job, mainly because he couldn't read French. He wondered who had asked for him.

He'd just gone around the corner, a block from his apartment, when he spotted Jess. She was alone and, once again, there was no sign of Britt.

"Jess. Wait up. I'm right behind you," he said. He didn't need to shout since she had incredible hearing.

She stopped and turned around, waiting for him.

He drew closer. "Where's Britt?" he asked before he noticed her short hair.

"Who eez this Britt?" the woman said.

Dear heaven, again he'd have sworn it was Jess. Even her gait was the same.

"I'm sorry, miss. I'm afraid I've mistaken you for my sister again. In fact, I was hoping to run into you tonight. I brought a picture of Jess, to prove to you that I'm not some crazy old man."

"Well, you might be middle-aged," she said looking him up and down. "But, hardly old."

He'd forgotten that part. He'd lived a long life and felt every one of his years.

He snatched the picture from his wallet and showed it to her.

She inhaled sharply this time and her arrogant demeanor slipped just a little as she stepped under a streetlight to get a better look.

"Not possible. You've taken a picture of me, somehow. This is a trick," she said, her eyebrows narrowing. "What are you up to?"

"I swear, that is my sister. She's in Paris, visiting, right now. If you would indulge me, I'd love for you to meet her. I think she's wondering about my sanity, too," he said, smiling pleasantly at her.

The doppelganger laughed. Even *that* was similar to Jess's laugh. "I suppose I could do that. I have to admit I'm curious. But not tonight. I have to go to work."

He wanted to reach out and touch her, to see if her flesh was cold, but that would be going too far. And if she was a vampire, as he suspected, it could be dangerous. Instead, he held out a hand to shake hers.

"I'm a bit of a germaphobe," she said, ignoring his extended hand.

Now he knew for sure. She didn't want him to feel the cold marble of her flesh. He'd been right about her. But what were the odds of Jess's lookalike being a vampire, too? Pretty darned slim.

"Would you agree to meet tomorrow night at the café where we first talked?"

She paused, eying him up and down. He should have noticed her couture clothing style. She dressed very fashionably in a short skirt with a top that frayed in odd places, and she wore four-inch spiked heels. Her hair was the same sable color as Jess's, but the style was shorter, and cut in different lengths. And close up, he noticed the ends were tipped with blue and purple.

"I guess so. Okay," she said, albeit reluctantly.

"Around ten?"

"Make it eleven," she said. He instantly knew why. It wasn't fully dark until ten, this time of the year.

"Wonderful," he said, then watched her stride quickly away.

She was barely out of earshot before he called Jess, telling her about the chance encounter again tonight.

"That's a bit of a coincidence, Regent," she said. "Could this woman be playing you? In a city the size of Paris, don't you think it's odd that you'd run into her again?"

"I think it's her regular route to work," he said.

"Right," she said, but didn't sound convinced. He couldn't blame her.

"I've scheduled a get-together at the café tomorrow night. Can you come?"

"We'll be there, Regent. This is one woman I cannot wait to meet."

BRITT COULDN'T WAIT either. But unlike Regent, it worried him that this woman looked so much like Jess. He downed the last of his coffee and put his cup in the dishwasher. Ever since a fringe group of the church had turned seventy-three-year-old Regent into a forty-something middle-aged man, he'd learned not to underestimate their capabilities. But could they create a woman vampire? A clone? And if they had, why?

For the first few days, while Jess had been in stasis, he'd spent a lot of time mapping the streets of old Paris during the day. He wanted to get a better feel of this city before they started prowling around at night. And he knew Jess well enough to know she'd want to check things out before long. She'd find local vampires one way or another.

And speaking of dark things, the fact that Regent had met Jess's lookalike twice, was of considerable concern. He was staring into his empty coffee cup when Jess strode into the room.

"Britt, do you want to go looking for those shadows again tonight?" she asked.

"Okay." He knew her well enough to know she was getting restless. She was ready for a bit of vampire ass-kicking action. That said, they both knew they had to be careful about starting anything unless they had to. Trouble usually found them, though. Deep down, did he really want a tame, boring vacation? Besides, they were going to be here for at least three months. He might have angelic DNA, but he believed he'd come from a lineage of warrior angels. He needed action, craved it. Finding what was behind those shadows might be exactly what they both needed tonight.

They were heading toward Pont Neuf where they'd spotted the shadows before, when Jess pulled two small bottles and a piece of paper out of her pocket. She held them up. "Holy water and a special prayer against evil spirits."

"Did you get this from Regent?" Britt asked.

"Nope, on the Internet," she said. "I ordered it the first day we were here, just in case something came up."

He stopped walking and gawked at her. "I'm sure *that'll* be something we can count on. Holy water from the Internet?"

She shrugged and looked a little embarrassed. "I know, but I didn't want to ask Regent. He'd only worry. If you want, I could spill a little on my hand to see if it really is holy water," she said.

"No way!" He grabbed the nearly opened bottle from her.

The fact that she'd even consider using holy water told him that she was catching the same vibes about these spirits as he was. Big, bad, dangerous vibes. "If this stuff is real, you'll get burned," he said seriously.

"Don't worry. I figured I'd hand off the bottles to you and be well out of splash range when you use them. I can't wait to see if it has any effect on those shadow things."

"Have you considered it might just make them angrier?"

She looked him in the eye. "I didn't know they were angry. Are you telling me you're getting some sort of message from them? As if they have feelings?"

"You could say that. I think they're dangerous," Britt said.

She tapped her chin. "I think they're dangerous, too. But I'm not getting the messages you are."

"I just wish this was happening on our home turf. We have no backup here. Who do we call if we end up with a corpse on the street, or a dead shadow?" he said. "We can't exactly kill something in Paris and dispose of the evidence without being noticed."

"I think we could figure out a way to dispose of the corpse if we had to. But do you really think a shadow can die?"

He sighed. "That might be our next problem."

They neared the end of the bridge. Maybe in their desperation for action, they'd blown the whole situation out of proportion. At least he could hope. But when he searched the sidewalk across from the bridge, his muscles contracted. Crap!

"Do you see what I see?" Jess said. "Over there?"

"I do. Those shadows near the building aren't natural. And they're close to the place we saw them before, aren't they?"

Jess nodded. "They seem to be growing bigger—or are there just more of them? Not good, either way."

"Definitely, not good," Britt repeated.

"I think we should report this," Jess said.

"Who could we possibly report it to?"

"Maybe the clergy? Regent could do it for us."

"Let's try the holy water first. If it has any effect, we'll get out of here and consult with Regent." No way was he going to burn her. "Move away, my love."

She took a couple of steps back. "Don't leave the safety of the bridge, Britt, just in case. They don't seem to like being near the river."

He kept his feet firmly planted on the bridge and tossed the bottle like a Molotov cocktail. It flew high into the air, allowing maximum splashdown upon contact with the cement.

The bottle smashed and holy water exploded in the center of the darkening mass. The shadows scattered so quickly, he could barely follow their movements. It appeared that not a drop of it hit them, because they slid into the cracks of the building at lightning speed, vanishing.

"I guess we won't need the second bottle," he said.

"I think we might." Her gaze remained pinned to the other side of the street. Nearly as quickly as they'd fled, the shadows were reemerging, pouring out from between the cracks and nearly covering the sidewalk for at least a block. They were practically roiling. "I think we just made things a heck of a lot worse. They brought reinforcements," she said.

"Dammit," he said between gritted teeth, more to himself than to her. "I thought the holy water might actually work."

"I think it worked too well. Let's go, Britt. Their anger is building so fast, I can even feel it now. We need to regroup and think of some other way to stop them."

"Wait a minute," he said. "Look! There's someone coming down the street. He's walking straight at the shadows, as if he doesn't even see them."

Jess waved her arms in the air. "Turn back," she shouted. "Turn back."

The young man looked at them like they were insane. "What have you two been smoking?" he said with a laugh, continuing down the sidewalk toward his possible doom.

"Can't you see what's right in front of you?" she yelled. "Don't go any farther."

He laughed even harder and staggered along his way.

"Why, in the name of all that's holy, didn't he listen?" Jess said, shaking her head. "What will happen to him now?"

"Oh crap," Britt said. The man was inches away from the swirling mass now. How could he not see them?

Then it happened. The stranger stepped into the middle of the darkest shadows Britt had ever seen. They swirled around the man's feet, but he continued walking, as if he neither saw, nor felt a thing. Before Britt knew it, the man was through it and going on his way, unaffected and unaware.

"What just happened?" Britt said to Jess.

"Maybe we're hallucinating? Could it be there's nothing really there?"

"One person might hallucinate, but two of us, seeing the same thing—I don't think so."

"What do you think would happen if one of us stepped into those shadows? Would we be as unaffected, or would it be different for us, because we can see them? Maybe we're blowing this out of proportion?" She made a move. "I'll go," she said.

Britt held up a hand to block her, even though trying to stop a vampire wasn't particularly smart. Still, he took his chances. "You will not. I'll go. You can save me if anything bad happens."

Even though she scowled at him, she said, "Go then." She handed him the last bottle of holy water. "If the holy water fails, I'll pull you out."

He crossed himself and looked skyward. Hopefully, they were overdramatizing this. His sense of dread was real enough, even though a stranger had just walked straight through them without realizing the shadows were there. "Maybe they're harmless. They didn't hurt that guy."

"You don't think that for a second, do you?" Jess said.

"No, I don't." In fact, the writhing mass spiked fear into his chest. He wasn't normally afraid. Why did these things affect him so fiercely? Maybe because their dankness, their soulless depths of despair and inhumanity, drifted off them in stark, invisible clouds.

The second his foot left the bridge and touched the street, the shadows reacted like a school of piranhas. They swirled toward him at lightning speed.

It definitely wasn't the same reaction they shown the fellow who'd waded through them a moment ago.

They were on him in seconds. As if fire ants were chewing at his feet and lower legs, pain overwhelmed him. He groaned but managed to shout to Jess. "Don't pull me out. They'll attack you!"

He dropped the holy water near his feet and the shadows skirted away from the liquid, but only for a second. Still, it gave him enough time to dive back onto the Pont to safety.

His sneakers were covered with black soot, or slime, and parts of the leather were eaten away as if by acid. Where there was no sneaker, his foot looked burned and his skin bubbled from the effects of the creatures. "Holy hell, it hurts. It feels like it's still burning."

"Hurry, let's go find Regent. He'll be able to help," she said. "If I know my brother, he'll have brought his herbs and potions with him, like the ones he uses on me when I'm burned by holy water. They have to work."

Britt attempted to walk, but stumbled. The poison continued to burn into his flesh, working its way through the sinew and bones of his feet. "Jesus, Mary, and Joseph," he groaned. "It's excruciating."

They had to take the long way around because the shadows were between them and Regent's apartment. They walked quickly, but not quickly enough for Britt. He was in agony and faltered several times. Jess supported him and kept him from falling flat on his face.

It was embarrassing to say the least. He'd been kidding when he said she could save him. He actually considered himself to be strong enough to be the one who did the saving, but Jess practically had to carry him the last few yards.

Reaching the entrance of Regent's building, she easily broke the security door with one twist of the handle.

Near the end of his strength, he felt as if he was looking at climbing Mount Everest. But with Jess's help, he managed the stairs. They burst into Regent's apartment without knocking and Jess dragged him to the couch.

"Regent, get your potions out. You need to find something to help Britt. Hurry."

Regent rushed out of his bedroom, his reading glasses in hand. "What's going on? Oh dear! What happened to Britt's feet? Was he burned by acid?"

"No, by evil shadows on the sidewalk," she said. "Can you help him?"

"Evil shadows?" Regent hesitated for just a moment, a strange look crossing his features.

"They're not vampires, Regent. They're something much worse."

"What in hell could be worse?" Regent asked, immediately moving to root in a cupboard off the kitchen. His reaction told Jess he was afraid. He only used curse words when he was terrified ... and considering the excruciating pain in Britt's feet right now, she knew he was petrified to look down. Had most of Britt's flesh burned off? If her brother looked, would there only be sinew and bone left?

Jess grabbed Regent by the shoulders. "Hurry, please. Since this was done by evil, you're the only one who can help Britt now."

"I don't know, Jess. It looks very bad." He held a bag of dried herbs in his left hand, but he looked unsure of his concoction.

"Just try something," Britt said, between gritted teeth. "Anything. It's the worst pain I've ever experienced. And you have no idea how much it hurts to die and be regenerated. But this is ten times worse." He finally couldn't hold back the agony and passed out.

REGENT CAREFULLY removed Britt's sneakers so he could apply his herbs. Jess bit back a scream when she saw what was left of Britt's feet. Looking at the burned tissue and visible bones, she couldn't believe Britt had been able to stay conscious as long as he had.

Thank heavens Regent had his herbs. Even though they'd never really helped her when she was injured, she prayed they would work on Britt. And though Britt had angelic DNA, he was definitely very human.

"Let's try to get what's left of his socks off," Regent said, sounding calmer now, maybe because he knew she was on the edge of losing it. And when she lost it, it wasn't good news.

Jess reached out to instantly yank them off.

"Wait! Don't touch them with your bare hands," Regent shouted. "You might get burned too. I have silicone oven mitts in the kitchen."

She raced in there, grabbed the mitts, and gently pulled off the strips of cotton that was all that had been left of his socks without causing any more damage to his horribly injured flesh.

Even while unconscious, Britt moaned.

"Damnation," she said, then bit her lip.

Regent started praying over him as he administered the herbs. A few minutes later, Britt started to come around.

Feeling impotent and unable to do anything, Jess got Britt a glass of water. She helped him tip his head to drink, but he was having a hard time getting past the pain.

He hadn't looked at his feet, and that was a good thing. They were horribly burned. And if she wasn't mistaken, it looked as if sharp claws had opened gashes on the insteps and down his Achilles tendons.

Regent continued to pray aloud while spreading holy oil on the horrific gashes. After he wrapped the herbs around Britt's feet, he covered them with gauze. Jess bit her lip. Regent's ministrations had to help.

Had it worked, or was the poison working deeper into Britt's system? She couldn't tell now that he was bandaged, but he seemed a little calmer. What herbs had Regent used this time? It could be frankincense and myrrh, for all she knew.

After Britt had either fallen asleep or passed out again, she paced around Regent's small apartment. Even though Britt might lose his feet, or worse, his life, they couldn't take him to the hospital. His wounds were paranormal, and no doctor's traditional medicine would have any efficacy on them.

"What do we do now, brother?" she asked. The pull of sunrise drained her energy and made her feel lethargic. She'd have to leave Britt and go back to her apartment soon. That would be agony in itself.

"We wait. I read something in one of the texts I'm studying about people dying like this during the French Revolution. Could it be the same thing? Could that dark time have had something like this going, as well as the plague?"

"How'd they fight it?" she asked.

"I don't know. But I believe a lot of people in the city died both before and just after the revolution. History put it down to the plague. But maybe, it was something much, much worse." Regent glanced at Britt, then looked away again in worry. "Don't worry, we're not going to let anything like that happen to Britt. We'll figure this out."

Jess glanced at Britt's flushed cheeks and paused to make sure he was still breathing.

She pulled Regent into the kitchen and set him on a chair. "Do you think Britt is just asleep, or is his condition worsening? Could the poison have put him into a coma?"

"I don't know, dear," he said. "We could always wake him to find out."

"As much as I hate to do that, I think we should," she said, yanking her long hair back over her shoulders. "I'm not leaving here if he's dying. I don't care what the repercussions might be to myself."

"Well, I do," Regent said. He approached Britt and knelt down next to the sofa. The second he touched his shoulder, Britt's eyes flashed open. "You okay, son?"

Britt nodded but didn't speak, his face instantly contorted in pain.

"Britt, do you want us to take you to the hospital?" Jess asked, knowing it would be an exercise in futility. Not that it mattered. She would stop at nothing to save him. "Are you feeling worse?" Worry was evident in her voice, but she didn't give a damn.

He looked at her and forced a pained smile. "No, I think it's working. I'm just tired, that's all, my love." He closed his eyes again.

Jess and Regent went back to the kitchen, where they could talk without bothering him. When Regent made himself a cup of tea, Jess noted her brother's hands were shaking. No wonder.

Regent took a long drink of his tea and looked at Jess. "How did this happen?"

Jess told him everything about the incident. "What do you think those things are?"

She knew her brother well enough to read his expression. He was keeping something from her.

"My question would be . . . why didn't they injure the man who walked through them, while Britt was attacked? And why do the two of you see them, when other people don't?" He took a long drink of his tea. "Tomorrow, when there's time, you and I need to talk. But not now. You'd better leave soon, before sunrise catches you by surprise."

She nodded, but she still had a bit more time. "We need to find out what these entities are," Jess said.

Regent leaned forward with a serious expression on his face. "There are volumes of old texts, written in languages and codes I don't understand, in the libraries here in France. But, as I mentioned, I have seen some texts in Latin that mention injuries like Britt's during the French Revolution. One particular script called it the work of the devil. Of course, back then, anything they didn't understand was the work of the devil. It might have been a reference to the plague. Since I can only read things in English or Latin, I'm limited. Most of the documents are written in French."

"We need to find someone who can speak French, someone we trust," she said, racking her brain for anyone she might know that could help. She jumped upright in her seat. "Sampson! He speaks French and Romanian, and he's got a degree in ancient dialects."

"I had no idea he was fluent in other languages," Regent said.

"I'm going to phone him tomorrow and get him over here." Jess leaned back on her heels. "When he comes, will the church allow him to help you?"

"As I said, we need to talk. But it's too late to start tonight, because you have to get home to safety, Jess."

"Wait. What is it?" Jess asked.

Regent sighed. "I'm not supposed to tell anyone, but I do know something about the shadows. I had no idea they were able to harm anyone, though. At any rate, I'll tell you what I know tomorrow."

Britt mumbled in his sleep, then groaned. Jess checked on him, but his eyes were still closed. "Do you think he's going to be okay?"

Regent reached over and touched her hand. "Honey, right now, the best things Britt has going for him are his angelic DNA, and the fact that he's still alive."

"And, he has you, Regent," she said. Regent might not think he had any special abilities, but he'd certainly proven he was special when he'd partially saved her soul.

Her watch vibrated on her arm. "Damn. It's nearly dawn. As much as I hate to leave, it's time I go back to the apartment."

"Go, dear. I'll keep an eye on him. Try not to worry."

"I'm sorry I have to leave you alone like this," she said, still looking at Britt on the sofa. "And worse, I hate to leave Britt when he needs me most."

Unfortunately, it was her penance to pay. She was a creature of the night, and had to abide by the rules of her life sentence or disappear along with the many vampires she'd killed.

Sometimes the thought of disappearing was almost sweet, but not tonight. She needed to be here to help Britt and Regent, and she'd damned well do her best.

She left Regent's place reluctantly. Who knew that being a vampire wouldn't be the worst thing that ever happened to her? That her life could continually get worse. . . . It seemed something always happened to remind her to be grateful for what she had, living as a vampire and hunting vamps side-by-side with Britt.

Could that vile evil eating into Britt kill him, or would his angelic DNA be able to heal his injuries as Regent hoped? He had survived death once before, but he'd had help that time.

On her way home, she passed the Arc de Triomphe. Usually, she kept going, but tonight, she walked toward it, almost as if she'd been lured there. She reached out and touched the stone, instantly feeling a vibration inside the arch. A feeling of power surged beneath the cold stone surface and along with it, a dark essence that nearly rocked her to the core. She pulled her hand away and rubbed it while she stared at the names of the fallen etched into the stone all around her.

Is that why this city resonated a sense of dread for her? Is that why those shadows crawled out from the brick? There'd been so many deaths in France over the centuries—from conquest, to plagues, and through more than a hundred years of war. Old cities held a sense of ageless trauma. Tonight, it seemed that evil leaked from the very pores of the walls of the arch. Had it always been this way? Or was this something new?

When strains of yellow filtered into the night sky, she forced herself away to continue on her way home. But for the first time, she checked all the rooms in her apartment before she locked herself into her newly made bunker.

She stayed in her clothes tonight, and figured she'd forgo a shower when she woke. She intended to head out directly to Regent's place, to find out if Britt had healed. Or . . . no, she couldn't think like that.

Before her body turned to stone and the world disappeared, she prayed that Britt would be okay.

Chapter Four

THE SUN HAD BARELY set when Jess left her room the next evening. She quickly drank her sustenance and made for Regent's apartment a few streets away.

As usual, at this time of night in Paris, the streets were bustling with tourists and citizens alike. It was agony to move at a regular pace instead of her vampiric speed.

She opened the still-broken security door and zoomed up the old, creaky steps, then barged into Regent's place.

She instantly cringed at the scent of onions and beef cooking, until she saw Britt seated at the table with Regent, having dinner. They were chatting over thick steaks and baked potatoes, and they each had a glass of red wine. Britt's feet were bare, and they were nearly healed. Pink scars marked the places where he'd been so badly damaged. Even his tissue had filled back in.

"It worked," she shouted, and both men jumped. She'd forgotten she could enter a room without anyone knowing she was there.

"Jess!" Regent grasped his chest. "You scared the living daylights out of me."

"Sorry." But she wasn't. She was overcome at seeing her beloved's current state of health. "Britt, how do you feel?"

He put down his fork and stood to offer his chair before he grabbed another one in the living room for himself. "I'm fine, Jess. Totally fine."

Normally she'd balk at being treated like a lady, but she'd take anything Britt wanted to dish out today. He was alive! "Was it the herbs and oils that worked?" she asked.

"Maybe," he said.

"Very minimally, if at all," Regent added. "After you left, Britt's blue light floated over him while he slept, hovering over his injuries for quite a while. I watched from the other room so I wouldn't interfere. It was quite something to see."

"Really?" Britt said. "I didn't realize."

Regent tipped his head. "I thought you were healing yourself consciously?"

"No." Britt scowled and looked a little frustrated. "I still have very little control over that part of my Fallen side. When my power is unleashed, it's as if it has a mind of its own and it does what needs to be done. Maybe my subconscious is aware of my abilities, but my conscious mind certainly isn't. If I have uber-DNA, there must be someone, somewhere, who can help me gain better control of it."

"There are passages in the Bible that talk about the children of the Fallen. Angels came to Earth and mated with human women," Regent said.

"According to my mother, my father was a construction worker. I seriously doubt there was much angelic DNA in him." Britt frowned.

"Your mother is still alive?" Jess asked, leaning forward and staring into Britt's face. "Why didn't you tell me?" Her bones felt like rubber. "She wasn't even at your funeral."

"I only met her once. I was raised in an orphanage. Maybe I understand why she shipped me off now."

"I notice you never say angel. You always say Fallen," Jess said in an attempt to change the subject. She'd find out more about his mother when they returned to New York, whether Britt agreed to it or not.

"Probably because I'm far from an angel, babe." He winked at her.

Regent laughed. He got up and poured himself a second glass of wine, then offered Britt another. "If you're both feeling up to it tonight, we're still meeting the woman who looks like you, Jess. She said she'd catch up with us at the café near Notre Dame, and I told her you'd both be there. But that was before Britt was injured."

"Yes, I think we should meet her," Britt said.

"Sure you're up to it?" Jess asked, hating that she sounded as if she could shatter at any moment. Having Britt's life hanging in the balance definitely showed her weaknesses to the world.

"I'm fine. It's as if nothing happened," he said, looking at his feet. "I might have a few scars, but the pain is gone and my strength has returned. Those things are *not* getting the better of me today."

Wary of sounding like a panicked girlfriend, she held her tongue. Was he truly healed? Either way, he'd never shy away from danger, any more than she would. It was part of who they were.

"What's this woman's name?" Jess asked.

Regent suddenly looked exasperated. "You know, I didn't even think to ask her. I guess it was partly because I was afraid I'd scare her away. She seemed pretty dubious of me, and given her undead proclivities, I didn't want to press her."

"You're sure she's a vampire?" Jess asked.

"Pretty sure," Regent said.

It was probably a wise choice not to press her, then. What time are we supposed to be there?" Britt looked at his watch.

"In an hour, actually. I told her eleven o'clock."

"Perfect—that'll give me just enough time to run out and buy a new pair of shoes," he said.

Jess glanced at his sneakers, where they'd been left at the front door. They were full of holes and claw marks, but all signs of the damaging soot was gone. "Sorry, I didn't think to bring you a pair of shoes."

"Don't worry about it. I needed a new pair of sneakers, anyway. I might as well buy them tonight."

"What will you wear to go to the store?" Jess asked.

"Regent and I don't have the same size feet, so I'll have to wear those torn-up ones." He frowned. "Any chance they'll still burn me?"

Jess picked one up and ran her fingers over it. "There's no residue left, just the holes." She put the sneaker down again. "I can't imagine what the poor shoe salesman is going to think."

"I'll tell him I'm an exterminator," Britt said, and Regent nearly choked on the sip of wine he'd just taken.

"At least your sense of humor is back. That's another good sign," Regent said, crossing himself and looking skyward. "Since we can't be sure if all of the poison is out of your system, I'll do up a package of my herbs to bring along. I want you to put them on your feet each night for a week."

"Is that really necessary?" Britt asked, grimacing.

"It is," Regent said.

"How will dried herbs stay on my feet?"

"Wear socks to bed. Stuff the herbs down your socks until they're on the tops of your feet." Regent grinned, as if he was thoroughly enjoying this.

Jess shook her head because Regent had done the same to her before. Yeah, now that Britt was better, Regent was having some fun at his expense.

"At the end of the week, I'll check you again. Hopefully, I'll be able to give you a clean bill of health."

"Great!" Britt took the last bite of his steak and washed it down with wine.

Jess helped clean up the dishes because she knew how anxious Regent was to go. She'd never seen him quite so eager to introduce her to another person. Hopefully, the whole thing didn't backfire, because he certainly had his hopes up. He really believed this woman might be their sister.

By the time they met Regent at the café, it was eleven o'clock on the dot. Regent was animated, and he was talking more than usual while he searched the streets for this mystery woman.

Jess didn't know what to think about having a lookalike. It was hard to believe another woman could fool her brother.

She and Regent both knew they had been adopted, and it was completely possible that they had another sibling out there. But another sibling who was also a vampire? Not likely. If this "sister" wasn't a vampire, she'd be well up in years. But according to Regent, she looked to be Jess's current visual age. Twenty-nine-ish.

The whole thing had to be a setup. But if it was, what would be the purpose of it? Why would someone undergo plastic surgery to look like her?

Regent's spine suddenly stiffened. The lookalike had arrived. Jess turned her head and her mouth dropped open. "Unbelievable!"

The woman stopped next to their table and appeared to be as stunned as Jess.

"Impossible," she said, harshly. "What is the meaning of this?"

Regent stood and offered her a chair. "I did try to tell you. Won't you have a seat?"

Jess observed the woman's fashionable hairstyle and perfectly applied makeup with navy-blue, lacquered fingernails that matched the highlights in her hair. Her clothes were expensive and had obviously been made specifically for her. Nothing off-the-rack for this girl. So why would someone go to the effort to make a Jess Vandermire lookalike, only to give her a different hairstyle and clothes?

Jess had to admit that, other than the superficial differences, she could be looking in a mirror. They were almost exactly alike.

And this woman was definitely a vampire!

"Hello," Jess said, giving Britt a nudge with her toe. Contrary to his prior comments about her having a double, his expression practically telegraphed the fact that he didn't like what he was seeing.

"Well," she replied. "I wasn't sure I believed your brother, but now . . . " She sat on the edge of her chair, as if she might run away at any moment.

Jess felt like doing the same thing.

When the waitress approached, Regent and Britt ordered coffee, but Jess and this other woman did not.

"May I ask your name?" Britt asked.

"Morana," she replied.

No last name, but it was a start. Regent made small talk, but Jess wasn't listening, instead focused on assessing the woman, who was doing the same thing to her.

"Is it possible you were adopted?" Regent asked, in his most hopeful voice. Regent was altogether too gullible when it came to this woman, which was surprising. He'd been around the block and, hell, he had a vampire for a sister. So gullibility wasn't common for him. But this lookalike had found a soft spot in him, obviously.

Jess wasn't jealous, just worried. Very worried.

"Yes, I was adopted," Morana said, narrowing her gaze on Jess. "But, I've never been told I have siblings."

"We haven't either. It's strange we look so much alike," Jess said, hoping Morana had some sort of explanation. "Where were you born?"

Morana looked pensive for a moment. "I just assumed I was born in Paris," she said. "But, to be honest, I've never actually asked."

Jess met Regent's gaze. Their story was pretty much the same. They'd believed they'd been born in New York, and never had a reason to question it.

"Are your parents still living?" Morana asked.

"No. They died years and years ago," Regent said, before Jess gave him a nudge under the table with her foot.

Morana's eyes narrowed suspiciously. "They must have died very young."

Was she digging to find out if Jess was a vampire? Even more suspicious now, Jess feigned indifference, shrugging. "We try not to think about it. And your parents?"

"I was raised by my adoptive father. He is elderly, but in good health."

"That's wonderful," Regent said, still sounding a little too exuberant. "Maybe he knows about your birth family, if you have siblings?"

Morana leaned back in her chair, still staring warily at Jess. "You don't honestly think we're related, do you?" she said with a soft French accent.

"No, I don't," Jess said.

"Given the adoption information and your looks, it's got to be at least a possibility?" Regent said.

Jess inhaled slowly. *Or she'd had plastic surgery.*

Jess had never seen her brother act like this before. He'd already accepted this woman as a sibling ... and he'd barely just met her. It wasn't like him, at all. Honestly, what were the odds that *both* she and Morana would be vampires? It was too much of a stretch.

Morana glanced at her watch. "I'd better go, or I'll be late for work."

Regent's hands fidgeted on the table. "Wait, before you go, can we plan to meet again? We don't even know where you live or your last name."

She stood. "I work at LaCave, under the city in the Kingdom of Bones. It's a favorite nightclub for cataphiles. And my last name is Longina."

Britt nearly dropped his cup. It clattered loudly onto the table. "Bones?"

"Yes, lots of them," Morana said with a gleam in her eye as if she'd picked up on Britt's phobia and found it humorous.

Britt shivered, but forced a nonchalant expression. "What are cataphiles?" he asked.

Jess was the only one who knew about his phobia and she'd keep it that way. He'd had a scare as a child, and was embarrassed to admit it had followed him to adulthood. At least that's what he thought had caused it. She had the feeling there was more to it than that.

"Surely you've heard of the bones under the city?" Morana said. "There are millions of disarticulated skeletons in the tunnels, along with miles of passages. Cataphiles are those who dare to venture into the catacombs."

Jess's gut twinged while she considered the shadows and the fact that millions of bones lay in the ground below them. Could that be why the dark entities were leaking out from the walls? Did they originate down there? And if so, why, after so many years, would they erupt from the tunnels now?

"I don't get why anyone would want to spend time down there," Britt said. "It must be like an underground graveyard."

Morana shrugged.

"We came to Paris on an extended vacation when my brother, Regent, was posted here a short time ago. So we haven't done a lot of sightseeing yet. I guess your club is something we've missed," Jess said.

"What are you doing here, anyway?" Morana asked, eyeing Regent first.

"I'm a Catholic priest, here on assignment," he said. He normally wore casual clothes these days, since he had no real reason to dress in his religious cassock.

Morana's cool features changed instantly. Her eyes widened and she froze in her seat. The expression on her face had been one of terror for about a millisecond before she hid it with a blank expression.

Jess noticed the change, as did Britt. If Morana was acting, she was damn good at it.

"I see," Morana said. "Well, in that case, I very much doubt we're related. I can't imagine being related to a priest."

Regent couldn't hide the fact that he'd been offended, which brought out the protective side of Jess. It'd give her actual pleasure to kick the woman's ass right now, but that would only upset Regent more.

Meanwhile, Morana didn't seem to give Regent's feelings another thought. "I'm out of here," she said, sounding bored, before she stood and walked away without a backward glance.

MORANA STRODE down the street as fast as she could. She needed to put distance between herself and those people. God almighty, how could a priest even want to be her brother? Was he crazy?

Her father would have an aneurysm if he knew she'd met a priest who believed he was her brother. Sinclair would try to make her stay at home. That was his modus operandi whenever he thought his baby girl vampire might be at risk. She scoffed loudly. As if she was afraid of a deluded priest, or that vampire who looked like her. Was it a trick? Why would anyone want to look like her? She had no wealth to speak of, and no real life to want to emulate. She worked at LaCave for entertainment, as well as a little extra fluff on the side, a neck bent her way, every now and then.

Still, it was worrying. Even if there was the slimmest of chances that what they were saying could be true, she couldn't see having a priest as a brother. And worse, he'd already seemed to want her as a sister, proof or not.

The fact remained that Jess Vandermire could be her twin. But, if she was also a vampire, she wasn't a regular one. Something was different about Jess, though Morana had no idea what it was.

Nearing the entrance to LaCave, Morana inhaled the scent of some fresh young things going down the ladder into the cavern in front of her. She grinned and followed them down.

BRITT DIDN'T LIKE that chick—not one bit. He didn't trust her, and he worried that Regent already seemed taken by her.

As a cop, he knew bad news when he saw it. And he'd seen plenty like her, vampire or not. He'd bet she'd been bad news long before she was ever vamped.

"Britt?" Regent said, as if he'd been reading Britt's mind. "What do you think?"

"Okay, I admit she looks like Jess," Britt said. "But, twin vampires, around the same age? Do you understand the odds of them both being twenty-nine? They'd have to have been bitten the same year. It's impossible to believe."

Jess cast a worried glance at Regent before she spoke. Britt already knew why she felt that way. She knew her brother had already fallen for this vampire, hook, line, and sinker. No matter how improbable, he honestly believed Morana was his and Jess's long-lost sister.

Unfortunately, Regent needed a reality check, and fast.

"Doesn't anything about this strike you as odd, Reej? Morana and I appear to be the same age. How could that have happened? And if she'd been created for some nefarious reason, how would anyone ever have guessed we'd show up in Paris? *We* didn't even know it ourselves until a very short while ago." Jess clamped her hands over Regent's and gently squeezed. "Doesn't any of this bother you?"

He patted Jess's hand. "Jess. We *were* adopted. We've always known that. Why do you deny she could be your twin sister?"

"It's just too convenient, Regent. We can't possibly trust her, and it might be better if we avoid her in future."

Regent looked taken aback. "I'm not sure I'm ready to do that yet."

"As a vampire, she's dangerous to you," Jess said.

Britt agreed, though he didn't say so. Surely Regent wasn't so taken with the thought of having a newfound sister that he'd take chances with a vampire.

"But if she's our sister?" Regent asked, holding his hands up hopefully.

Sensing Jess's frustration, Britt stepped into the conversation. "Regent, we can check her out, you and I. *But*, before we say the word 'trust', we need to find out more about her. I think it'd be best that you don't meet her alone in future. You should at least have one of us with you."

"But . . ."

"No buts. Please agree to this," Jess said.

Jess smiled her thanks at Britt and his heart squeezed. She was so beautiful, inside and out.

That other creature was only like Jess in one way—her looks. She didn't have Jess's heart. And for some reason, he could see through Morana. Unlike Jess, she looked conniving and cruel. Jess's inner richness and forgiveness showed through, marking her as different from her supposed sister.

Morana had an agenda, he'd swear to it. Worse, he knew he could take a stake to her and wipe her out without guilt. She exuded the same kind of evil as the vampires they took out in New York. Unfortunately, Regent's guileless hope put a damper on that possibility, and the fact that they were in another country meant he couldn't start an incident.

But if she gave him one moment's reason, Morana could kiss her ass goodbye.

Chapter Five

STILL SEATED OUTSIDE the café, Jess surveyed Britt and Regent from across the table. "Morana's obviously not that keen to claim us as her long-lost family, so I don't think we should worry about it, either."

"But what if we are related to her?" Regent asked.

"Oh, Regent, are you really that desperate for another freaking vampire in your life?" Jess asked, trying to tamp down the despair growing in her gut.

"Jess, you know I love you. But, if we have another sister, I'll want to know her too—no matter what her issues."

Jess inhaled and exhaled slowly. Regent was truly the most kind-hearted person she'd ever known. His goodness knew no bounds. But if he kept it up with this vampire, he might end up very badly hurt or worse.

Trying to be more understanding, Jess shrugged. "Will you be okay if Britt and I check into her background then? I have a contact in the French police force, someone who worked with me in New York a few years ago."

"Who is he?" Britt asked, sounding suddenly jealous. That wasn't like him at all.

"*Her* name is Veronique LaFontaine," she said and watched Britt's expression flip to embarrassment.

"If you feel you have to," Regent said.

Jess stood. "I do. And for now, will you please be careful around Morana? Don't meet her alone again. Promise me."

Regent looked a little disappointed, but he pressed a hand over his heart and said, "I promise."

"Good. Let's go, Britt."

Britt sat upright in his chair. "What? Right now?"

"Of course. The sooner, the better."

Regent drained his coffee and stood slowly, grabbing onto the side of the table as if he needed the support. Jess almost reached out to help him, but he would never have allowed that.

"Want us to walk you home, first?" she asked, forcing her voice to sound casual, not concerned.

"No. I'm fine. I always enjoy my evening stroll," he said. "I think I'll walk down the Champs-Élysées before I head home. I enjoy seeing the sights."

Jess was about to warn him about the shadows, when Regent said, "Don't worry, I'll go the long way around. I'll be sure to avoid the left side of Pont Neuf until things are clear."

She nodded. "And, I'll let you know if we learn anything from Veronique. Either way, we'll be in touch tomorrow."

"Good night," Regent said.

After he left, Jess asked the waiter for directions to the police station.

After going two blocks, Britt slowed his pace. "Did this French cop work on the vampire-hunting team while she was in New York?"

"No. She was on assignment with two other investigators in my department. I met her because she was always on night duty. The person she'd been tracking had drug deals running at night near the shipyard, and he hung out in vampire clubs."

"Did she know about you?" he asked.

"Maybe," Jess said. "I never told her, but I had the feeling she already knew there were vampires around. She didn't come right out and say it, but she dropped a few hints. I didn't validate her statements, though. Maybe I should have."

A few blocks later, they arrived at the Prefecture de Police, where Jess asked for Veronique, then showed her New York police force credentials. The officer sent the two of them down the hall with directions to Veronique's office.

Jess knocked on the doorjamb since the door was open. Veronique was leaning over some paperwork, and by the look of her dull brown hair, she'd been running her fingers through it... a lot. Same old Veronique Jess remembered. "Hello?"

The policewoman jumped out of her seat, a startled expression on her face. "Lieutenant Vandermire?"

"Actually, it's captain now," Jess said with a grin.

"Congratulations. And how wonderful to see you," Veronique said, grabbing Jess and giving her a kiss on both cheeks.

"It's good to see you too, Veronique. May I introduce my lieutenant, John Brittain."

He held out his hand, but Veronique grabbed him and kissed his cheeks, too. He looked a little flustered by that. Maybe she should have warned him. Veronique was full of life, and as good a cop as she'd ever met. In a different world, they'd have probably been good friends.

"Please," she said. "Please, have a seat."

They sat around a table covered with perps' mug shots.

"You seem to be up to your eyeballs in work, Vee," Jess said.

"You have no idea. It's crazy here lately. I don't know what is going on." She clapped her hands together. "So, what brings you two here. On the job?"

"No. Vacation, actually," Jess said. "My brother Regent was sent over here to work for the church. I think I told you he was a priest?"

Veronique nodded. "He's elderly, is he not?"

Luckily, Veronique had never met Regent in person. Jess might have told her his age, though. "Not that old, actually. Middle-aged."

Veronique frowned. "*Mon Dieu*, my memory is bad. I thought he was in his seventies."

Jess let that comment slide and hoped to hell Veronique would assume she'd made a mistake.

"What brings you here at this time of night?" Veronique asked, glancing at the clock over her door. "You may be on vacation, but you both look like you're on the job."

"We're not working," Jess said. "But we do have a favor to ask. The thing is, I met someone here who looks exactly like me. I wanted to find out if you knew anything about her?"

"You mean, you want to know if she has a record?"

Jess nodded. *That's exactly what I meant.*

Veronique gave her an odd look. "I will definitely do a search for you, if you'd like. Do you have her name?"

"It's Morana Longina." Jess dug into her pocket and pulled out a fork, making Veronique's eyebrows arch inquisitively.

"This is a piece of cutlery Britt swiped from the café where we met her tonight. She didn't eat, but she kept touching the fork. I'm not sure if you have the time or resources to check this for me. . . . But I was hoping you might." Jess sighed. "I know it's not much to go on."

"Not much at all, but you know I love a challenge," Veronique said. "I'll check EURODAC to see if anything shows on her prints."

Jess stood.

"It was nice to meet you, Monsieur Brittain." Veronique winked at him. "I have the strange feeling this won't be our last meeting."

"Honestly, we're just on vacation," Jess argued, although she understood what Veronique meant. Dyed-in-the-wool cops like her didn't take lengthy vacations. They found it too hard to leave the job behind. She clenched her teeth. She'd love to tell her friend about the dangerous shadows in the old part of the city, but if she did that, she'd have to also explain about vampires, angels, and other paranormal entities she wasn't allowed to talk about as part of the New York City Special Forces unit.

Once they were back outside again in the soft Parisian night air, Britt grabbed her hand and squeezed it. He'd dressed in civvies tonight—jeans and a T-shirt—not his fighting clothes. They probably looked like typical lovers strolling the streets of Paris as they walked along.

"How are your feet now?" she asked casually. "Do you have any residual pain or problems from your attack last night?"

"None," he said. "Though I might be getting a blister from these new shoes." He looked at her wistfully. "I wish I knew more about my Fallen abilities, Jess. That blue light comes in handy, but it'd be even better if I actually knew how it worked."

"Even though we don't understand it, it seems to help you when you most need it. That's almost as good as knowing," she said.

"For a vampire who's supposed to be dark and broody, you're pretty optimistic tonight, doll," Britt said. "And . . . on an optimistic note, why don't we go home? We have a little catching up to do."

"But what about the scenery?" she asked, pointing at the small boats moored along the Seine. She loved to torture him.

"There's only one scene I'd like to see, and that's you, naked in my arms," he whispered against her ear just as another couple passed them on the street.

"What do you say we put a rush on and get home quickly, then, handsome?" she said, still feeling the tingle of heat on her earlobe.

Minutes later, Jess locked the door and turned to find Britt already removing his shirt.

BRITT BRUSHED HIS mouth against hers, barely a touch, but it heated her instantly. He didn't mind her cool flesh, but when it became warm at his touch, it was a definite turn on.

"We've been so busy getting resettled here, we haven't had time to ourselves. We have some making up to do," he said, pushing her gently against the wall and pinning her there while he nibbled on her earlobe.

"If that's a promise to spend more time with me, I'll hold you to it," she said against his hot mouth, then licked a path to the carotid artery in his neck.

He let her go there, knowing it was erotic for her. Not that he'd stop her, if she needed some blood to maintain herself.

Groaning, he broke away from her magnificent body long enough to draw her into his bedroom. He had the biggest bed. The bed in her bunker was a super-single, another point of contention for her. She missed her king-sized bed at home, even though she only experienced it upon lying down and waking up.

He liked the way she sighed while he unzipped her black skirt and let it fall to the ground. God in heaven! She was wearing the barest of G-strings. Red! Did she know this was going to happen tonight? Maybe he wasn't the only one with plans for tonight.

"Nice," he said.

"Wait until you see the rest," she mumbled, yanking off the pale yellow angora sweater that had accentuated her firm breasts and tantalized him all evening.

She always knew how to make him crave her. And crave her he did.

Under the sweater, the red lace, see-through bra that was so flimsy it was barely there, took his breath away, and was nearly his undoing.

"I'm glad you're doing lots of shopping here," he said, barely containing his lust.

She ran her hands down his back and cupped his rump, pulling him against her. "Are we just going to stand next to the bed, or should we get more comfortable?"

"Comfort is not what I had in mind for you, my love. I intend to make you scream with pleasure."

"Wow. That'd be something, if you could make a vampire scream."

"Is that a challenge, baby?"

He took his time undressing while she eyed his body, making him grateful he'd stayed in shape. He'd always worked out, even in his darker days when he'd been close to alcoholism, before he'd been recruited to the vampire-hunting team and turned his life around.

He pulled her into bed and kissed her until all he could envision in his mind was her luscious body. He rolled on top of her, pinning her to the bed, taking his time kissing her face, her neck, every sensual spot, until she'd started purring under his ministrations.

She wasn't screaming yet—but it was a good start.

What he was doing must be working, because her eyes were turning dark and her teeth partially extended.

Sweat broke out on his back and dripped down the sides of his face, but he kept the momentum going. She wasn't helping him keep his cool by moving erotically against him. It was all he could do to hold his own.

It wasn't until the moment she screamed his name that they went over the edge together.

Sated.

Satisfied, and totally in love with this woman, he fell onto the bed beside her and pulled her luscious, naked body on top of him.

"I love you, Jess," he said. "With my heart and soul."

She nuzzled her face against his, and kissed his neck. "I feel the same way, lover. Only I can't exactly promise my soul, since I don't have much of one in the first place."

"Darling, you have more soul than most humans," he said, running his hand across her beautiful hip and down her tight rump.

"Britt, I know I'm one of the undead, but somehow, when you make love to me, I actually think I can feel my heart beating. Pounding, actually. You're amazing. I'm so thankful that we are together. You make me feel almost whole."

"You're more whole than any woman I've known."

She lifted her head, and stared at him with her beautiful, now green eyes. "And just how many women are we talking?"

He laughed. "Not *that* many. I was married, so at least one," he admitted.

"Just one?" She shook her head.

"Well, maybe two," he said, then pulled her close for another kiss. He'd never get enough of her.

Since he'd become one of the Fallen, he didn't need as much sleep. After their hot and sensual bouts of lovemaking, he often got up and took a shower, then went out for breakfast while Jess was in stasis. This morning, after exiting the shower, he stood outside her room with one hand on her door. He could open it—he had the code—but somehow seeing her in stasis in that room felt wrong. He didn't want to see her in any type of a crypt. In New York, he always waited for her to wake inside her massive bedroom. He'd sit there, waiting for the lights to slowly illuminate seconds before she'd animate. He loved her. He didn't believe she was truly dead. It didn't matter that she had no pulse.

But he didn't feel comfortable doing that here in this dungeon of a room. And he didn't think Jess would like it, either.

Finally, he pushed away from her door, letting his gaze linger there for a few seconds before stepping outside into the morning sun. Heat warmed his skin and the air was scented with some sort of floral aroma he didn't recognize. After a quick glance back at their building, he made his way to his favorite place for breakfast.

Since he had plenty of time to kill, he took his time enjoying his breakfast of sausage, eggs, and espresso before making his way to Notre Dame to meet Regent.

He entered the beautiful church, genuflected and crossed himself, then made his way to the area where Regent worked. He rapped on the massive oak door and waited.

"Come in, Britt," Regent said, crossing the room and leading Britt deeper into the old structure. "Follow me. I have another office in a mostly unused part of the church. I guess they wanted to keep me out of the way."

Britt frowned. "Why would they do that?"

"I'm beginning to wonder myself. Yesterday, I found some old texts dating back to the French Revolution when religion was outlawed. I believe it's documentation that proves a couple of Vatican sects broke off from the church and began their own form of religion right here in Paris during that decadent time when moralities were tested."

"That's all very interesting, but—" Britt looked around to make sure they were alone, before saying, "Aren't you supposed to be researching the shadows?"

Regent glanced over his shoulder. "I'm supposed to be finding a lost piece of script that links to the shadows, but so far I've had no luck. But I'm not supposed to have told you anything, so we can't talk about it here."

"Maybe there's more to it, Regent. Maybe there's something they haven't told you yet. After all, you have very specific talents and knowledge in a subject most people know little about—say, vampires?"

"If that's the case, I have the feeling we won't find out until the time is right," Regent said.

If Jess's brother was hunting for something that would put him in the line of fire, his job could become extremely dangerous. No wonder Jess wanted to be here. It didn't surprise him that she had had a sixth sense where her brother was concerned. She'd known he'd need her. And so, here they were.

Not only were there shadow creatures swirling on the streets at night, but they'd yet to come across any vampires in the city, other than Morana. He had the feeling life would get very interesting once they found the local vamp contingent.

After he left Regent, Britt walked the streets most of the day, trying to figure it all out. The more he thought about it, the more his gut reacted to Regent's chance meeting with Morana. He didn't believe in coincidence . . . which meant they really needed to find out what that woman was up to. Sure, the shadows were dangerous, but she was a vampire. They couldn't risk turning their backs on her, either.

A feeling of dread trickled into his gut when he thought of Morana Longina. And he'd learned, long ago, to trust his instincts. Something was off in Paris. He just had to find out what.

Chapter Six

THAT EVENING, BRITT sipped his coffee while Jess drank her sustenance. Though he was tempted, he avoided letting his mind wander toward more lustful thoughts. He didn't want to sidetrack his plans tonight. "Did you sleep well, doll?"

"After our romp, I slept like the dead," she said.

He rolled his eyes. "What are your plans tonight, babe?"

"I thought I'd go by and check on Regent. You coming?"

He hesitated. "Why don't I let you and Regent have some time without me tonight?"

She cast a curious look his way. "Okaay. . . and . . . what are *your* plans?" She leaned against the doorframe between the kitchen and the living room in that come-hither pose that drove his libido into full throttle instantly.

Hell. Maybe his plans to covertly spy on Morana could wait.

"Nothing big," he said, hating that he'd told her a little white lie. "But, if you have other ideas, I could change my plans." He grabbed her and pulled her onto his lap before he ran his hands up her back and into her hair, kissing her tenderly.

"Which are?" she asked.

"You're using womanly witchcraft to get to my deepest, darkest secrets aren't you?"

She laughed. "I'm a vampire, Brittain. I've certainly never been called a wanton witch."

"Well, that's not exactly how I meant it to sound either," he said.

"I'm teasing you, silly." She patted his chest, then slipped off his lap in order to pull on her boots near the front door. "As much as I'd like to take you up on your offer, I really need to check in on Regent tonight."

Of course, after their shadow encounters, Jess would need to make sure her brother was safe. Still, he knew she wouldn't like him wandering the streets alone at night.

Britt, however, needed to find out more about Morana. There was more to this situation than anyone knew. He was sure of it. So, he'd do his best to check her out. Still, the only way to be certain if she really *was* Jess's twin, would be to have their VNA tested. And the only person he'd trust to make that judgment was Dr. Sampson Case, Jess's forensic vampirologist. That was one more reason for Sampson to make a trip to Paris.

Britt waited near the café where Morana had been twice spotted by Regent. Either she'd done it deliberately or she really took this route to her job every night. If she came by tonight, he'd follow her and find out about this job of hers.

It wouldn't be easy to trail a vampire without her knowledge, but he'd learned a few techniques while on the job as a black ops vampire hunter. The air was scented tonight with heavy perfumes, colognes, and French cigarettes; they would all help hide his scent.

He waited in the darkest recessed corner of the café, where trailing plastic vines and an umbrella hid him in plain sight. He drank a glass of red wine while he waited. He'd checked his watch about ten times before he finally spotted her coming his way.

After she passed him, he slipped down the street behind her.

So far, she hadn't given any signs of noticing him. She might be going to work, considering she'd dressed in the same retro-chic garb that seemed to be her style—a mini-skirt with a loose blouse hanging low on the sides and high in the back. Her heels were red and six inches at least.

Her fingernails matched her shoes. Her hair had red tips tonight, and she was smoking. He'd never seen a vampire smoke before, but he was glad she did because he was pretty certain it masked her ability to catch his scent on the breeze.

For a while, he thought he might have given himself away, because she took a circuitous route through alleyways before descending into a debris pile that was once a set of stairs leading to a section of the city that looked like it should be condemned. He halted and slipped into a recess when she slowed near the entrance of an alley. She looked around before entering, but as far as he could tell, she hadn't spotted him. She disappeared into the side of an old brick building.

He waited a couple of seconds before following her into a tiny opening. It led into a tunnel with crusty old safety lights on the wall. He climbed down rusted steel stairs that looked like they might have once been used for tunnel repairs decades ago.

It didn't escape him that he'd most likely run into human bones down here. Dammit, he hated his phobia almost as much as he hated the bones that put him into a cold sweat. When he was a kid, Halloween skeletons had terrified him. He had no idea how or why it had started, but he still cringed at the thought of them to this day. And *real* bones were even worse.

When he hit the cave floor, he spotted the first skull, then a second and third, followed by more disarticulated bones in the muted glow of the lights. His skin turned clammy and the hair rose on the back of his neck. Of course, this was one of the many entrances to the Kingdom of Bones—his worst freaking nightmare. He shuddered and asked himself if he could actually do this. "Crap!"

Morana had slipped away while he was trying to get hold of himself. The tunnels went off in too many directions for him to guess which way she'd gone.

Just then, he heard laughter and clanking of feet climbing down the rickety stairs behind him. He waited while a group of women, most likely in their late twenties, literally descended on him.

"Hi," he said, expecting they'd give him the cold shoulder and move on without talking to him.

"Hi, yourself," one of the women said, giving Britt an interested twice-over. "You're American?" she said in perfect English, with only a hint of a French accent.

"I am. And I don't know where I'm going," he said, hoping they'd tell him what was so interesting down here.

"You're going to LaCave alone?" the female gasped. "*Mon Dieu, monsieur*, that is not wise. There are several hundreds of miles of tunnels down here. You might never find your way out again."

"It's exciting though, isn't it? It's the most popular bar in the city." A curvy blonde with heavy makeup pinned her heavily defined eyes on him. "We've been coming here since we were sixteen. The atmosphere down here is the best."

"That's what I've heard," Britt lied. "Since I don't know how to find the bar on my own, would you mind if I came along with you?"

"*Bien sur*," she said. "We'd never turn down a handsome man like yourself. Please, join us."

One of the women said something in French and they all broke into laughter. Britt didn't care if it was at his expense; he only cared about finding this mysterious club. It got discernibly darker as they moved deeper into the tunnels. One of the women turned on a halogen flashlight she'd been carrying in her pocket. The hallway illuminated ahead of them, highlighting dark eye sockets in the skulls planted in the walls—eye sockets that seemed to watch them with dark intent.

"Jesus!" he said before he realized it.

"It's spooky, isn't it?" a redhead said. "That's part of the excitement, you see?"

Hell, he didn't find it exciting. This dark and unnatural place with carefully planted skulls' unseeing eye sockets made his skin crawl.

"It's not too much farther," the blonde said. "Watch your step though. The ground is uneven ahead." She grabbed his hand and held it the rest of the way. He went along with the game.

Doing this without Jess made him edgy. Hopefully, though, she'd understand, especially if he learned something about Morana.

Before reaching the opening of the cavern where the bar was supposedly located, deep bass music reverberated through the very rock and bones themselves. His stomach twisted.

"This is it," the blonde said, excitement in her voice again. "What do you think?"

"Impressive." But all he could focus on was ignoring the skulls that watched him from the walls.

The club, situated inside a cavern, was larger than he expected. And it was lit from ceiling to floor with every kind of theatrical lighting one could imagine. A fully equipped bar built of marble and brass was located in the far right corner of the room. Throngs of people sat at tables, while others writhed on a built-up dance floor in the center of the cave.

At least eight bartenders worked the bar, and Morana was one of them. She hadn't lied about her job. One point in her favor.

She hadn't spotted him as far as he could tell, so he stayed with the group of women, who pulled him along with them to meet their other friends.

"What is your name?" the blonde who'd held his hand in the tunnel asked.

"Britt. My friends call me, Britt," he said.

"I like it," she said, pulling out her lipstick and reapplying it liberally without a mirror. He'd always been curious about how women did that without smearing it everywhere.

"What are you drinking?" he asked her and she practically purred at the offer.

"I'm having the LaCave specialty—a Longina Long Island Iced Tea. It's made with a special brand of Chinese Tea that has long-life properties."

"Speaking of Long Island, I'm from New York, myself," he said glancing at the bar and wondering what else Morana put in the iced tea that was named after her. If everyone was drinking it, it must be okay. Maybe she thought it was ironic that people believed Chinese tea could give them a longer life, when she lived forever.

"You're from New York? How exciting," the blonde said.

After they received their drinks, the others in the group introduced themselves to Britt in broken English. He couldn't possibly remember everyone's name, but he did try. After all, they were his cover.

"My name's Sylvie. Are you seeing someone?" the blonde asked point blank.

He nodded quickly. "Practically engaged."

"But you're here alone?" Her eyebrows went up suggestively.

"She had to be somewhere else tonight," he said.

"Her loss," she said. "And our gain."

He shrugged in a noncommittal way. She could think what she wanted as long as he blended into the crowd.

"Curious men are my favorite," she said suggestively, leaning closer to him.

Maybe he shouldn't have shrugged. He moved his chair slightly when she wasn't looking. There was no sense giving her ideas. He had no intention of going that far for cover.

The evening went on, with most of the women in the group laughing and telling stories about things that had gone on at work. He appreciated that they'd included him. It turned out to be a great way to watch Morana and her co-workers.

Suddenly, a firm hand closed on Britt's shoulder and he glanced up to find Jess smiling down at him, though her eyes were sparking with irritation.

"Jess." He jumped out of his seat. "What are you doing here?"

She forced a smile, but none of the humor reached her eyes. "I might ask you the same thing, lover."

Without thinking, he'd given himself away when he slid a sideways glance toward Morana who was still mixing drinks like crazy. He might as well tell the truth now. "Just doing a little surveillance. I thought you were visiting Regent?"

"I went over there, but he's in some sort of meeting tonight, so I decided to find you."

One of the women who'd been drinking too much waved at Jess as if she were a long-lost friend and urged her to take a seat.

"Thanks, but we have to go," Britt said. "It's nice to meet all of you."

The blonde pouted. "I'm sorry we didn't get to know each other better," she said, more than a little tipsy and oblivious to Jess standing next to him.

Jess glared at her, then slid a cool glance at Britt. Her arms were crossed over her chest, looking as if she'd like nothing better than to kick his butt right now. And if he wasn't mistaken, her green eyes had turned a shade darker. He'd better get her out of here before her teeth grew.

"I simply needed a cover, Jess," he said, daring to touch her elbow in an attempt to lead her away from the unwitting human who'd so stupidly hit on him in front of Jess.

Jess glanced back at the woman as they walked to the other side of the room. She remained silent for mere seconds, but it felt like hours before she said, "What have you learned?"

Morana hadn't spotted them—strike that—she hadn't given the impression of having seen them. But she probably had.

Britt still had his beverage in hand. He took a long drink and glanced around for a table to set it on.

"What are you drinking?" Jess asked him.

He held up a tall glass with a sprig of mint on the top. "Would you believe a Longina Long Island Iced Tea with some sort of special Chinese tea that promotes long life?"

"Not like she'd need any of those properties, herself."

He took another drink. "It's good, too. Besides being named after her, I've noticed Morana's the only one who mixes them." He leaned toward Jess in order to nuzzle her ear and sneak in a whispered message at the same time. "Let's go for a stroll around the room. Maybe we can get an idea of what she's up to."

"Maybe she's up to being a bartender and that's the extent of it," Jess said.

Britt pursed his lips. "You don't really think so, do you? I don't know what she's doing, but I doubt she's earning enough money to buy those clothes as a bartender."

"And—" Jess said. "Wait. How do you know how much things cost here?"

"I saw the price tags on your last few acquisitions. You left them in the living room."

"Sneaky."

"Not purposely. The price tag was on the top. The amount nearly took my breath away."

Jess laughed. "You keep forgetting, I can afford nice things if I want them."

"Still, don't you wonder how Morana is able to buy her wardrobe, considering the wages she's most likely earning here?"

She touched his hand and he instantly wrapped his fingers around hers. "Maybe she has another job, or maybe her father keeps her afloat. There could be many other ways she earns her money."

"Crap, I think she might have spotted us," he said.

"You really don't trust her, do you?" Jess said, sliding her fingers up his shirt and distracting him in the way only she could.

He kissed her long and hard.

"You and I have a thing about walls, don't we?" she said against his mouth.

He groaned, remembering their very first encounter. "Those kinds of memories can get you into trouble, lady."

"One can hope," she said in a stern voice, then slid out from underneath his arms. "Since we're in public, we'd better focus on the project at hand, since you think it's so important that you came without me."

He respected the hell out of her professionalism, even though tonight she wore a pair of designer jeans with holes in them and a sequined knitted top hung loosely over her breasts. She also wore heels, not unlike those of her doppelganger. "First time I've seen you out without your leathers."

"They are certainly more comfortable than this get-up."

"How'd you know I'd be here? And another thing—how'd you find the place?"

"I knew you'd be doing some checking on my so-called twin, over there," she said. "I know you well enough to have figured that out."

"And, finding this place?" he asked. "It's not easy to get to."

"No it isn't, but I asked around. Morana had told us the name of the bar. Once I got close, I just followed the crowd."

Just then, Morana confirmed that she had, indeed, seen them. She stepped up to them, forcing a peevish smile. "You two can't keep your hands off each other, can you?" she said. Maybe she was jealous that Jess had found love.

"Hi Morana. We were just going to come over and say hello," Jess said.

"Really?" She sounded cynical.

Jess always gave Regent credit for her partial soul and her happiness, which had increased even more since Britt came along. Britt loved being a part of her salvation. But what had Morana's upbringing been like?

If Jess and Regent really were related to this cold vampire, Britt could see how their tight relationship could be a bone of contention for Morana. She seemed to be the jealous sort, anyway.

"You've been here nearly two hours with those other women, Britt. I'm surprised you didn't come over and say hello," Morana said.

"Sorry about that. It was hard to get away."

"At least, until Jess came along, it seems," Morana said in a snide voice.

"Of course," Britt said, letting his gaze wash over Jess.

"Britt says the Long Island Iced Tea is very good," Jess added, obviously trying to decelerate the elevated tension.

Morana raised a finely shaped eyebrow at him. "Yes, it's my own creation."

"Not your typical Long Island Iced Tea," he said. "Your choice of tea is quite different. It adds an exotic flavor to the drink."

"Doesn't it though," she said.

"Are we holding you up from your job?" Britt asked, suddenly tired of playing this game. He found her sarcasm and leering stares hard to endure.

Jess jabbed him in the ribs with her elbow. "He didn't mean that, Morana. Obviously, you're on a break. Would you like to join us?" She looked around. "We can find a table, I'm sure."

"The tables are all full. That's the way they are every night. Thanks for the offer, but Britt is right. I do have to get back to work. I just wanted to ask why you showed up here."

"We're following you, of course," Britt said and forced a laugh.

Morana glared at him.

"We're not," Jess said. "Don't mind his odd sense of humor."

Morana gave Britt a hard stare, then nodded. She turned and strode back to the bar.

"Britt, why are you deliberately rude to her?"

"Easy. I don't like her."

"You don't even know her," Jess said.

"I don't have to. She gives me the creeps."

"Well, until we hear from Veronique, why don't we cut her some slack?" He could hear the unspoken words in her voice: *for Regent's sake.*

"I'll try," he said.

Her cell phone buzzed. She pulled it out of her pocket and read the text on her screen. "It's from Regent. He's not free yet, but I still think I'll wander over that way and wait for him." She looked into his eyes. "You coming with me?"

"No. You still haven't had your one-on-one visit with your brother."

"And you still don't have any dirt on Morana, do you?"

He shrugged his shoulders, then kissed her again. "You love me though, don't you?"

"I do," she said.

"I won't do anything I shouldn't," he said.

"Such as?" Jess asked, tucking her phone back into her pocket.

"Call her an evil bitch vampire."

Jess sighed. "Well, you certainly know the type."

He hated that he'd made her think that she was ever the type. "You are not an evil bitch, my love. You never have been, and you never will be."

"Knock on wood," she said. "I don't want to tempt fate." She allowed her eyeteeth to grow just a fraction and flashed them at him. "I guess these are just love toys."

"Don't tease me," he said. At least he knew how to make her feel better. "Speaking of vampires, I wonder how it is that Morana is able to hold down a job. Where does she feed?"

Jess sighed and her fangs disappeared. "I have the feeling you're going to try to find out."

"Damn straight," he said.

"Just make sure you're not her next delicacy."

"As if." He shuddered and she laughed. "Say hi to Regent for me, doll."

"I'll do that. And, Britt, don't go all undercover ops on Morana yet, okay? Maybe she really is my sister. If that's true, Regent wants us to at least give her the benefit of the doubt, as hard as that will be."

Damn it. He shrugged and nodded in weak agreement.

After Jess left, Britt hung around for a while, but his heart wasn't in it any longer. He kept thinking about Regent's feelings being hurt if he went too far.

It seemed to him that Morana's co-worker, the other bartender, was also a vampire. He had a goatee and earrings from his lobes to the tip of each ear. He wore a purple silk shirt, expensive-looking dress pants, and his blacker than black hair and heavy makeup made him look like he was mimicking the human Goths who visited the bar. But he was a Goth of a different sort.

He'd ask Jess later if she'd noticed the guy. He and Morana seemed pretty tight, too, but not in the romantic way. Partners in crime, maybe?

Britt yawned, then stretched his back. He'd had too many drinks, which was unusual for him these days. He felt a little tipsy, even. He glanced around the room, noting that the group he'd followed in had already left. That meant he'd have to trail someone else back out of the caves, so he didn't get lost.

He glanced at his watch. It was four in the morning. He'd had enough of this place for one night. Besides, Morana had disappeared into a back room a while ago. He watched the other vampire for a time, fairly certain he'd been correct about the guy, who seemed aware of his scrutiny and had become somewhat nervous. That piqued Britt's interest, but not enough to for him to think about doing anything about it tonight. He'd learned how to ID vampires while hunting the streets of New York, and he was pretty damned sure the bartender was one of them. He'd check on both of them another night.

Not knowing his way out of the tunnels, he impatiently waited for someone to leave. When no one did, he decided to backtrack and find his own way out. Just in case, he checked his cell phone for a signal. Three bars. If he got lost, he could call Jess, or the authorities, as embarrassing as that would be.

Back in the dark tunnel lined with skulls that now seemed to be grinning at him, he swiped at the instant moisture on his brow while he tried to ignore the sounds of ancient creaking bones that made it nearly impossible for him not to panic. From somewhere close by, a gust of stale air washed over him. He couldn't believe people found it exciting to be down here with millions of bones from graves that had been emptied over the centuries. Were their owner's souls resting easily? Was that why he found this so disturbing?

He picked up his pace and rounded an unfamiliar corner. Damn it! This area was darker than he remembered. Had he taken a wrong turn?

He walked several feet and as he went, it got darker and darker. Finally slowing his almost panicked steps, he considered turning back. But which way did he go? He'd passed several tunnels that branched off from this one. Oh hell! He was lost.

Running a hand along the wall in order to make his way in the dark, he couldn't help touching the ancient bones. He shivered and pulled his hand back. He'd rather trip and fall on his face. No sooner had that thought crossed his mind, he stepped on something and nearly toppled over it. What the hell? Had there been a cave-in that had left debris on the tunnel floor?

Wondering why he hadn't thought of it sooner, he yanked out his cell phone and used it as a flashlight to see what he'd gotten himself into. When he pointed the light at the ground, his stomach instantly balked and he swallowed hard.

He'd nearly tripped over a body sprawled on the cave floor in front of him. "This is *not* happening," he said, his teeth glued together while the woman's dead eyes stared blankly at the ceiling and the stench of blood nearly made him puke.

JUST BEFORE MIDNIGHT, Regent left Notre Dame. The meeting tonight had been a surprise, and it had lasted for hours. Two cardinals and several priests had attended in a room at the back of the church. He'd never expected to be privy to the kind of information that had been shared tonight, but he'd finally learned the whole truth about why they'd brought him here. For the first time, he was glad to be one of the chosen. They needed everyone they could get.

One item discussed hadn't been a surprise to him. As a priest, he knew there'd been a papal palace in France. The Palais des Papes, or the Palace of the Popes in Avignon, had hosted popes for more than three hundred and fifty years in this country. The building was now a national museum. Given the information he'd learned tonight, he had to question the original reason for building the palace in France. According to the church's historical records, vampire outbreaks had occurred in Europe during the time of the palace's construction, and during the French Revolution, there'd been a concerted effort to rid the country of the Catholic Church and religion itself. The think-tank of priests he'd met tonight had hinted that evil entities were currently attempting to recreate the same state that had existed during the French Revolution. A takeover of humanity by evil beings. Bloodless, cold monsters that had conjured shadows to invade every nook and cranny of civilization. No door could hold them back. Nothing but religious buildings, running water and iconography could even slow them down. The only safe havens in the past had been the churches, although they learned that some Parisians had starved to death inside their safe zones back then.

Most of the priests had never encountered anything like the creatures that were now building forces inside Paris. If the missing script had been able to fight off the evil centuries ago, no wonder it was so important that they find it now. Regent had also seen the shadows when he strolled the city at night, though it seemed that his being a priest had kept them at bay. For now. They simply slipped into the cracks whenever he neared them.

That's why he was here. He'd assumed as much when he arrived and spotted his first shadow. After all, he was most likely the foremost authority on paranormal entities within the priesthood. But even if they were counting on his expertise on vampires, the shadows were something else—something he didn't understand. He had no idea of the scope of the looming cataclysm facing the city, but the situation must be dire, given the important people in this room tonight.

He took a deep breath and hoped to heaven that things weren't as bad as he suspected. After the session ended, he strode away from the church before sending a text to Jess, agreeing to meet her at the same café where they'd met with Morana. It would be unlikely they'd see her tonight. It was late, and she'd be at work.

Jess was already there when he arrived.

"Regent," Jess said, and he did a double take. "Whoa, Jess. If your hair were different, I'd have thought you were Morana. That's not your usual style of dress."

Jess glanced down at her clothes and waved at them in a dismissive way. "I got these so I'd blend into the bar scene where Morana works," she said.

Regent's heart quickened in hope. "You were there?"

"Only because I figured that's where Britt had gone."

"And, had he?" Regent asked.

She sighed. "Oh yeah, he doesn't trust her for a second. As a matter of fact, he's still there right now. I don't know if he's doing the right thing, but I've learned to trust his instincts. I guess it can't hurt to find out more."

Regent dropped onto the metal café chair, looking mentally exhausted. When the waitress came, he ordered an espresso.

"You sure you want an espresso this late at night?"

"After the meeting I had tonight, I don't think I'll be able to sleep for a week," he said.

"What's going on?" Concern etched into her features.

"For one thing, I've learned more about the shadows," he said, glancing over his shoulder. "I can't talk here, though. I've been sworn to secrecy." He sat and thought for a minute. "Come to my apartment later. We should have enough seclusion there." Though he still wondered if he was being monitored by the church. *A definite possibility given what he'd learned tonight.*

Jess glanced around. "So, Reej, I'm guessing you've learned why you're here."

He nodded. He and his sister were always on the same wavelength. "I think so, and for once, I'm in agreement with this posting, even if it does scare the life out of me."

His team of highly educated priests had some serious issues to take care of, but for the time being, he couldn't divulge everything he knew. He could, however, tell Jess enough to help her figure out what the shadows were. Besides, she'd need to know in order to stay safe.

He took a deep breath and considered telling her another tidbit of news he'd garnered, something he'd learned about their adoption. She wouldn't like it.

He cleared his throat. "Jess, yesterday, I contacted our family law office. You know the same one that Mom and Dad's family used for generations . . ."

"Why did you do that?" she asked.

"I figured they might still have a record of our adoption. After all, they've been serving Vandermires for a very long time."

"And?"

"They did some digging, and found the records. They told me where we came from originally."

Jess frowned at him. She always seemed to know when he was holding back. "Well, dear brother, spill it."

"We weren't born in the U.S."

Her mouth dropped open. The same way his had, when he'd been told.

"What does that mean?"

His espresso arrived, steaming hot. But he drank most of it in one gulp. "We were born in Rome."

Jess stared at him for what seemed an eternity before she said, "You've *got* to be kidding."

"I'm afraid not," he said, rubbing the back of his neck and staring into the tiny cup left with nothing but crema. "We were born in Europe. That makes the possibility of Morana actually being our sister a lot more feasible."

He lifted his gaze and saw the realization in Jess's eyes. She obviously didn't like his news one bit.

Fear that they knew nothing at all about their lives before the adoption slithered in his gut. Why had they been separated by continents? And who would split up twin girls?

MORANA FINISHED her shift at the bar early, leaving Britt behind in the club. Usually, she hung around and made sure everything was done to her satisfaction, but not tonight. She wanted to give Britt the slip. She had Jess Vandermire on her mind and she couldn't think straight. That never happened to her and she didn't like it.

Normally, she'd cruise Paris for a few hours before sunlight, then head home to her secure room in the basement of Sinclair's simple-looking old farmhouse. But it was far from simple. It had levels she had yet to access.

Why would her adoptive father have hidden chambers below their century-old home? And why didn't she remember growing up? She had no idea what her childhood had been like, what she'd done, where she'd lived. As long as she could remember Sinclair had been giving her a drug to help her age, then another to keep her calm enough to interact with humans. Had those concoctions also taken away her memories? She had a brief snatch of something every now and then, but nothing concrete.

She'd forgotten to ask how old Jess and Regent were when they were adopted. She'd put that on her agenda for the next time she ran into them. And damn it all, she hated that they seemed to be fixated on her. She hadn't appreciated Britt and Jess coming to her place of work. Especially since Jess's human boyfriend had snuck in with a group, obviously hoping to spy on her. She'd seen him the second he stepped inside her place. And she'd make sure he'd be sorry for his devious attempt.

She blew out a breath and adjusted her hair just as a tall, long-necked brute walked toward her on the sidewalk. She could practically see his pulse working his carotid artery from here. He smelled a little too strong of French cologne, but she was used to that.

Vampires in France didn't take blood from humans anymore. Or, at least, they weren't supposed to. Fuck that!

She stepped closer to the light so he'd see her figure, and she pushed her mouth into pouty fullness. He smiled at her. His mistake.

"Evening, handsome," she said, realizing she'd been conversing with Jess and Regent so often, she'd taken to speaking English more often than French.

"Hello, beautiful," he replied in French. He'd been drinking. Funny that the cologne had masked that fact until he got closer. Usually, she'd smell alcohol a long distance away.

He was even bigger and brawnier close up. Morana smiled at him and lured him to a dark corner of the street with a beckoning finger.

Most likely he thought her a prostitute, but she didn't care. He was a means to an end.

The human grabbed her breast without even asking her name. Would Jess be shocked by her behavior? She hoped so. For some reason, she wanted to be the exact opposite of the woman who looked enough like her to be her twin. She doubted Jess had ever done anything this dirty. Morana smiled at that thought, causing the human to grunt and start feeling her up harder, no doubt assuming the smile was for him. He was no more than a pig in rut to Morana, but he was also a source of hot, delicious blood.

He'd just planted a hand between her legs and had started moving up to a place that he assumed would be hot and ready for him. He'd have been in for a surprise if he'd actually made it that far. She pulled him against her and bent his neck as if to kiss it. The fool was so willing. And so very, very stupid.

Chapter Seven

EVEN THOUGH HE'D seen his share of dead bodies, Britt recoiled at the sight of the glassy eyes and torn flesh near his feet. Her thorax had been ripped open and bared for all to see. Her arms had been slashed from wrist to elbow, showing gut-wrenching views of sinew and bone, and by the blood saturating her clothing in the lower abdomen area, he was pretty sure she'd been slashed down there, too.

Worse, it was the blonde woman he'd been drinking with in the club. The one who'd had the hots for him. What was her name? It escaped him right now. A wave of dizziness warped through him. What the hell? He'd been dizzy ever since he left the club. That wasn't like him at all.

The light from his cell phone flashed off and he nearly dropped it while fumbling to get it back on again. Weird sounds reverberated in the dark tunnel; scuttling sounds and the creaking of stone in the walls intermittently broke the eerie silence when a vehicle drove on the street overhead.

He had a strong feeling of another presence in the area. It was as if someone was standing just beyond the circle of light his tiny cell phone had created. The killer?

Meanwhile, he heard footsteps coming down the tunnel behind him. Fumbling with his cell phone again, he managed to get the light back on.

He waved the light back and forth while leaning heavily against the freaking bones in the wall. If he staggered now, they'd think he was drunk. Sweat broke out on his forehead and he felt nauseated. "Stop. Don't come any closer."

If he was in New York, he'd have this crime scene in hand. But here in Paris, he didn't even know the emergency phone number. Could he get the operator by dialing zero? He felt like an idiot. An ill-equipped, supposedly tough-cop-slash-idiot.

To his surprise, it was the police moving toward him with a very bright flashlight now shining in his eyes.

"Arretez!"

Britt held up his hands. "Do you speak English?" he asked. "I'm a cop from New York City. I was trying to find my way out, and I just came upon this dead woman."

"Don't move," the officer said in slow English. Below the bright light, Britt could just make out the business end of a handgun pointed at him.

His gut twisted. Great. Just great. And how did they know to come here? He didn't have to be a cop to know he was the immediate suspect. Worse, he'd also been seen spending part of the evening with this woman and her group. Her name swam around in his cortex, but wouldn't surface. What was wrong with him?

The police officer shouted something at him in French this time.

"English!" Britt said louder this time. *"Anglais!"*

He heard a female voice behind the officer who held the spotlight on him.

When the officer scanned the corpse at his feet, Britt also looked down. The light from his cell phone hadn't allowed him to see the complete scene with such clarity. And again, his head started to spin.

He was standing on bloodied ground inside the crime scene. He fought to keep from passing out. God almighty, he had no idea what was going on.

Veronique LaFontaine stepped forward with a smaller flashlight of her own. She shouted orders at the officer in French, and the cop lowered his gun.

"Mr. Brittain? Is that you?" she asked.

He sighed. "It is."

"What are you doing here?" she asked in a slow and casual way that proved he'd been right. He was definitely suspect number one.

"I was checking out the underground bar. I'd just decided to head back home, when I became lost and stumbled across this poor woman. How is it you got here so fast? I just found her myself," he asked.

"Do you know her?" Veronique asked, avoiding his question.

Britt hesitated and inhaled deeply. "In a way. I met her tonight in the club. In fact, I spent a couple of hours with this woman and her friends."

"What is her name?" Veronique's monotone French accent was starting to irritate him. He'd been on this end of the guilty stick before, and he'd been innocent then, too. But he knew this could go very badly for him, especially in a foreign country.

Veronique pulled out a small pad and began writing. "You haven't told me her name," she pressed.

He racked his stunned brain. It was as if the drinks had done something to his mind. Yet, he didn't think he was drunk. "It's . . . Michelle. No, Sylvie, I think. Yes, that's it."

Veronique suddenly looked disturbed. She didn't like the fact that Britt knew the woman's name. Hell, if he was in her position, he'd be thinking the same damned thing. Guilty.

"Can I move yet?" he asked.

"One moment," she said. "The forensic team will be here very quickly. What do *you* think happened here?" Veronique continued.

"I think someone killed her," he said dryly. He knew better than to antagonize the only person who could help him in this situation, but goddammit, right now, he couldn't help it.

"Did you see anyone else in the vicinity when you found her?"

"No."

"Did you hear anyone else?"

"No." But he had the feeling someone was there.

"Why do you think you didn't run into someone else?"

"I have no frigging idea."

"Could it have been because this isn't the tunnel that leads out of the club?" Her voice was soft. Too soft.

"I told you, I got lost on the way out, okay?" He inhaled deeply and rubbed the back of his head.

The forensic team arrived shortly after that, and the interrogation was halted. Britt waited while all of the pictures were taken and evidence retrieved before he could move out of the way. He had to leave his shoes behind as evidence.

"I'm afraid I'll have to take you in," Veronique said.

"Kind of figured that," he grunted, but didn't try to overstress his innocence. That would make him look even guiltier.

Veronique drove him to the station wearing only his socks, but didn't make him sit in the cage. She remained quiet most of the way.

"Do I get one phone call?" he asked, feeling rather stupid since he didn't have an effing clue about Parisian law.

"Of course. But wait until we get to the station, please."

"Sure." He sighed.

If only Jess had stayed with him. He was beginning to think he didn't belong in France. First, he'd been attacked by shadows, and now, he'd been implicated in a murder. What the hell? He looked at his black socks, now covered in dust and probably bone particulates from the tunnels under the city. A shiver slid down his back. He fought the urge to pull off his socks and toss them out the window. That would only make him look even guiltier.

"Why do people like to hang out in that grisly mortuary down there?" he asked.

"Pardon?"

"You know. Cataphiles?" He ran a hand through his hair. "What's the allure down there in that grisly tomb of a club?"

"It's a tourist attraction, *monsieur*, as I'm sure you are well aware. We try to think of the bones with respect."

She had no idea how much he hated bones. Had all of those people—the ones who'd been buried in graveyards since the year twelve hundred—expected to end up as part of a wall in the catacombs of the city? Not likely. The idea of rotting bodies falling out of their graves centuries before freaked him out, but seeing the dried-out bones in the walls had really messed him up.

"I meant no disrespect to the dead," he said, because there were obviously worse things coming out of the walls in this city.

"How long have you known Jess?" Veronique asked, changing the subject. And for once, he was glad she'd stopped asking about the dead woman. Or was this just another approach?

"We've been partners for the past three years. She recruited me."

"And what were you doing before that?"

Ah, double-hell! He should have seen this question coming. "I was a taxi driver."

Veronique stopped at a red light and frowned at a driver swerving erratically past them. "Captain Vandermire recruited a taxi driver as a member of her unit? That's a little strange, *n'est-ce pas?* What special talents do you have?"

If he could talk about vampires right now, he'd fill her in completely, and she might understand him a lot better. But he was sworn to secrecy by the force. "I actually was a cop before that."

Any chance she'd let that tidbit go?

"A cop turned taxi driver? I'm confused." She beeped her horn, and dove into the heavily used traffic circle near the Arc de Triomphe. This had New York City's horrible traffic beat by a mile.

"I was wrongfully accused of something. My name was cleared, and I returned to the force."

"Accused of what?"

Her inquisition style impressed him. She was soft-spoken, conversing with him in intimate tones, making him feel as if he could tell her anything. He imagined that many a poor sap fell for her superb technique. But not him.

He gritted his teeth and remained silent. She eyed him again and said a little more sternly. "Accused of what?"

"Murder." Crap. Might as well hand her the nails for his coffin. "But I was innocent."

"Yet you lost your job over it? I'm wondering if you were truly innocent, *monsieur*, or you simply had friends in high places?"

"I think I'll keep my mouth shut until I get a lawyer," he said. He should have done that sooner, but given their connection with Jess, he'd actually thought he might be able to trust her to believe him.

Veronique's hazel eyes held a sharpness he hadn't noticed before. She might be a friend of Jess's, but that didn't mean a thing when it came to him. He'd been found at the scene of a crime, and right now, he was her prime suspect.

Britt didn't wait. He pulled out his cell and called Jess.

JESS ENTERED THE Prefecture de Police with Regent in tow, asking for Veronique when they got to the front desk. They found her in her office going over her notes. When she lifted her head to look at them, Jess's muscles tensed.

"Father Vandermire, I imagine?" She got up and shook Regent's hand while eyeing him suspiciously. "I'm sorry, Father. I expected you to be older."

Regent pulled his hand back and shifted uncomfortably before shooting a nervous glance at Jess. "It's nice to finally meet you, Captain LaFontaine. Jess has told me so much about you." He cleared his throat. "I think I'll wait in the outer office while you ladies talk." He turned and left her without looking back.

"Have a seat, Captain Vandermire."

Uh-oh. No more first-name basis. This didn't look good for Britt.

Jess sat. "What's going on, Vee? Britt says he stumbled across a body in the tunnels, and that you think he's the killer."

Veronique brushed back her shoulder-length hair. "I wish I still smoked," she said, avoiding the obvious question.

"I was with him earlier, you know," Jess said.

Veronique's obvious fatigue shifted to interest. *"C'est vrai?"*

Jess nodded.

"Why didn't Monsieur Brittain inform me of this?"

"Maybe he forgot about it? I left him at the club to go see my brother."

Regent had moved into the hallway to wait for her, but they could both see him through the window in Veronique's office.

"I'm sure you realize your alibi doesn't work very well for him."

Jess's gut spiraled into a dive. "It wasn't meant to be an alibi. Britt is one of the top police officers on the New York City Force. He doesn't kill people. He saves them."

"Except when he was accused of murder and kicked off the police force, apparently," Veronique said in a cool, questioning way.

"He didn't kill anyone. The person wasn't even really...dead." Crap, she couldn't believe she'd just divulged that. The fact was, the person hadn't really been alive to start with. He'd been a vampire all the time. But she couldn't very well tell Veronique that.

"I'm confused. How could this be? How could a cop be accused of murder if the person wasn't dead?"

"Well, he appeared dead, you see."

"He was in a coma?"

"Not exactly, but something like that."

Veronique threw her pen onto the desk, and Jess froze. This conversation was going south, fast.

While Veronique rubbed a hand over her face, Jess stretched her neck back and looked at the ceiling, noting it was full of pencils. Veronique had been throwing things, too.

"The way things look right now, I'm afraid your friend, Monsieur Brittain, is going to have to stay here."

"You're making a mistake, Vee. Britt did not kill that woman."

"And you know this, how?"

"I know him. He's not a murderer."

Veronique shook her head. "Good. Hopefully, the evidence will prove him innocent. Until then, he stays here."

Jess clamped her teeth together. She had little recourse. It went against protocol, but she was going to find out if she could share some very, very controlled information with the French Captain. She stood and pulled out her cell phone. "Do you mind if I make a phone call to my boss? There's something you need to know, but I can't tell you unless I get permission."

Veronique nodded, but she was frowning. "I knew there was something more going on here," she said.

Jess talked to the chief for about fifteen minutes in the hallway. He was reluctant at first, but given the fact that Britt was in serious trouble, he decided the truth might help. "But make sure you swear her to secrecy, understand? We can't have this getting out," the chief said.

"Understood, sir," Jess said and hung up.

She returned to the office and shut the door behind her, leaving Regent in the hall where he preferred to wait.

Veronique sat with her elbows on her desk. She'd shoved her hair back behind her ears, and had a fresh pen in her mouth like it was a cigarette.

"If I share secret information about the New York police department, can you keep it between us?" she asked.

Veronique yanked the pen out from between her teeth. "Possibly. It depends on what you're going to tell me."

Jess sighed. "I hope you agree, because I'm putting more than one person's ass on the line by sharing this with you." Then Jess proceeded to give her a bare bones rundown of their black ops secret unit of vampire hunters in the New York City Police Department. She told her Britt's ex-partner had been a vampire. Britt couldn't have killed him because technically, he was already dead.

Veronique's expression didn't change. She took in the information with a blank countenance that surprised even Jess.

Jess considered the fact that Veronique might think she was insane. That wouldn't help Britt, either.

She had no recourse. She lowered her head and let her teeth grow and her eyes darken. But when she raised her head to prove there were vampires, Veronique was smiling.

Chapter Eight

STANDING IN ONE of the tunnels, Morana waited at the back of the crowd. The scent of blood permeated the air. The police had stopped her patrons from leaving, taking statements, before letting anyone pass.

She looked around. Where was her co-worker, Diesel? The scent of blood would be too strong for most vampires to handle without giving away their true nature, so she hurried back to the bar to warn him to stay inside LaCave until it was safe.

She pulled the bar doors shut behind her and looked around the place. Diesel wasn't here. Strange. She was sure he'd been at the bar when she'd left. In fact, everything should have been cleaned up by now. But it wasn't.

She started jamming dirty dishes in the dishwasher angrily.

If the police didn't manage to finish up before sun-up in two hours, she'd be staying the night here. But that was fine. There were many secret passages—places no humans could find—and she'd set herself up with a little security nest years ago, just in case. On the other hand, if they were monitoring who came and went, she'd have to leave via the same route as the humans.

She pushed the button on the commercial dishwasher and set it to work, then put her special blend of tea away in the locked vault. When she turned to wipe off the countertop, Diesel was sitting on a stool, staring at her.

She didn't react. It took a hell of a lot to scare her. "Where the shit have you been?" she asked.

"I might ask you the same."

The way Diesel's spiky blue-black hair swept off to the side always reminded her of a cartoon character. "I came back to warn you not to go into the tunnel. There's a dead girl down there and a lot of blood."

Diesel looked coldly into Morana's eyes. "How is it you can handle the scent of all that blood without giving yourself away to the cops?"

"If I told you, I'd have to kill you," she said, making an attempt at humor.

He didn't catch on to humor easily.

"Seriously, Morana. Do you have some trick that I don't know about? If you do, you really should share. Aren't I your friend?"

Not that good a friend, buddy. "If I had some deep, dark secret, of course I'd share," she lied. She was good at lying.

"Riiiight," Diesel said, dragging the word out in a way that told her he didn't believe a word of it. Maybe he was smarter than she thought.

Diesel leaned over the bar then glanced back over his shoulder, most likely to make sure the room was empty. "How was she killed? Did a vamp do it?"

"How should I know? I didn't get that close," she said. "Sometimes humans are worse ghouls than us. They can't wait to get a look at a gruesome corpse. Besides, I was pretty far back. I just came here to warn you."

"Do you think the cops will question us?" he asked.

"Probably."

"What about the other bartenders, and everyone else in the club?"

She pulled at the gold ring at the top of her ear. "Too late. Everybody's gone. The killer, too, most likely," she said, eyeing him suspiciously.

Diesel slapped a bejeweled hand onto the bar. His fingers bore pewter rings of the most descriptive sort. Skulls and crossbones, types of metal that glistened like oil. "Fix me a drink, will you?" he said, gruffly.

Morana glared at him. This show of bravado was unusual for him. *And it's not like he can't make his own drink.* "The cops could walk in here at any moment. Do you really think you should be sitting here, drinking a glass of warm blood?"

"I'm thirsty. I'll hide it if they come in."

His eyes were getting blacker and his fangs had started to protrude.

She'd have to weigh things out. Of course, they could always explain away the vampire trappings as makeup for his nightshift. The blood, however, wouldn't be so easily explained.

"Oh hell, all right. I'll get it for you." She went to the cavern wall and opened a locked panel that was almost invisible to the naked eye. She yanked out a bottle of blood and poured two fingers into a glass, then slid it toward him. "Down it!"

He drank quickly while she closed the panel. As soon as he finished, he reached over the bar, opened the dishwasher, and shoved the glass onto the top rack, then turned it on again.

He hadn't finished too soon. Almost immediately afterward, the police came in, asking questions. Diesel had a drop of blood on his lip and Morana wiped her own to tip him off.

He caught on and swiped his mouth clean.

"Good evening," Morana said to a tall, slim detective with blond hair and blue eyes. The thing she liked best about tall men was that their necklines were columns of muscle, with arteries just waiting to be tasted. This man's neck was especially long and lovely. She'd have liked nothing better than to sink her teeth into him while he screwed her brains out.

"*Bonjour, madame,*" he said.

"It's *mademoiselle, cherie,*" she replied, making a flush rise up his neck. Hmmm, maybe she'd get to taste that neck, after all.

"Have you heard about the murder in the tunnel?" he asked.

"We were told that there was someone dead out there, but we have no idea who it is," Morana said. "Right, Diesel?"

He nodded quickly.

The cop described the dead woman. She realized it was the blonde who'd been making a play for Britt before Jess turned up.

"I know who you mean. She was effervescent," Diesel said. "And, yes, we probably both waited on her at the bar. She was very thirsty."

"Did you see her sitting with a tall, dark-haired man this evening?"

Morana whipped her head around to stare at the cop again. She knew exactly who he was talking about. "You mean, John Brittain?" she asked, maybe a little too innocently because Diesel narrowed his eyes and glared at her.

The officer glanced at her before turning his attention back to his notepad. "Exactly. Do you know him?"

"I know his name, at least. And yes, he was with a group of partiers. He spent most of his time talking to a blonde woman who fits your description. You didn't mention whether she had big . . . ?" She held her hands up as if to cup her breasts.

"Yes, that's the one," he said, flushing again. She read his nametag. It was Bourgeois.

"Did they seem to be a couple?" he asked.

"I don't know. He spent quite a while with her," Morana said, avoiding the bit about his friendship with her own possible twin sister.

She certainly didn't want to implicate herself in any way. Being arrested and stuck in a cage with the possibility of sunlight flowing in during the day wouldn't be good for her skin.

"Where are the other bartenders?" Bourgeois asked.

"They always leave an hour before closing," she said. "Diesel and I finish up the last hour alone."

"We will need their names, as well," the detective said.

"If you give me your email address, I'll send them to you, as soon as I can," she said. "It'll take me some time to gather them up."

He looked like he'd balk at that suggestion. She narrowed her gaze on him for a second, coming close to showing her stubborn side. She didn't have time to do office work. It was getting too close to dawn.

He waved his hand to dismiss the urgency. "That'll be acceptable," he said.

He grilled both of them for a while longer, but since they had no further information to offer, he finally turned to go.

She shared a relieved glance with Diesel, just before the officer paused near the doorway. Suddenly, he made his way back and held out a hand to her. She betrayed nothing while he handed her his card. "My email address," he said. "And my phone number."

She smiled at him coyly. "Yes, thank you. I'll definitely get back to you."

He looked her up and down, his gaze resting on the curvaceous outline of her breasts. "Please do that."

After he left, Diesel shook his head in disgust. "Christ, he was practically salivating over your chest. Were you compelling him?"

"No. And for your information, I don't have to compel men to make them notice me." She pushed up her breasts and inhaled. "And, I'm great in the sack."

"Well, since I'm not into your type, I didn't notice," Diesel said, sounding miffed. He'd had a crush on her since day one, and she knew it. She liked having a panting vampire at her beck and call. She'd have sex with him some day. But for now, he was too useful as a wanting and willing best friend. Up to this point, she'd never actually had sex with another vampire. She imagined they'd have pretty impressive stamina, but she didn't want to share her special blood with any of them.

"I'm going to bed," Diesel said, as if he couldn't bear another minute in her presence. She grinned again. Oh yes, she'd have him lapping at her if she allowed it.

They needed to leave. She knew the police would be monitoring the place, and if they hung around, the cops would be curious. She didn't need any more cops sniffing around her bar.

"C'mon Diesel, let's leave together," she said. "We need to let the police see us exit the tunnel."

"How do you know they're watching the place?"

She tipped her head at the other vampire and shook her head. He could be a little slow-witted at times. "Oh, they're watching. And, they will be for a while. So don't get too thirsty over the next little while or you'll be caught."

Diesel frowned at her. "I didn't kill that girl!"

"Okay, take it easy. I'm just trying to protect you."

He slammed the club door shut and locked it behind them. "Sometimes, I could really dislike you," he said.

She reached over and slid one hand along his upper thigh. "You don't mean that."

She heard his teeth gritting. Poor bastard.

BACK AT THE precinct, Jess was still waiting for Veronique to appear shocked or afraid at the sight of her vampirism. Instead, the captain merely picked up the phone and dialed.

"Don't forget. You promised to keep this secret," Jess said, eyeing Veronique as she waited for someone to answer the phone at the other end.

"Calm yourself, Jess. You'll understand why I'm doing this in a moment." A moment later, someone obviously came on the line. Veronique spoke quickly and it sounded to Jess as though Veronique had summoned someone to her office.

Jess quickly reverted back to her human form when the office door opened. She'd deny anything she'd told Veronique, if she had to.

A ruddy-faced, plump man with thick shrub-like hair entered and shut the door behind him. *"Oui?"*

"Pierre Sirois, I want you to meet Jess Vandermire. She works for a special unit of the New York City police force."

Jess was about to deny everything when Pierre turned his gaze on her and his eyes went directly to her mouth. Was he checking for fangs?

"What's going on, Vee? You promised secrecy."

"This is a secret *we're* also about to share, my friend," she said. "We have a very similar unit to yours. Pierre here is my second in command."

"Non!" Pierre said. "You're kidding me. You have a vampire unit in the United States, *aussi?*"

Jess inhaled deeply. She'd only been sanctioned to talk to Veronique about this, but if they had the same kind of unit, it would be a wonderful opportunity for the two countries to share intelligence. "I'm asking you to keep this in the strictest of confidence," she said to Pierre.

He nodded vigorously. He looked almost excited at the prospect.

"Yes, of course. And we would ask the same of you."

Jess nodded. Sure, vampires came from Europe, but she'd honestly never considered that another police force might have a similar unit. Why hadn't she considered it? When she got home, she'd definitely create a task force to find other units like this in the world. She hated being at this kind of disadvantage.

"I wanted to talk to you about it when I was in New York," Veronique said. "I thought you might be working on such a project, but I wasn't sure enough to risk it."

"I wish you had. Think of the intelligence we could have shared."

"*Oui*, but we have stringent rules about that. The promise of reciprocity changes things, now."

"The thing is, John Brittain is my lieutenant," Jess said. "He's the best human vampire-hunter in North America. He has abilities that are unique."

"And they are?"

"I cannot share that information with you. Let's just say, he'd never murder a human."

"So you also think this was a vampire killing?" Veronique asked. Jess didn't like the way Veronique asked the question. It was almost as if she suspected Jess, herself.

"I'm afraid I have no idea. I haven't seen the body," she said, making sure her voice held enough contempt to warn Veronique not to push her too far.

"*Oui, je comprends*. But it's the gruesome nature of the killing that makes the vampire unit interested in what's going on in the catacombs."

"On the phone, Britt told me the woman was sliced open with precision. Vampires aren't known for using knives," Jess said. "And I can tell you that Britt is definitely not a vampire."

Veronique nodded. "I agree. He doesn't have the traits I look for."

Jess wondered what those traits were, but she doubted Veronique would share, so she didn't bother to ask. "Then, why do you think vampires might be involved?"

Veronique sighed. "The catacombs hold power over people. We have to consider they might also be a haven for other dark entities. With that in mind, we keep our eyes and ears open whenever something unusual happens down there."

The words *other dark entities* made Jess think about the shadows. Was Veronique's team aware of them, as well?

She had to keep that a secret for now. In order to tell the whole story, she'd have to admit that Britt, the progeny of a fallen angel, had managed to save himself from the horrible injuries the shadows had caused him.

"Are there other evil entities besides vampires down there?"

Veronique's expression quickly became closed and her mouth pursed. "Probably not."

"But you hinted earlier that there might be."

Veronique's face screwed up. "There's something about the tunnels lately. It's a gut feeling on my part—something feels wrong. It's not very scientific or even professional, if you want to think of it that way. But, sometimes, I wonder if there are other dark things lurking down there. I've tried to convince the Prefecture de Police de Paris that we should close the catacombs. Stop the tourists' visits. But no one will listen to me. The business of the catacombs is too lucrative, and the more we try to stop cataphiles from going down there, the more cachet it has."

Even though Jess understood that, right now she was more concerned about Britt's situation. "Do you honestly believe Lieutenant John Brittain murdered that woman?" she asked, making sure Veronique remembered his rank.

Veronique rubbed her eyebrow and stared at the file on her desk. "I'm sorry, but until I have more evidence, I must hold him."

Jess inhaled and gripped the sides of her chair. "Then we're not going to get along," she said. She started to rise.

Veronique held out a hand to stop her. "But what about sharing information?"

"Sorry, Vee, but as long as my lieutenant is wrongfully accused, there'll be no sharing of anything. And if you don't release him soon, there'll never be an arrangement between our units. I would have thought my credibility and the fact that I just told you the truth about my unit, might create an understanding between us. But the fact that you still insist on holding a cop, the most honest person I know, is cause for reassessment. I'm not sure I can trust you."

Pierre shifted in his seat and his anxious expression turned on Veronique.

Obviously, Jess had information they badly needed.

"Let's not be too hasty. We are comrades in arms. We fight the beasts. We should really work together," he said.

Jess shook her head vehemently. "Nope. I'm done here."

She lurched to her feet and strode to the door. Before she'd yanked it fully open, Veronique had cleared her throat and jumped up to meet

Jess near the door. "Jess, you're putting me in a very bad situation."

"No, I'm not. If you don't show some faith and trust, all thoughts of our working together are over."

"*Merde!* Take him, then. But I want to see him here tomorrow. Maybe he saw someone else interacting with the woman during the evening."

The muscles in Jess's shoulders released a little tension. "You've made the right call, Vee. Pierre. Please release Britt right away."

Veronique walked to the door. "Follow me. We'll go together."

Pierre's expression had transitioned from worry to relief. They obviously had something big going on and needed help—she'd bet her fangs on it. But since they weren't ready to tell her about it yet, she'd use it to her advantage to spring Britt from jail.

"Everything okay, Jess?" Regent asked, as they walked out into the hall.

"Yes, we're going to get Britt now. Why don't you come with us?"

He looked tentatively at Veronique for a second, then nodded.

Jess touched Regent's shoulder. He stood up and, together, they followed Veronique. There was no sense trying to hide himself and his youth. Vee had already seen him and her curiosity had subsided. It wasn't as if she didn't have more pressing matters on her mind.

In the holding area, Britt sat inside a nine-by-nine cell. Jess and Regent waited impatiently for Veronique to open the door, but she seemed to take forever to find the right key. Britt's head was tipped back against the cement wall and his eyes were closed, his mouth an angry thin line when the door creaked open.

Jess's tight shoulders relaxed just a little when he took the shoes she'd brought, at his request. His feet were bare and his socks were balled up on the bench beside him.

"What about the charges?" Jess asked Veronique, as Britt stepped into his footwear without putting his socks on again. That was odd.

"I haven't actually filled out any paperwork," Veronique admitted.

That meant Britt had never been formally charged. She could let him go without a shitload of paperwork. Had they been planning to release him for lack of evidence anyway? Could she have just been manipulated into giving them information when hadn't had to?

Her jaw tensed.

She had to face it. She'd likely been played. And that meant they were desperate. But what was behind that desperation? The shadows? Or something worse?

Chapter Nine

AS THEY LEFT THE precinct, Jess bit her lip against saying something she probably shouldn't. Britt looked somewhat frayed around the edges. It had to be hard on him, being accused again of a murder he had nothing to do with.

Even though he didn't seem affected by his incarceration, she knew better. He was a good cop, who could keep his emotions in check when he needed to. And almost as if he wanted to prove that he was okay, Britt dominated the conversation as the cab drove them back to Regent's apartment.

After the driver screeched his vehicle over to the curb, Jess tossed the right amount of euros at him and they disembarked. Jess silently vowed to buy or rent a vehicle soon.

On their way up the stairs to Regent's apartment, she glanced at her watch. "We can't stay long."

"Just long enough for a cup of tea," Regent said.

Again, odd behavior; first from Britt and now from her brother. Usually, he'd insist she go home right away to avoid getting caught by the rising sun. And he'd been too quiet this evening. Had he been rattled by Britt's arrest? He'd mentioned that something had happened at his secret meeting, but with the night's events, he'd never had the chance to tell her about it.

Whatever it was, she could tell it weighed heavily on him. So yes, she'd definitely stay long enough for a cup of tea.

Britt sat at the tiny kitchenette while Regent poured him a steaming cup. Jess spotted a few packets of blood in the fridge when he opened it. "How'd you manage to get that?" she asked.

He grinned at her. "I'll always have what you need, dear sister."

She squeezed the bridge of her nose between two fingers. "I hate that I'm such a burden for you. You shouldn't be worrying about me. You should be living your life, doing what you want to."

"I do live the way I want to. And I haven't regretted one moment of our lives." His face flushed. "You know what I mean, of course. I'd have preferred that you'd never been turned into a vampire, but you were, and we went on from there."

Too worked up to sit at the table, she dropped into a lotus position on the floor near the door. She leaned against the wall and watched her two favorite men going through the motions of drinking tea and trying to come to terms with what had happened that night. Both of them seemed traumatized in their own unique way. And even then, Regent was doing his best to help Britt and she adored him for it.

The minute they put their cups down, she said, "Okay, spill it, Reej."

"What's really going on?" Britt asked, the dull expression leaving his eyes.

Regent clasped his hands on the table. "I had a meeting tonight. Something very important happened," he said, staring into his empty teacup. "I'm not supposed to tell a soul about what was discussed. But..."

Jess stifled a grin. She knew Regent was serious, but honestly? He'd been a priest who hunted vampires for decades, and he'd kept that from the church. "We won't tell anyone. You know that."

"I know."

"Okay, then. What the hell is it?" Jess asked.

Regent frowned. "You're not going to believe what the meeting was about, or the real reason I was brought here," he said.

Was it Jess's imagination, or had Regent's shoulders straightened just a little? Had he finally been recognized for his obvious abilities?

"So... spill it!" she said.

"It's starting to look as if they brought me here... because of my experience with vampires. Somehow, they've learned about what we've been doing with vampires for years! That's why they need me. They think I might be able help, especially since a couple of priests have been attacked and seriously injured."

Jess lurched upright. "Really?"

"It's worse than that. Ever since the incident, the two priests haven't been themselves, so to speak," Regent said.

"What does that mean?" Britt demanded.

"They've been mentally and physically taken over. And, they're our very best exorcists."

"You're saying that vampires targeted the exorcists?" Jess's blood stalled in her veins.

"No. Shadows," Regent said.

"So, what you're saying is that they took out the only people who could do them harm?" Britt said.

Regent nodded. "Those men are part of a contingent of specialized priests. They have an innate talent, and are very successful at their jobs. Which means . . . they won't be easily replaced. Few priests have that kind of gift."

"It looks like you were lucky, Britt. Maybe your DNA protected you from being possessed," Jess said, looking at the man she couldn't live without. "Otherwise, more than your feet could have been damaged." There'd been no sign of residual damage, but Sampson hadn't arrived to check his physiology yet. She stared into Britt's eyes clinically. The news about the shadows possessing humans was huge. This wasn't good at all. "You are yourself, aren't you?"

Britt gritted his teeth. "Honestly? Until my feet healed, I was having some weird thoughts that I didn't tell you about. I was able to ignore them, though. And luckily, after my flesh healed, I was free of those ideas, too. If they'd tried to possess me, they failed."

Jess exhaled. "Good."

"What about the priests? Will they be okay?" Britt asked, a touch of survivor's guilt evident in his tone.

"I certainly hope so, son," Regent said very seriously.

"Whatever is going on—we'll help you get through this," Britt said.

Jess loved the fact that whenever he spoke to Regent, it was with friendship and respect. Britt's voice held a gentleness that he reserved for her brother alone.

She loved Britt more than she was able to properly verbalize. "Your specialized group would probably like to know Britt can fight off the shadows," she said. "But that would mean divulging secrets to an organization we can't totally trust."

Regent exhaled. "Sad, but true. But of course I'm not going to tell them anything about either of you." He winked at Britt. "But what happened to you after you were attacked by the shadows does give me a little bit of knowledge they don't have."

Regent loved being a priest, but lately, he'd learned things about the fringe sects of the church that might have soured his ideals a little. Not that he'd ever admit it out loud. But he wasn't the same trusting priest he used to be, and Jess was relieved to hear it. At the same time, she didn't want him to lose his faith.

"The church is made up of people, humans who are fallible. You know better than anyone that a few weak men don't represent the whole church. It is still as strong as the faithful beneath its roof," she said.

Britt shared a glance with Regent before both men looked at her. "Do you realize how intuitive that statement was?" Britt said. "Do you know how much soul you need in order to have those kinds of thoughts?"

Jess bit her lip and didn't speak for a couple of minutes. The last thing she wanted was for Britt and Regent to think she was more than a vampire. She wished Britt had spoken the truth. But she'd merely conditioned herself to say those types of things for the sake of her brother, so he wouldn't know how dark and unfeeling she was. Finally, she said, "Don't go all mushy on me. And don't forget *what* I really am." She crossed her arms over her chest.

"I know exactly *who* you *are*, Jess. Not *what* you are."

She'd expected that from Britt. It was one of the first things that had made her fall for him. Most people didn't see past the teeth and the cold flesh. But he did.

Enough of the syrupy, uncomfortable stuff. She let her arms drop and shifted her gaze back to Regent. "So, what do the priests think is happening? Do they have any ideas?"

"A few," he said, rubbing his hands together, more animated than usual for this time of night.

"If the shadows are the reason the church brought me here, it's a good thing they've got me researching in the archives. I've found information I'd have never known otherwise. As I mentioned to you before, these shadows seem to have made an appearance during the time of the French Revolution. And maybe even before that. There might have been a very good reason for the church to have seated a pope in both France and Rome at different times in our history."

Jess's knees suddenly weakened. It would've sucked the life out of her, if she'd had any life to give. "That sounds worse than bad, Regent. From what I remember from my history, we're talking about pretty dark times in France's history."

Regent's expression turned sober. "I know. But if we can figure out how they were stopped before, we might be able to do it again."

"Surely, it can't be that easy," Britt said.

Regent shook his head. "It won't be easy at all. No one is exactly sure what type of evil apparitions these shadows are, but if they're the same entities that existed in the seventeenth century, we're going to have a battle on our hands. They nearly won the last time. But they didn't. Unfortunately, right now, we have no idea why not."

Britt turned in his seat, and Jess came over and sat on his lap, her arm resting lightly around his shoulder. It didn't escape her that Regent fairly beamed at the sight.

"I'd bet my eyeteeth it has something to do with the bones under the city," Britt said, shuddering. "I get an overwhelming feeling of dread down there."

"Hey, if anyone's betting eyeteeth, it should be me," she quipped. Then she grew more serious. "But I do think you're onto something. And I think the vampire unit of the French police know about it, too. My guess is that they're worried enough to consider bringing us in on it, but they have to decide if they can trust us, first."

"Great way to earn our trust, by arresting me," Britt said, frowning.

"I know. Worse, they might have actually played me." It was embarrassing, to say the least, but at the same time, she had to admire their skills. "They got me to tell them about our vampire-hunting unit in New York City. I have the feeling they'll be asking for our help soon."

"Do they think the murders in the catacombs are connected to the shadows?" Regent asked.

Jess shrugged. "I'm not sure. All they seem to know is that the victim was just plain murdered and brutalized."

"I hope she was murdered first," Britt said, lines of fatigue and sorrow evident on his face.

"That poor thing," Regent said, crossing himself then lifting his cross to kiss it. "I'll pray for her everlasting soul so that she may reach the protection of heaven." His eyes closed in a quick prayer.

"I intend to find out who murdered her," Britt said. "Having met her, I know she was naïve and looking for attention. She should have stayed with her circle of friends. So why didn't she?"

Jess bit her lip. "There will always be people like her who need protection from people like us. We'll see that her murderer gets what's coming to him, Britt."

Knowing Britt, he blamed himself for not being able to save the blonde. The fact that he'd known her for a short time made it personal for him. She wasn't just another victim.

Jess got up and strode to the window. Lighter hues were appearing on the horizon. "I think it's time we go. Even though my watch hasn't warned me yet, the sun is about to come up."

Britt met her at the door without another word. Regent, too. She allowed her brother to hug her. "Keep us apprised of what you learn, little brother. Britt and I will do nighttime surveillance to see what we can come up with, in regard to the shadows. We'll let you know if we find anything. But be careful, Regent! If they're attacking priests, you're at risk too."

"I promise." Regent said. "Now get going, you two. I don't want you to be caught outside at dawn."

Jess hated to leave him, but her brother was a grown man and he had skills she didn't always give him credit for. She didn't like being overprotected, and neither did he.

Outside, with a knowing glance, she and Britt separated. It was a game they played—to see who could get back to the apartment first. Jess jumped up the side of a building and took to the rooftops, thoroughly enjoying the race. She always beat Britt home, and she almost felt sorry for him. Almost.

BRITT WAS EDGY. He'd arrived back at the apartment, but Jess wasn't there yet. What the hell had happened to her? She always won. Images of the shadows proliferated in his mind and he went to the window, just in time to see spears of light beginning to shoot into the heavens. Solar rays that could burn Jess alive.

In a panic to find her, he strode back to the door and wrenched it open. Holy hell, he should have stayed with her. He'd just stepped into the hall when she opened the stairwell door and headed toward him. "Jess! You scared the crap out of me," he said. "Where were you?"

"I ran into Morana. I let her know that Regent and I were actually born in Rome. Hopefully, that will be enough to prove we're not related. She swears she was born in France. She hates the idea of us being twins as much as I do. And I have the feeling she'll do some digging to find proof of her birth, just to verify that there's nothing between us but a slight resemblance."

"Bet that was a fun conversation. How does she plan to prove you're not related?"

Jess shrugged. "She said she'd asked her adoptive father."

"I'd sure like to meet that guy," Britt said, unable to hide the dislike in his voice.

"Why?"

"To see if he really exists, for one thing."

"You really don't trust her, do you?"

"Doll, think about it. If Morana's really your twin, wouldn't that make her parent a centenarian?"

"Of course he would be. You're right," Jess said, and she looked almost angry that she hadn't considered that angle.

"We need to find out if the man really exists. Maybe he's a vampire too?" She strode into the kitchen and got herself a bag of blood, poured some into a glass, and turned away from him to consume it.

He sighed. "I guess it's possible. I heard about a guy in Mexico who . . ."

Jess raised a hand to stop him cold. "Don't humor me, Brittain. We both know birth records in places like that are virtually nonexistent, especially for a man who's more than a hundred years old."

"True."

She wrapped her arms around him and pressed her face into his chest. "Too bad my time is running out tonight. I'd suggest a little stress reliever in my room." She winked at him. "I don't think I'll be able to remain animated long enough, though."

He nodded. "Raincheck?"

"Anytime, my love."

When she let go of him and strode toward her room, he couldn't take his eyes off her. He'd never tire of watching her.

"You going to bed, too?" she asked, leaning against her doorframe, and etching the image of her magnificent body into his brain. The sun was nearly fully up, and he had to switch off the lust because he had work to do once she went into stasis.

"I'm not really tired."

She frowned, her concern instant. "Be careful if you're going out. Don't forget you're still a suspect. Don't do anything that might make things worse for you."

"I was never formally charged, remember?"

"That doesn't mean that they won't finish the job if you get in their way."

"Don't worry, my darling," he said, blowing her a kiss. "I'll be careful. And, you'd better hurry inside or you'll still be standing there when I return."

She sighed. "If only I could go with you."

His heart twisted. She rarely spoke like that. And when she reluctantly shut the door between them, he could tell that she hated having to leave him to his own devices. He rubbed the back of his neck. Maybe someday he could save her. He'd managed to save humans once, and even though he'd been told it was a one-time only deal, he had to hope it could happen again—for Jess.

He was going out all right. He had a killer to find.

WHEN MORANA arrived home an hour before dawn, Sinclair was sitting at the dining room table with a half-empty bottle of Amaretto in front of him. How could he drink a bottle of that sickly sweet stuff? But then, as far as she could remember, she'd never had anything but blood, as far as sustenance went.

"Papa," she said. "Why are you still up?"

"I worry about you, my love," he said. "I don't like you working at that bar. It's too much of a temptation for you."

She tossed him an irritated look. He had to be at least in his nineties, or maybe more. So how was it he appeared to be only in his sixties? Maybe Sinclair had devised elixirs for himself, as well as her. After all, as a Watcher, he'd learned enough to have come up with a formula that would keep the beast inside her under control most of the time. All the time, as far as he knew.

She'd never divulged the whole truth about the effect his miracle drug had on her, even though he asked often. She made a face. She couldn't remember anything about her childhood. Any memories of being turned into a vampire had been wiped clean from her mind somehow. Sinclair had put it down to amnesia, caused by trauma, and told her it was a blessing she didn't remember. Still, she wanted to know how she'd died. Who had done this to her?

She did remember him bringing her lambs and baby goats to feed from when she was a teenager. Along with the goats' blood, he'd used an elixir to help her grow. Unfortunately, those memories only reminded her that she still needed his help. Sometimes, he pushed her too hard to act like a human. He was lucky she hadn't ripped his throat out by now. She needed him to keep making her elixir. Otherwise, she'd have very little use for him.

Sinclair had big plans for her, he said. Only he hadn't bothered to consider that she might have goals of her own. For some reason, he thought she was destined to have control over the other vampires in France. It was true that he knew enough powerful people that he might actually be able to make it happen. But did she really want that?

Maybe it was his goal to rise within the Watcher community. She needed to find out more about this secretive group of his. Over the years, he'd managed to keep her in the dark about the Watchers. All she knew was that he was one.

Merde! She wanted to be on her own, to become the true vampire of her heart, but for now, she had to wait. She was getting closer to finding the recipe for the elixir that she craved so badly. Once she could make it herself, she'd have no need for her father.

"Papa, do you know anything about my biological parents?" she asked, knowing those type of questions always irritated him. She used to do it all the time, but had long ago given up.

He straightened in his chair, a frown marring his glazed-over expression. "Why are you asking?"

"I met someone the other day who looks exactly like me."

Sinclair Longina's bleary-eyed gaze went cold-sober in seconds. "Where?"

She bit her lip. She didn't want to believe that bitch was truly her twin, but seeing the wary expression on his face, she realized it might be true. Papa obviously knew something.

"What is her name?" he asked gruffly.

She folded her arms over her chest. "What difference does it make? She can't possibly be my twin sister, right?"

Sinclair's shoulders slumped and the blood drained from his face. "Twin?"

"It appears so. But you know all about her, don't you!"

Sinclair shook his head vehemently. "My darling daughter, you have no sister and no brother," he said.

Fuck! Sinclair had slipped up. She hadn't mentioned the brother. At that, she seated herself at the table and poured her father another glass of his liqueur. "You look thirsty, Papa." Usually, liquor made him a little more loose-lipped, but she'd never learned enough to actually do anything.

"No more drink. I'm going to bed," he said, fiddling with his glass of amber liquid. It didn't escape her that his gaze barely left the glass. Maybe he was afraid the alcohol might loosen his tongue. She could compel him to answer—at least she should be able to—but she'd never tried it on him. She stared at his face, at his brown eyes that always looked at her with adoration. He'd wasted his time loving her. She had no compassion, no desire or need for his love. For some reason, he didn't seem to care that she was a vampire. In fact, he'd gone out of his way to save her from herself. She laughed inwardly. The poor man had nearly worked himself to death when she was a teenager. And humans thought teenagers had angst! Hah!

Would he have managed to control her if he hadn't been a Watcher? He'd always told her he had special abilities. She thought he'd said that just to scare her into doing whatever she was told when she'd been younger. As painful as the growth elixir had been, it was worth it. It bothered her that she'd forgotten so much of her childhood, though. "Papa, how old was I when I was bitten?" She softened her voice, instantly irritated that he wasn't fooled by her attempt.

"Why do you want to know? It was a dark time. You've forgotten, and that's a good thing, my love. So I will not speak of it."

Sheesh, whose dark time had it been? Hers or his? She tapped her fingernails on the table and searched for another way to get something out of him. But it seemed that once she'd mentioned a twin, he'd closed himself off. She wasn't going to find out anything tonight. But she had learned something. Now, she knew for sure that Jess and Regent Vandermire were her siblings. Not that she'd ever admit that to them.

Still, she couldn't help wondering about her father. How much did he really know? She'd learned very little about Sinclair over the years. Who, or what, did he watch? For a long time, she assumed it was only vampires, since she was one. But lately, she'd begun to question whether the Watchers were interested in something else. They usually met in France, but sometimes Sinclair travelled to Rome. If she hadn't been so self-absorbed, she might have found out . . . if she'd given a crap about him, that was.

"Have you had your monthly infusion?" Sinclair asked, blinking his red-rimmed eyes in a weak effort to clear his mind.

"Yes."

"Where did you get the goat? I didn't see a carcass in the back. Actually, I haven't seen any for a while."

"I can kill them in the fields, Papa. Why would I bring them here? It would make our neighbors curious."

He sighed a little. "Yes, that's good thinking, *ma Belle*. And the mixture? Do you have enough, or do you need more?"

I always need more. But she'd certainly lost her taste for goats. Lately, she'd been craving her drug-infused blood more than she used to. It gave her a feeling of immortality. The mixture or the serum, as he called it, and the last blood pumping through the heart of her prey, gave her a high like nothing else could. Not even biting a human during sex was so good. It was the ultimate in arousal. Her father had no idea what his drug did to her and for her.

"I have enough for a little while, but maybe you should make me some more, Papa."

He frowned. "Why?" He started to shift in his seat, as if uncomfortable. He seemed to have forgotten about going to bed now that she'd asked for more of the drug. He obviously didn't like this conversation.

"Lately, I've found that I need a little more in the blood mix," she lied. She didn't need more—she just wanted more. "You really should give me the recipe, Papa. Then I could make my own and I wouldn't have to bother you."

He shook his head. "I can't. I'd be breaking a sacrosanct promise."

"The Watchers again! Who are they? Why won't you tell me?"

"I can't tell you. I'm sworn to secrecy. That's one part of my oath I intend to keep, at least. I'm not supposed to use my knowledge to help you the way I do either, my love, but. . . ." He spread his hands on the table. "What kind of father would I be if I didn't help my child?"

"But I'm not your child, am I? I'm someone else's child. Someone who had other children, a boy and a girl? Why were we separated?"

Sinclair's hands curled into fists. "I don't know any of that. I can't help you."

"Tell me, Papa. Telling me the truth can't be any more difficult than raising a vampire. I couldn't have been an easy child." Nor was she an easy adult.

Sinclair snorted at the same time that a tear formed in the corner of his eye. "You have always been my joy."

Morana wanted to scream. No wonder she could never get through to the man. He was delusional. How could he feel that way about her? She inhaled, holding back a shriek of anger. Too bad she needed him. She didn't dare anger him to the point that he'd quit on her.

But if she got the recipe, she wouldn't need him any longer. She could become powerful on her own. Damn him.

He went to a locked safe and let the biometrics scan his iris. When the safe opened, she virtually salivated.

He took out one vial and squeezed it tight in the palm of his hand, then relocked the safe. She couldn't even break in. It had been set up so that a single attempt would result in the safe self-destructing. Her father knew her too well and had covered all of his bases.

He kept her under his control and wanting. She hated him for that.

Chapter Ten

BRITT MADE HIS way to the catacombs again. Since the club didn't open until well after sunset, he intended to do a bit of investigating on his own.

There were no signs of the police outside when he arrived. He did a perimeter check on the street, looking for other openings to the catacombs that the killer could have used.

No doubt cataphiles knew of other ways in and out, and the police would likely be aware of those locations. He was probably wasting his time, but he *had* to do something.

"John Brittain," a familiar female voice called to him from across the street. "What are you doing?"

Shit! It was the one person he wanted to avoid—Veronique LaFontaine. Slim with messy brown hair, her eyes widened in a surprised expression he didn't believe for a second. Nor did he miss the underlying sharp intelligence in her gaze. She was obviously trying to hide what she really was—a dedicated, determined cop. He'd bet her baggy slacks and wrinkled white blouse were part of her camouflage.

Had she been following him? "Morning," he said.

"Don't 'morning' me! What the shit are you doing?"

He almost grinned at the way she said shit. It sounded like *sheet*. But the last thing he wanted was to antagonize her. "I'm trying to prove I'm not a killer. Since I'm a decent investigator and profiler, I thought I'd take a look around."

"Really?" she said, in her soft French accent. That voice sounded so feminine and trusting, but he knew she wielded it like a guillotine, ready to drop on him at any moment.

"Where's Jess?" Veronique asked, then obviously realized her mistake. "Oh, I see."

"Do you really?" Britt asked. "Jess is the best person I know. Don't mistake her for anything else."

Veronique's irises sparked with anger. "I happen to admire her very much, Monsieur Brittain. I knew she was a vampire when I met her in New York."

He inhaled sharply. "How?" He noticed she deliberately ignored his rank.

"I have ways," she said. "We worked on a case together."

"But that case had nothing to do with vampires, did it?" Britt said.

"No. I was following a felon from France. He frequented vampire clubs, so Jess was assigned to be my U.S. partner, most likely to protect me from the real vampires I'd encounter. At first, I didn't trust her, but over the time we worked together, I saw her integrity, and I once caught her taking out a vampire in an alleyway. She has some impressive skills."

"Did she know you saw her?"

"No."

Britt frowned. He found it hard to believe that Jess hadn't realized this woman had caught her in the act. Was Veronique lying?

"Strange," Britt said, hinting that he found her statement to be less than plausible.

Veronique looked him up and down. "So. You are a profiler?"

"I used to be."

"Well, why don't you tag along with me today? Maybe you can spot something that I've missed."

Britt's heart leapt at the thought, but he wasn't fooled. If she still thought he was guilty, she'd assume he'd be trying to find a way to cover things up. And then she'd have him. It was a common technique—one he'd used on occasion.

"Great idea."

"Good." She started walking.

"Where are we going?"

"To the catacombs. Where else?"

"Okay." He followed her into a passageway he hadn't spotted earlier. As he'd suspected, there were probably plenty of entrances in the city.

Her planned excursion into the catacombs might explain Veronique's attire. It was clammy and cold down there, and even more eerie in the beam of the flashlight she'd pulled out of her pocket. No bones were visible yet, but he still broke out in a cold sweat. Dammit.

They'd taken a circuitous route to the site of the killing, Veronique impressing him with her knowledge of the tunnels. At the crime scene, the body had been removed, but forensic tape had been positioned and a policeman jumped to his feet as they approached. He'd been sitting on the ground with his back against the stone wall. He saluted the second he saw Veronique.

"Anyone try to get down here?" she asked the cop in English for Britt's benefit. He appreciated that.

"Non," the officer said, glancing at Britt and then his watch before switching to English. "But this place is creepy."

"Oui, je sais—I know. I've been down here too many times not to be aware of that fact. It's unnerving at times," she said, giving the man's shoulder a pat before leading Britt to the spot where the victim's blood had seeped into the ground.

She flashed the light around, and Britt looked at the ground closely. This time, he saw more than he'd been able to with the minimal light of his iPhone. There'd been blood, but not nearly enough of it, given the condition of the woman's body. Maybe the soil was fine and it had sunk in quickly? He scraped the floor with the toe of his shoe and realized it was hard-packed clay.

Meanwhile, Veronique continued her search, flashing her light on the walls and up at the ceiling.

He knew what she was looking for. "Very little arterial spray," he noted out loud.

She nodded. "And, if she was cut open first, there should be spray."

"You think she was already dead when she was sliced? But why?"

"Just some sick fuck who wanted to get his jollies?" she said, casting a suspicious look his way.

He didn't give her the satisfaction of getting angry at her attempt to rile him. He'd have blood on more than his shoes if he'd killed that poor woman. Besides, he spotted something glistening a little farther down the cave. It had caught in the light of her flashlight when she'd moved it over the walls.

"I saw something down there," he said.

"What?"

"I don't know. It was shiny. Could be anything, but it's worth taking a look."

Veronique passed him the light. *"Après vous,"* she said.

"That's the first thing you've said in French that I understand," he said, then went silent as they circumnavigated the spot where the body had lain. He got to the location where he thought he'd seen something. But there was nothing. What the hell? "I swear there was something shiny down here."

"Look again. Maybe we're at the wrong angle," she suggested. "Try shining it nearer the wall."

He did so. *There!* He saw it again.

"Did *you* see it this time?" he asked.

She shook her head. "No."

Shit. If he found something that she couldn't see, it would just make him look even guiltier. Maybe he should pretend it wasn't there.

No. He couldn't do that.

He moved a couple of feet and shone the light directly on the spot where he'd seen the reflection. At first, he thought he saw a candy wrapper, so he moved closer.

Veronique said, "Don't touch it, in case it's evidence."

As if he'd do that. "It looks like the foil part of a gum wrapper," he said.

Veronique pulled out an evidence bag and gloves. She deposited the foil into the bag and tucked it into her pocket.

He grimaced. "I was hoping we'd find something worthwhile."

She patted her pocket. "You never know. This might have fingerprints on it."

He doubted it.

Glancing at the cave floor, it was clear why they'd considered this a vampire attack. There wasn't enough blood, given the victim's extensive wounds, unless she'd been dead before she was sliced open. Or, perhaps, she'd been killed elsewhere. But if that was the case, how had she been transported without leaving a blood trail? Besides, she'd been in the bar with him earlier, at least until Jess had shown up. So she couldn't have been missing more than half an hour before he'd found her body. . . .

Veronique had to be considering the same things. If she thought like him, she'd be looking for another tunnel leading to the actual crime scene.

"Let's go up again," she said, rubbing her arms against the cool dampness. "Even in summer, it's like a cold room down here."

He followed her up, even though he really wanted to remain and search other tunnels.

"Join me for a coffee," she said. It wasn't a request.

He nodded. They took a small alley and she led him to a café on a secluded street obviously not frequented by tourists. It was packed with locals.

Veronique ordered two coffees along with croissants and cheese. Britt's stomach actually growled at the thought of food.

Veronique must've heard his gut protesting. "Hungry?"

"I haven't eaten in a while," he admitted.

"Why. Is your conscience bothering you?" she asked.

He gritted his teeth. "No. I just haven't eaten breakfast yet this morning."

"Why not?"

"I wanted to do some checking while Jess sleeps. Besides, it's not unusual for me to forget to eat when I'm on a case."

"I feel it's my responsibility to remind you you're not on a case. This is France, not New York City."

He didn't respond.

The waiter brought steaming cups of coffee, along with the lightest, flakiest croissants he had ever seen. He bit into one. "These are amazing!"

"This is where the real French food is served," she said, crunching into her own croissant that she'd buttered and piled high with a soft cheese that smelled pungent and nutty.

They both stopped talking long enough to eat. Britt had the feeling Veronique hadn't eaten in a while, either. "I'm surprised to see you still on the job, Veronique. Weren't you up all night?"

"I caught a couple of hours' sleep after you left," she said.

He doubted that.

"There is something I must ask. Why are you and Jess really here?" she asked.

Britt crammed the last bit of croissant into his mouth and savored the buttery taste, then washed it down with his coffee. Before speaking, he raised his hand to order another round. Then he turned his attention back to Veronique. "Jess told you. We're here on sabbatical. Jess didn't want to leave her brother over here all alone. That's the truth, whether you believe it or not."

"He seems like he can handle himself," she said. "He's an adult, after all."

"Oh, he can. But they've always been a team." He paused. He wasn't about to tell her that Jess didn't quite trust the Vatican's reasons for sending Regent here. "Besides, she'd never been to France, so we decided that taking some time off would be good for both of us."

"You and Jess are a couple?" Veronique's eyes narrowed on Britt. She was probably trying to figure out why he was interested in a vampire.

"I am deeply in love with Jess," he said.

She tipped her head. "Good. Let us hope you haven't done anything to make her regret that."

"You really think I'm a murderer, don't you?"

"Right now, I see no other alternative. And, considering your job, you could get away with something like this quite easily. Nobody would suspect a crack vampire hunter."

The server returned with the second order of coffee and croissants. Britt needed the interlude to get his temper under control. He didn't want to say more than he should.

He took a deep breath. "I can see I'm going to have to prove my innocence to you."

She nodded, picking up another croissant and taking a bite. "If you can," she said, her mouth full.

He sighed. How was he going to do that? He sure as hell couldn't offer a DNA sample, since he had angelic DNA in his blood. Sampson had told him that wouldn't be a good idea . . . unless he wanted some uncomfortable questions after. "I wish I had some idea about how to do that," he grunted.

Veronique downed the last of her coffee. "You can come into the Prefecture tonight and look through some mug shots, for starters. If you recognize anyone who might've been talking to our victim, it'll go a long way in proving your innocence."

"I'll do that," he said. "What time do you want me there?"

"I go on duty at ten p.m.," she said, brushing a few crumbs off her pants.

Britt rose from the table and threw down enough euros to cover the bill. "I'll see you tonight."

Veronique stayed in her seat while he stalked off. There'd be no more searching today. He'd go home and try to sleep. It was going to be a busy night.

AT SUNSET, JESS woke slowly as she always did. Only, in New York, her windows changed from black to opaque as the sun set. Here, there were no windows, making her feel as if she was in a crypt. She hated that feeling. If she and Britt were going to stay here for three months, she'd have to find another place and retrofit it to her specifications.

Lying flat on the uncomfortable bed waiting to be reanimated, she heard Britt moving about in the apartment. The offending odors of coffee, bacon, and eggs assaulted her nostrils as she came to life. He always cooked himself a big breakfast on Sunday. She closed her eyes and waited for her fingers to be able to move. Lately, it seemed her body regenerated at a snail's pace. Finally, she was able to sit up.

Britt had already eaten by the time she had her shower and got dressed. She wore a sundress today, which was rather ironic, considering the sun was bad for her health . . . and it was night. But she couldn't resist—she'd had fun shopping at the establishments of the few French couturiers who stayed open late. The silky fabric glided over her skin, so light, it was barely there.

Normally, she dressed much more like a vampire than a human.

"Jesus, Jess. You should warn a man before you wear a sexy get-up like that. I could've had a heart attack." Britt jumped to his feet and approached her.

"I think you're going a little bit overboard."

"Oh, hell, no, I'm not." He pressed himself against her to prove his point. She grinned against his neck, making sure he could feel her eyeteeth. Just to prove hers.

"Not a good time, my love. I must quench my thirst. Making love right now might make me lose control." She went to the fridge and poured herself some sustenance.

He sighed and looked at his watch. "I guess I don't have time, anyway. I have to go down to the police station and look at mug shots tonight. I ran into Veronique LaFontaine today and she asked me to come in."

"Dammit, I told you to avoid the cops."

"I don't think it was a coincidence, Jess. My guess is that she was following me."

"Why does she want you to look at mug shots if she thinks you're guilty?"

"Maybe she's giving me enough rope to hang myself," he said, shrugging. "But at least, this will give me a chance to see if can recognize someone who might have actually killed her."

"I'll come too. I wasn't at LaCave as long as you were, but still, I was there." Jess finished up and put her glass in the dishwasher.

"Sounds good, my love. Shall we go?" He held the door for her and patted her rump on the way by.

She drilled a daring look at him, knowing the effect it would have on him. He was the one who'd started this game, after all.

Ten minutes later, they reached the station. "I'm starting to regret agreeing to this," Britt said under this breath, his shoulders instantly slumping at the sight of the long table full of binders.

She felt the same. They'd be here forever.

She sat beside him and searched through page after page of unfamiliar faces. In New York, she'd at least know a few of them. Being here, so far out of her element, made her a little homesick.

At midnight, Britt closed one of the many binders he'd gone through and leaned back in his hard wooden chair. He cursed under his breath. "This is hopeless. There's no way in hell this can possibly help me prove my innocence."

Veronique entered the room, and apparently heard his comment. "You just got very lucky. You're no longer a suspect, Monsieur Brittain, another victim has just been murdered while you were sitting right here in the precinct."

Jess jumped out of her seat at the same time Britt did.

"Damn it," he said. "Did you catch the killer?"

"No, but my man caught sight of him. He'd already killed the woman, but hadn't yet finished slicing and dicing."

"It's a serial, then?" Jess breathed.

Veronique nodded. "I'm afraid so. And, since you're innocent, John Brittain, and a self-proclaimed profiler, I would appreciate it you'd consult with me on this case."

Jess's anger ratcheted up. Veronique had some nerve.

Britt reached out and squeezed Jess's hand, most likely in response to her building annoyance.

"Actually, I'd be very happy to help you catch the vicious bastard who killed that poor woman and nearly got me incarcerated."

"Jess, will you help as well?" Veronique asked.

"No."

Veronique looked taken aback by Jess's abrupt comment. It obviously wasn't what she'd expected her to say.

"Okay," she said, then turned to Britt. "I do appreciate your willingness to help, especially after accusing you of the murder."

Britt nodded, but his face remained unreadable.

Jess, on the other hand, was still too angry with Veronique to forgive her.

"I'd probably have thought the same thing about you, if I'd found you in that compromising situation, Captain," Britt said.

"You're damned lucky he's agreeing to help you," Jess said between her teeth. "I don't like the way you run your team, Vee. If you were in New York, I'd have given an officer of the law the benefit of the doubt before I accused him of murder."

"If you recall, I didn't actually charge him. But, you're probably right, Jess. I could have handled this a little better. My problem is that I see things in black and white. I don't work in the gray areas. I'm considered too strict by my own staff, and I do regret causing a rift between us. I truly respect what you do."

Jess stared through her on her way out. She hated being angry at her friend. And Veronique was a friend. Sometimes the evil vampire in Jess made her into a bitch. Hopefully, Veronique understood that.

Britt followed. "I don't blame Veronique for thinking I was guilty. Isn't that why you went to her in the first place? Because she's above reproach?"

"I guess you're right. I shouldn't hold her responsible for hauling you off to jail and throwing you in a cell."

Britt coughed to hide a grin. "Glad you're forgiving her."

"Oh crap, you know I will eventually. I still respect the hell out of her because she's one of the best."

"Right. So why didn't you want to help in the tunnels?" He knew it was more than just a grudge against Veronique.

Jess stopped walking but didn't make eye contact.

"Holy hell, it's the blood, isn't it? I should have thought of that." He grabbed her shoulders and looked into her eyes. "You're feeling less than a cop because you don't trust yourself to go in there with all that blood."

Jess bit her lip and her fingernails dug into her palms.

After rubbing her arms for a second and getting no response, Britt backed off. "Okay. I understand. Still, there's no need to punish yourself for it. You can do other surveillance while we're working in the tunnels. Finding the killer is more important than analyzing the remains, anyway."

Jess made an irritated noise. "Don't humor me, Brittain. We both know that finding clues at the murder site is often the only way to find the killer."

JESS FELT USELESS while Britt worked in the tunnels the next few days . . . and nights. She was out of her element here. Wandering around the streets gave her a chance to familiarize herself with certain sections of the city, but there was so much more to see and find. She had an omnipresent sense of the many souls who'd been lost here over the centuries. She wondered how the older vampires managed to get past it.

On the third evening after Britt left to meet with Veronique, Jess decided to catch up with Regent to hear about his recent trip to Avignon.

She felt a little calmer when she reached Regent's apartment and saw that his lights were on. Climbing the stairs quickly, she knocked then entered, noting the door had been unlocked. She gritted her teeth. Her brother had to be more careful. On the other hand, locks wouldn't keep out a shadow.

"I came to hear about your trip," she said, joining him on the sofa. He turned off the television, fairly bursting with excitement to tell her his news.

"I actually went to the Palais des Papes," he said. "I didn't expect to be given approval, but it came within hours. Would you believe a limousine was sent to drive me to Avignon? And when I got there, I was left to look around on my own. That was highly unusual, but I was happy I could wander where I liked."

"How'd you manage that?" Jess asked. Up until now, it seemed the church had kept a pretty tight rein on her brother. He was rarely allowed outside Notre Dame or the library during working hours, which bothered Jess to no end.

"Somehow, I got a special pass. My membership in the secret group seems to have helped."

Jess got up and wandered away from Regent, looking out the window. Was it an act of desperation on the part of the church? Had they been unable to locate the script, so they decided to let Regent go off on his own? Maybe they were smarter than she gave them credit for. Regent had very good instincts. If he wanted to go to Avignon, there must have been a reason for it. She leaned forward. "Did you find anything helpful?"

His mouth twitched into a sort of a smile.

She sat opposite him and waited. He loved telling her long, convoluted stories. She always forced herself to listen, for her brother's sake—he did so much for her.

"At the *palais*, I walked down the long halls and looked into rooms. I had no idea what I would find, but I'd hoped to come across something that might tell us what happened during the revolution."

Jess nodded. "You weren't looking for the script?"

His gaze shifted and he broke from his reverie just long enough to shake his head, as if it would be unlikely to find anything like that there. "There were paintings on the ceilings. As well as familiar angel-slash-demon gargoyles that were so cleverly hidden, one might almost miss them, I spotted a lot of iconography that seemed out of the norm for a papal palace. Of course, I had the benefit of being able to search in places the public isn't allowed.

"What do you think the gargoyles symbolize?" Jess asked.

"Knowing what had happened to Britt, I believe they represent the children of the fallen angels."

"Interesting. I bet Britt would love a private tour there, too then."

"I would have asked about the gargoyles, but I didn't want to let anyone know how interested I was in them. I had to keep my knowledge of such things out of their purview. I'm sure my superiors think I know more than I'm telling, which is technically true. But we don't want the church to start asking questions about Britt. For some reason, up to now, they haven't asked about him, even after he'd exposed himself as one of the Fallen to Cardinal Vasilli in New York City."

"Maybe this is a different group?"

"Maybe," Regent said, but he looked doubtful. "But if Vasilli didn't report his findings to the church, it begs the question—why not?"

"And it proves we need to be careful here, Regent. At the very least, until we know what you're getting yourself into."

"Don't worry, dear. I intend to be very careful. Now to finish my story . . . I was allowed into areas the public couldn't go, even into the richly decorated back rooms. I found a small alcove that looked much more rudimentary than the rest of the building. It was in an area well offset from the tourist route. It was the rough-hewn stone in the alcove that caught my attention. It seemed so out of place, I had to look closer."

"Why?" she asked. Her blood would run cold right now if it wasn't already ice.

"It was as if I was somehow drawn there. I had to go. I looked the alcove over. There might have been a crucifix hanging in there at one time, if the lighter shade of stone was an indication. Maybe there'd been a shelf below it? Someone had prayed here. But why? Why there, when the magnificent church was so close?"

Jess couldn't sit still any longer. She started pacing around the room while she continued to listen.

"I was just about to leave when I spotted a tiny flaw in the dark corner of the alcove. It seemed out of place. And yet, I felt as if I'd been led to that spot. I don't know why, because, really, it looked the same as every other part of the stone. But when I touched it, a tiny door opened, and an ancient book slid forward just far enough that I could grasp it and pull it out."

"Really?" This was a surprise. Regent had often had a sixth sense when it came to vampires. Maybe his gift was more encompassing than she realized. He'd felt there was something behind the wall and he'd found an opening. The odds of that happening were astronomical.

"It was lucky I'd worn my priest's robes. I slid the yellowed book inside my vestment and, without a second thought, turned to leave. I decided that if there was nothing special about this book, I would return it to its rightful place later. After I closed the door, the opening disappeared immediately, as if it had never been there. I've never seen such good camouflage."

"And yet you managed to find it," she said. "I guess that explains why your heart rate is elevated and your cheeks are flushed," she said. "Was the book that exciting?"

"I don't know, I haven't looked at it yet," he said. "I waited for you."

"But . . . ?"

"This is the weird part, Jess. You know I'm not one for hocus-pocus, but I'd swear I was led to that place and shown the secret button that opened a door to this." He pulled the book gently from his vestment, and ran a hand over the aged burgundy cover that sandwiched yellowing, archaic-looking pages. An odor filled the room suddenly, an aroma of history.

"I can't believe you actually stole it," she said, not trying to mask her admiration. "And, from the Pope's Palace, no less."

"It's not the Pope's Palace any more, but you could put it that way," he said, not sounding as guilty as she'd have expected. "The thing is, I think it was meant for me."

"I've never known you to hint at anything even remotely connected to things that border on the paranormal . . . unless it's a vampire." She laughed. "Maybe there's hope for you yet. Let's see what's inside."

His hands virtually shook as he cracked open the first page. The lettering was beautifully written in quill pen. There was colorful scrollwork and hand-drawn images at the beginning of each paragraph. But the language was completely unknown to both of them.

"That's weird," she said. "I've never seen anything like it."

"Is it Cyrillic, do you think?"

Jess shook her head. "No. I don't think so."

Regent thumbed through the rest of the book before gently placing it on the coffee table. "Great. How am I ever going to figure it out?"

"You'll find a way, brother. Of that, I have no doubt."

He pulled off his collar and set it on the table. "I need a drink," he said.

She frowned. She hated to see disappointment stabbing at him. He thought the book had been meant for him. If it was, why couldn't he read it?

"I mean lemonade." He pulled a pitcher from the fridge and poured himself a glass. "Where'd you say Britt was?"

It was a weak attempt to take his mind off the book, but Jess wasn't fooled.

"I didn't. You didn't ask," she said, forcing a teasing note into her voice. She'd do anything to help her brother get over his disappointment. He'd had such hopes that finding this book meant something big. And maybe it did. It just might take him a while longer to figure it out. "You'll be happy to hear Britt's off the hook. There's been another murder. So now, he's helping the French police find the serial killer."

"Serial killer? That doesn't sound good." Regent lowered himself onto the chair next to her. "As dangerous as New York is, Paris seems to have more darkness than we realized."

"Maybe we're just opening our naïve eyes for the first time," Jess said. "We've lived in a fairly young country our whole existence. Even though we knew vampires existed in Europe forever, we didn't really understand their place in society here."

"And we still don't," he said. "They seem to be the least of the troubles here. It's the shadow creatures the church is worried about—not the vampires."

"True," Jess said. She'd never admitted it before, not even to herself, but she felt their evil pull whenever she saw them. They were dark, powerful entities and they seemed to be building in number. No wonder the church was frantically searching for a way to stop them.

"From what I've learned, they're believed to be demons," Regent said. "And it gets worse, my love," he said. "I've been invited to observe the two priests who've been possessed by them."

Jess crossed her legs and leaned forward. "Demons. That's a new one for us. Like demons from hell?"

"Where else?" Regent said seriously. "The committee I'm on is working to find a way to eradicate them, but so far, they haven't even been able to help the possessed priests."

Jess cringed. She didn't like Regent being on the front lines of anything so menacing.

"If these things take hold of the city, it won't be long before there won't be anywhere safe on the planet," he said.

"*Great*—another potential apocalypse. All in a day's work for us, I guess. Are you going to be doing research again tomorrow, or will you have time to focus on figuring out that stolen book? It might very well be the key to stopping all this."

"I didn't steal it," he mumbled. "It was shown to me."

"Sure. Sure," she said, trying not to crack a smile. "I'm proud that you'd do something this daring. I didn't know you had it in you."

He rolled his eyes. "What would I do without you, dear? You never let me get away with anything. Okay, I stole it. I'll say a few extra prayers tonight for forgiveness."

"A few?"

"A lot," he said.

Jess stood. "Keep me posted on anything you learn about the shadows. I'm going to do a little searching of my own tonight."

"Without Britt?"

Jess smiled at her brother, but inside, she felt hollow. Regent was well aware that she'd grown used to working side-by-side with Britt. But right now, she felt cut out of the action. "Of course. I'm more than capable of looking after myself."

"I know," he admitted, grudgingly. "Better than most."

Jess looked around his tiny apartment, looking for anything that could initiate a change of subject. "I'm thinking of getting a bigger place for the rest of the time we're here. Would you like to share with Britt and me?"

Regent paused for thought, then replied, "Thank you, but no. I have a feeling the church is keeping an eye on me. If I were to stay with you, it would put you under their scrutiny, too."

Okay, so he'd just validated a concern she'd had about him being watched. It seemed he was well aware of what was happening around him. And he had things under control. She shouldn't have expected anything less. "Why do you think they are watching you?"

"I think they believe I have more talents than I actually do."

"They might be right," she said. "I think you're capable of amazing things, Regent. Look how many times you've managed to heal me with your concoction of herbs."

Regent snorted. "But you always said they did nothing for you."

Jess's hands rose questioningly in the air. "Who knows for sure?"

"You'd best leave, dear, since you seem intent on patronizing me tonight," he said in an unusually serious tone. One that he never used on her. He got up and walked her to the front door.

"It's only because I love you so," she said, worried by her brother's comments. Regent was always the one with upbeat witticisms. Normally, he'd do anything to help her stay positive. Not seeing him being his normal, happy self jarred her to the bone.

With everything he'd learned about the demons, he should, at the very least, be excited to be involved in the fight against them. Regent wasn't afraid of anything evil. At least, if he was, she'd never seen it. He hadn't been unnerved by anything they'd faced in the past—and they'd come up against some pretty mean characters.

Maybe he was simply down because he couldn't decipher the book he'd found.

Regent forced a smile and squeezed her hand. "And I love you, too, dearest."

But was he afraid of demons? Even though Regent had been a crack vampire hunter in his day, he was an old man on the inside. His body might be capable of fighting, but she wasn't quite sure his mind was there yet. Maybe it was more of a mental block than a physical one. She wasn't sure.

She was just about to leave when someone knocked on the door. Stepping aside, she watched as Regent opened the door to a man in his forties, who stood there, a bottle of wine under one arm. He entered without invitation, so he must know Regent fairly well.

"Gaston," Regent said, his expression brightening. "I'd like to introduce you to my sister, Jess."

Gaston took Jess's hand and shook it. Normally, she didn't allow people to touch her, but she didn't see a way around it without being rude. This man held her hand long enough to be curious about her, but he didn't react or comment on her cold flesh.

"It's a pleasure to meet you, Jess," he said in a mild French accent. "Regent and I have been enjoying each other's company since he arrived in France." Gaston smiled. "In fact, he's the only chess partner I've had in a long time who can occasionally outwit me."

"Occasionally?" Regent already sounded lighter than he'd been a moment ago, and that made Gaston okay in her books. His lack of concern about her cold flesh was a worry, though.

Regent had a friend in Paris. Except for Sampson Case, he usually avoided personal friendships over the years because of her lifestyle. Maybe she'd only imagined his low spirits a moment ago.

She stepped outside into the sultry Parisian night where lights glittered along the Champs-Élysée, where cafés and clubs were still running full tilt. She walked toward Pont Neuf, wondering if the shadows would be lurking there again tonight.

From what they'd observed so far, the shadows seemed to stay low to the ground. So, if she stayed above them, she might be able to check them out without putting herself in danger.

She crossed the *pont* and then the sidewalk before checking to make sure no one was watching. Then, quickly, she scaled halfway up the brick wall. It was enough, though, to see the shadows roiling out of the cracks of the brick below her. They must be able to sense when there were people in the vicinity. So why hadn't they bothered the man who had walked straight through them the other night?

Or maybe they had?

What if they'd possessed him?

Jess's gut churned as she watched them pooling below her on the sidewalk, unformed shapes that reminded her of mercury in their fluid movements. If they were demons, she saw no profile that would make her think that.

A piece broke off from the writhing black pool then slithered and crawled a short distance away. A single entity on its own? She moved along the walls, jumping from one building to another, following the lone shadow that continued to move away. It didn't interact with pedestrians, and it unnerved her to think it had a destination in mind.

Before long, she had a good idea where the shadow demon was going. It turned and melted into a crack near an opening to the catacombs, the one closest to where the first young woman had been murdered. It was also the place where people entered to go to the bar.

She watched and waited outside. It didn't return.

Crap. She had to know what that thing was up to, so she dropped to the ground and entered the cavern opening, completely aware that she'd never be able to see the damned thing in the dark, even with her vampiric vision. She leaped down the stairwell into the tunnels, avoiding the ladder completely. The minute her feet hit the tunnel floor, she moved toward the site where the woman had been killed. She'd been here twice, so she knew the layout.

A minute later, she heard a familiar voice. It was Britt. That meant that the latest victim had been found around here, too. She strode toward his voice, watching very closely for the demon. So far, there'd been no sign. But then, given the darkness down here, the place could be crawling with shadow creatures.

She met Britt and Veronique on their way out. Britt smiled when he saw her. "Jess, this is a surprise."

Veronique scowled. "I thought you weren't interested in helping?"

"I changed my mind," she said.

Britt watched her closely and got quiet. He knew something was up. Of course, he had no idea what, but his instincts were that good.

She wished she was as good as he was at reading signs.

"Welcome aboard, then," Veronique said, oblivious to the vibes Britt had so quickly picked up on.

Jess sighed. "Since we're here, I'm curious to know where the body was found."

"Back there." Britt indicated the direction with his head. "It was obviously the same psycho, though, this time, he didn't finish. One arm wasn't slit open all the way."

"Weird modus operandi," Veronique said. "Not many serial killers work in this way. It's certainly not a copycat."

"Thank God," Britt said. "It takes a maniac to do what this perp is doing."

"Absolument," Veronique agreed instantly.

"Was there any DNA on the first body?" Jess asked.

"Rien. Not a hint, other than the victim's," Veronique said. "Very frustrating. And, once again, this victim had been patronizing the bar. I'm thinking of shutting that damned place down."

Jess instinctively balked at that suggestion. "If you do, this maniac will just begin killing somewhere else. At least here, we have a chance to catch him." Out of the corner of her eye, a shadow writhed from the wall to the ground and slithered away. Had it been listening all along? Was it capable of that?

This situation was getting more menacing by the minute.

Chapter Eleven

JESS AND BRITT left Veronique behind in the cavern consulting with her forensic anthropologist, a woman who was probably very competent, but she'd have nothing on Sampson.

Britt cleared his throat. "I think we should be together from now on, Jess. We work better as a team."

She didn't get the sense that he was worried about her. He actually thought they'd do better if they worked in tandem. "I suppose you're right—we should stick together. Especially since we don't have a handle on what exactly is wrong here."

"Good. I think you'll be able to withstand the catacombs. You managed well enough tonight," he said.

She hated to tell him she'd most likely just been distracted by the shadow. But for now, she'd let him believe she could do it.

They left the catacombs, and were back on the street, when suddenly Morana stepped out from a recess in the wall. "What do you think is going on down there? Do you think it has anything to do with vampires?"

Jess raised an eyebrow and didn't respond to her questions. "Hello, Morana," she said, not hiding the fact that she didn't like that Morana had obviously been listening to them.

"I know what you are, just as you know what I am," Morana said. "Isn't it strange that we are both vampires and yet our brother is not?"

"*If* we are your siblings," Jess said, wondering why, all of a sudden, Morana was talking as if she believed it was true. "If we are sisters, how did we manage to be turned at approximately the same age?" Unless Morana was much older than she looked. *And thank God she didn't question Regent's age.*

Morana shrugged and chose not to share anything else. Jess suspected Morana knew exactly why they were the same age, or at least why Morana *appeared* to be her age. "How old are you, Morana?"

"Twenty-nine. And you?"

"Twenty-nine, forever."

Morana grumbled something Jess couldn't make out. It was probably in French. "Morana, if I told you I have the world's foremost specialist in vampire physiology on my staff, would you believe me?"

Morana stared hard at Jess. "Maybe."

"His name is Dr. Sampson Case. If you agree to have your VNA tested, we'll have our answer once and for all," Jess said, finally.

"VNA? What's that?"

"It's like DNA, only for vampires," Jess said.

"Interesting," Morana said, pausing to think about it. Finally she said, "Let's do it then."

"Good." Jess took a slight step back and bumped into Britt's chest. She should have realized he was there. He was always there for her, and for the umpteenth time, she thanked her lucky stars that she had him in her existence.

She couldn't call it life, because she didn't have one of those. She was death. But when she really thought about it, death actually defined her. She'd become something positive. And, as hard as everyone on her team worked to help her achieve those things, they deserved everything she could give them.

A noise on the roof above alerted Jess, and she sensed what it was immediately. A vampire . . . and not a friendly one. She glanced quickly at Britt, and his hand was already inside his jacket, reaching for his stake.

"Don't move," Morana said. "He might go away."

Jess laughed. "They don't usually go away unless we send them back to hell."

Gasping as dramatically as any actor, Morana asked, "Is that what you do in your country? You seriously kill your own kind?"

Jess instantly stopped paying attention to the vamp on the roof and turned her gaze on Morana. Short of telling her to stop the dramatics, Jess bit her tongue and measured her words. "I do. If you have a problem with that, you can leave."

Morana didn't take her eyes off the roof as she replied in a caustic voice, "There are a few vampires in France I wouldn't mind getting rid of, now that you mention it. I've never actually considered killing them, though, since the elders would frown on it. I'm not sure how you get away with it in your country."

"Maybe because we don't have any elders to speak of."

Morana's gaze left the roof for a split second, excitement evident in her eyes. "That would be a definite plus." The smile that crossed her features looked about as evil as any she'd seen on vampires in New

York. In an instant, Jess believed Morana wanted the same thing as those heartless creatures—self-gratification and power. If that was true, Regent would be devastated to learn that Morana was bad to the bone.

Worse, she might have just decided to become a landed immigrant.

The vampire overhead didn't drop down among them like Jess expected. This one climbed down the side of the building like a lizard. Or a bat.

He was thin, gaunt, and had stringy black hair that fairly dripped onto his shoulders. His eyebrows were massive and curled at the points like a mustache with wax on it. His teeth were bared for their benefit.

If vampires didn't run around killing other vamps in this city, what did this one want?

She inhaled and tipped her head ever-so-slightly back to peruse the roof again. Vampires lined the roof. No wonder he wasn't nervous about being outnumbered—he wasn't alone.

"Stand down, Britt," she said under her breath. "This is one fight we won't win the normal way." Luckily, if things got ugly, Britt could easily wipe them all out with a mere thought.

"What do you want, Vin?" Morana asked the vampire, venom evident in her voice.

"We want it known that we had nothing to do with the killings in the catacombs."

"Why are you telling us?" Jess asked, instantly curious. Why would they care what anyone thought?

Wait a minute—she knew exactly why they wanted this information known. They feared retribution from the black ops vampire hunting unit of the Paris police. Apparently, no matter how much Veronique denied it, someone still killed vampires in the city.

"There's no need to send out hit squads," the vampire said. "We're complying with the rules of engagement set out by the hierarchy."

"The what?" Jess asked. *Hit squads?* "Who is the hierarchy?"

"The oldest of us. They've always been the leaders and they've managed to keep a fragile peace with humans in the city." He turned to Morana. "You tell her, Morana. Tell her the truth," Vin said.

Morana hissed out an irritated breath. "Vin, you always were a bastard. Now you're a simpering coward, as well."

The vampire stretched his shoulders back and seemed to grow in height until he hovered over Morana.

Jess took a fighting stance, just in case.

"I'm no fucking coward, bitch, and you know it. Someone is trying to cause a war and we're not going to be part of it."

"Why are you telling this to me?" Morana asked, looking at her blood-red fingernails as if she didn't give a damn.

"Not you. That one, who looks like you." The vampire pointed an ancient finger at Jess. "She is the one working with the police."

Morana's head snapped around, and she narrowed an angry gaze on Jess. "She is?"

"I am," Jess said. "What's wrong with that? Britt and I are police officers."

"My own sister!" Morana said.

"That's yet to be determined," Jess reminded her. Sampson would verify the facts for her before she'd trust one word this woman said.

"Sister?" Vin said. "Does the council know about this?" He looked panicked suddenly. "You're not twins? You can't be."

Morana looked like she might go helter-skelter on him. Jess suspected the vampire had let something slip that Morana didn't want them to know. What was the council? Vampires, with some sort of pact with the police? If so, they'd never managed anything like that in North America, where vampires were still too young and savage. But with the olde ones? Maybe that's how they'd existed so long.

Jess stepped forward, hoping to decelerate things before they blew out of proportion. "I'll pass on your information," she said to the vampire.

She didn't have to look at Britt to know tension was galloping through him right about now.

To her surprise, the vampire named Vin backed off. "We have nothing to do with the others, the dark ones seeping out from the ground. They're not part of us. Tell them that," he said to Jess again.

"No one cares about your insignificant vampire frat house or whether you're joining another group," Morana said with a vampire-enhanced voice that surprised Jess.

The vampire rounded on Morana again. "You've suddenly gotten a little too confident, haven't you? If you continue acting like this, you'd better have some heavy hitters backing you, bartender." Vin loomed over Morana for about two seconds, then slid a quick glance back at Jess, as if he didn't want her to see him like this.

For a second, Morana looked like she wanted to slice him open. Both Jess and Britt readied themselves for whatever might come next.

Instead, Vin shot straight into the air and landed on the roof again. The vampires lining the rooftops stepped back and were gone.

"Neat trick," Jess said.

Morana stomped toward Jess. "I think you and I need to talk."

"I agree," Jess said.

"Does everyone in France know you work for the police?" Morana said. "What kind of vampire hunts her own kind? It's hard for me to accept that you could be my sister."

"I kill vampires who are a threat to humanity," Jess said. "It's my job, and my reason for being. I'm making the planet a better place."

"Better for who?" Morana asked. "Humans? What about our kind?"

Britt's hand slipped over Jess's and squeezed in an attempt to calm her. He knew she could easily go ballistic at a comment like that. "We *are* evil. We don't deserve to be saved," she spat.

"*Merde!* You really believe that, don't you?" Morana said.

"It's the truth."

Britt squeezed her hand again. "Morana. It sounds as if there is some sort of peace pact here in France? Is that true?" he asked.

"In a way," she said.

Unfortunately, it also sounded as if she didn't agree with the peace. Her eyes were dark, and her teeth had lengthened since Vin had gotten in her face.

The hardest part of this for Jess was that she realized she could be looking at a reflection of herself. One she hated.

"It's a peace that was etched out by the oldest ones. Some of us don't agree with it. Going hungry to maintain a peace with our food source is no existence."

"Why do you have to go hungry?" Jess asked. "I have my own blood supply from donors."

"Cold blood from a bag," Morana said, her mouth turning cruel. "Only the lower classes of vampires do that here. We have clubs with willing patrons. We take warm blood from our food sources."

It was Jess's turn to squeeze Britt's hand this time—for added strength. "How do you stop the bloodlust from taking over?"

"Who says we do?" Morana replied caustically.

"You kill humans?" The muscles in her back clenched. She couldn't let this woman exist if she willingly took human lives, sister or not. She'd be an abomination.

Out of pure instinct, Jess extricated her blade and stepped toward Morana.

"With the high and mighty morals you have, surely you wouldn't kill your own flesh and blood?" Morana said. "Regent would never forgive you."

Jess narrowed her eyes. Morana was a calculating bitch who knew exactly what to say to stop Jess from kicking her ass.

"Whether you're a vampire or not, Regent would be very disappointed in you right now, Morana. I'm glad he isn't here to see this." Jess turned on her heel to leave.

"Don't run away angry," Morana cried out like a spoiled child. "I don't kill humans, but I am a damned vampire, okay? Surely you can't blame me for my anger. Sometimes it's hard to control."

Jess slowed, trying to think of Regent. "I'll tell you the truth right now. If I give you one more chance, it will only be for *my* brother. If you screw with me again, I will kill you!"

Morana's eyes were black. Jess thought she'd have to break her promise to Regent because it looked like things were about to go south—fast.

Then, all of a sudden, Morana switched back to her normal self, looking repentant. "I'm very sorry."

You're quite the actress, Morana.

"When will you bring your forensic anthropologist over to prove our relationship?" Morana asked. Her voice had taken on an innocent tone that was so not her. Jess had watched her working behind the bar. There, she'd had little patience for her human clientele or her vampire co-worker. The fact that she flashed her lashes at Britt before turning to Jess made Jess's gut clench.

"Vampirologist," Jess said through gritted teeth. "I've already sent for him. As far as I know, he'll be here tomorrow."

Morana clapped her hands in mock appreciation and Jess felt like retching.

"Good. We need to get this thing sorted out. I don't know about you, but I want to know the truth."

Hell, yes, Jess wanted the truth. The sooner she could distance herself from this calculating vampire, the better. There was no way this evil bitch could be her twin sister. Wouldn't she somehow *know* if it was true?

"How can I reach you?" Jess asked. "When Dr. Case arrives, that is." She expected a phone number, at least.

"You know where I work," Morana said. "You can find me there every night."

"Right." Jess glanced at Britt. He'd been unusually quiet through the whole episode. She appreciated that he'd been there for backup, but had let her handle possible family matters on her own. Damnation, could she really have a sister?

Morana glanced at her watch. "Speaking of which, I'm going to be late. I'll catch you both later," she said, actually having the nerve to look Britt up and down, as if he was a tasty treat she'd like to nibble on before she left.

Not if we see you first. Jess couldn't stop her teeth from grinding together. "We wouldn't want you to be late for work."

Morana narrowed her gaze on Jess now. "Jealous much?" She wore a leather ultra-mini skirt tonight and a low-cut V-neck purple chiffon blouse with a ruffle that had been popular in the sixties. She looked amazing. Truth be known, Jess felt frumpy in comparison and uncharacteristically jealous at the way Morana had just eyed her boyfriend. *Crap!* She didn't want to give Morana the satisfaction of getting under her skin.

"If you have time, come to the club later. We have a band playing tonight—the Dead Zone. They're very good, by all accounts." She winked at Britt and sashayed off, making sure her hips waved seductively as she went, as if their antagonistic conversation hadn't even happened.

Jess glanced down at her fashionably tatty jeans, simple white T-shirt and leather jacket. Maybe she should think about how she dressed while she was in France. On the other hand, she shouldn't feel the need to compete with a woman who looked exactly like her.

"Jess," Britt said as they strode down the sidewalk at a faster clip than most people could manage. "Slow down. Someone might see us."

She slowed immediately. This thing with Morana—was she her sister or wasn't she?—was making her crazy.

"Thanks for the reminder," she said. "I'm letting her get to me."

"I'm not surprised. Everything you thought you knew about your family has been turned upside down. But don't worry. We'll figure it out." He grabbed her hand and squeezed. "Listen, do you really believe the vamps have a pact with the police here? Why else would they ask you to pass a message along for them?"

She hadn't even been thinking about that. *Damn it!* She'd been too focused on trying not to kill someone who might be her sister. But she had to get a grip. She was here to help Regent, to stop the shadows. And she couldn't let Morana distract her.

Suddenly, Britt staggered, his hand broke contact, and he caught himself by planting a hand on a wall. "Damn, I hate this place. Who knew I'd crave battling good ole New York vampires?"

"What's going on with you, Britt? Do you think the shadows affected you?"

"No. It's not that. I'm just a bit dizzy."

She slowed again, when she realized she'd inadvertently sped up. "You okay now?"

"Yeah," he said, sheepishly rubbing the back of his neck. "The feeling has passed. But I've been thinking . . . I don't think we can trust anyone, even Veronique. She's holding back on us, too."

"Maybe she still considers you a suspect?"

"It's not likely, since I was with her when the second killing happened, and they were obviously committed by the same person."

They approached Pont Neuf, where the shadows had done a number on Britt's feet and ankles. She wondered how he'd react to being back here again. She eyed him surreptitiously. If he was nervous, he didn't show it.

"I've been meaning to tell you . . . I came to the tunnel tonight because I followed a shadow to the crime scene," she told him.

"What?" His shoulders stiffened and he turned to her.

"I followed a shadow. It went through the wall at a catacombs opening near where the body was found. I have the distinct feeling it deliberately went to the murder site. That's how I found you and Veronique."

"That puts a different spin on the murders, doesn't it? Or a different spin on the shadows. Do you think these things are capable of making a murder look like it was done by a human?"

"They certainly did major damage to your feet."

Britt sighed. "True. But whoever killed those women physically attacked them with a weapon. The shadows don't have that capability, as far as we've seen. Maybe they're just drawn to death?"

"Maybe. I did have the feeling they were following me, at one point," Jess said. She looked into Britt's eyes. Did he know something about the dark entities that she didn't? He seemed quite sure the murders hadn't been done by the shadows.

"Wait a minute, Britt. Regent said two priests had been possessed by them. What if the killer is a possessed human? That would make our serial killer a *lot* more insidious."

Britt's jaw tightened and his mouth became a thin line. "Oh God, Jess, I hope that's not what's happening here." He ran a hand across the back of his neck. "Shit! This place is turning out to be my worst nightmare."

"Why?"

"What if I actually *did* kill that first woman? I was sure I didn't, but what if I'd been possessed without knowing it? I remember feeling particularly dizzy that night. Could that be an effect of possession?"

"But both victims died the same way," she said. "And you were with Veronique and me at the time of the second murder. I doubt the shadows would possess you, then leave and take over someone else. I have the feeling the possessed don't get off so easily."

His shoulders loosened just a little. "But if these things are controlling the murderers, it makes sense that the killers would use the same methods, right?"

Jess's insides churned. Dropping into stasis at dawn would be a reprieve from all of this darkness, especially if Britt actually had been involved against his will. She straightened her back. "No. I don't believe it. You weren't possessed; you're stronger than that," she said, hoping her words were comforting to him.

Please, God, let it be true. He couldn't live with that on his conscience.

When they got back to the apartment, she said good night and went into her sealed room. She climbed into bed and everything went black. No consciousness. No conscience.

As a penance, she'd been told she had to stay like this forever. She'd never be one of the lucky vampires who could be saved by a fallen angel, her fallen angel.

Just as her life began to fade, she felt a cold tear run down her cheek.

UNFORTUNATELY, when Jess awoke the next evening, she felt the same sense of panic she'd had when she'd died at dawn. Her world was spiraling out of her control. When they'd lived in New York, Britt awakened her with a kiss most mornings. But he'd never done that here. Why not? Was it because her room was an airtight mausoleum, or because he was rarely home when she rose? He'd been distracted since they arrived here, and it wasn't just because of the shadows, or the murders. He'd reacted to France in an almost visceral way from the moment they'd landed. He'd felt something was off in this city, as did she. Worse, she'd noted it was affecting him physically. He'd become distant and far too serious.

She was sure he wasn't aware that he'd changed, and she wasn't about to tell him. She didn't want to throw him off stride. But something about Paris had thrown him, and she intended to find out what. She'd give him his autonomy. . . but she'd be here if he needed her.

She'd barely had time to dress after her shower when the phone rang. She picked it up. "Hello?"

"Jess, it's Sampson. I'm at the airport. Can you pick me up?"

"Britt and I will be there in a few minutes," she said. Then she hung up and threw on a silky dress that made her feel just a little bit less of a vampire.

It would be good to see Sampson. She'd missed him. He was part of her inner circle, and she trusted him with her life.

"Britt, Sampson's at the airport. He needs us to pick him up," she called out, expecting him to reply. No one answered.

Sniffing for the familiar scent of his soap, she hurried down the hall to his room, knocking before opening his door. The bed hadn't been slept in again. Did he not sleep at all, anymore?

She glanced at her watch and sighed. He was probably still on the case and looking for clues. The fact that he'd been implicated in a crime didn't sit well with him. He'd never gotten over being framed for a murder he hadn't committed in New York City. And she knew he wasn't going to let it happen again.

It went without saying that she'd help him prove his innocence.

But there was something else that was bothering her—the church had put her brother directly in the path of the shadows. Would they be sentient enough to know that he was studying them, trying to find a way to defeat them? And where did Morana come into this? Jess didn't believe for a second that Regent had found her by accident. The coincidences were piling up.

Shoving her cellphone into her pocket in case Britt called, and pushing all of her worries aside, she got into the SUV she'd rented and met Sampson at the airport. He beamed at her when she arrived to pick him up.

"I'm so happy to see you, Jess. How are you?" He looked her over in surprise, most likely at her more feminine attire.

She brushed her hands over her hips. "I've only been gone a week, you know. I'm fine."

Sampson picked up his luggage and nodded seriously. "You look great. But what's wrong?"

She'd told him when they'd spoken on the phone that she needed him urgently in Paris. But she hadn't explained why. She hadn't wanted to tell him over the phone line. Only, it looked like Sampson had thought there was something physically wrong with her.

"I'm sorry I couldn't explain why we needed you here," she said.

"Not a problem. Now that I know you're okay, that is. Everyone else is okay, aren't they?"

"Yes, Britt and Regent are fine as well."

He heaved a breath. "Okay, what's going on, then?"

"I'll tell you on the way to Regent's place." They walked to the parking area where she'd left her rental SUV with darkened windows.

"Regent's place?" Sampson asked.

"Yes, you'll be staying with him while you're here. He has a spare room, and he'll enjoy your company." Jess hesitated a moment. "And, to be honest, Sampson, I'd feel much better if he had someone to keep an eye on him. The church has him involved in some research that could prove to be dangerous. He needs surreptitious backup."

"I'm not exactly the fighting type," Sampson said, sounding concerned that Jess might expect him to suddenly become a vampire hunter. He raised his arm and proved it by showing his lack of muscle. "I'm a medical man. That's my strong suit, I'm afraid."

"Don't worry. We're not expecting you to join a black ops team or anything." She grinned at Sampson. "Just be there and keep an eye out for Regent. If you have any concerns, contact me or Britt. We'll take it from there." Then she proceeded to fill Sampson in on what was going on.

By the time they pulled up in front of Regent's apartment, Sampson looked concerned. "I'll do my best to look after him, Jess."

She stared straight ahead. "There's another reason I needed you to come."

"Yes?"

"I need you to verify the VNA of a possible twin sister."

Sampson's mouth dropped open. He clamped his hands onto his bald head and said, "What did you just say?"

"I might have a twin here in France. She's also a vampire."

"What are the odds of that happening?" Sampson said, almost stuttering.

"I know. That's one of the reasons I need your expertise."

"Isn't Regent going to wonder why I'm here? I'm guessing he doesn't know I'm going to keep an eye on him, because the Regent I know would never agree to that."

Jess had the good grace to at least look sheepish. "I'll stress that I want you here as my personal physician. I'm sure that'll be enough for him. Besides, he knows I need you to check my lookalike's VNA against mine. He'd never agree to being coddled, but I have the feeling he's lonely. I'm sure he'll be fine with you staying here. You two can catch up on your chess games."

Sampson's eyes widened. "You mean he doesn't even know I'm going to be his guest?"

"Maybe I should have mentioned it, but I didn't," Jess said. "It'll be fine."

Sampson let out a long breath. "Okay, I'm your man. Let's go shock the heck out of your baby brother."

Jess laughed. "You are the most amazing friend," she said.

Sampson's eyes widened even more. No wonder. She'd never actually called him a friend outright before—an oversight on her part. He'd looked after her for years, and she valued his friendship. She should have let him know that before.

Suddenly, Sampson smiled so wide, it was if the sun had come out. She'd finally done something right.

She knocked on Regent's door, and then let herself and Sampson in. "Regent, I have a surprise for you," she called.

"Sampson," Regent said. "Nice to see you."

Jess waited for the two men to exchange greetings. "Listen, I was thinking. . . . instead of putting Sampson up in a hotel, could he stay with you? You have two bedrooms, right?" she asked pointedly.

"I do." Regent grinned at Sampson instantly. "Of course you can stay here with me."

"Perfect," Sampson said, then went out to grab his suitcases.

"I'll show you your new laboratory tomorrow," she said to Sampson once he got back inside.

"That'll be fine," he said, rubbing a weary hand across his eyes.

"I'll make a nice hot cup of tea," Regent said, putting water in a pot and setting it on the gas burner. "And then we'll let you get to bed."

Jess left the two men making plans for Sampson's stay.

She walked a distance from Regent's apartment before she slowed and leaned on a post where she could watch the river. She had a basic plan for tonight. It was time to talk to Morana, face-to-face. They needed a long, truthful talk about their upbringing. No more tap dancing around Morana's biological possibilities. She wanted the truth.

She'd convinced herself that changing into club attire was merely so she wouldn't stand out, but now that she saw herself in the mirror, unease seeped into her. She'd put on a red leather mini dress that opened in a seductive teardrop to expose her belly button, and four-inch spiked red heels. Forcing herself to do it, she pulled her hair up to make it look shorter. The resemblance was really uncanny. She thought she looked more like Morana than herself. And that galled her more than words could say.

BRITT HAD ALMOST reached their apartment when Jess stepped outside. When he saw her, he tried to swallow, but his mouth had gone dry. *Holy hell!* She was gorgeous in that outfit. Something akin to need slithered in his gut. He didn't even want to think about other men looking at her while she was dressed like that. He'd never seen that much of her shapely legs outside of the bedroom. And those heels were going to kill him.

He didn't have to wonder where she was going. He knew instantly: LaCave. Britt's hand rasped over his unshaven chin. He'd have to change his clothes and shave before he joined Jess tonight.

The fact that Jess hadn't spotted him was unusual, though. *Geez!* Was it even Jess? If it wasn't, he'd been drooling over the wrong woman. And that just made him sick.

Instead of changing his clothes, he took a shortcut that should allow him to catch up with her. Finally catching sight of her again, he picked up his pace. His jeans, white polo shirt, and leather jacket would have to do for the nightclub scene. He ran a hand through his hair and set his gaze on the most beautiful woman in France. There was no way that could be Morana.

Jess turned the corner a moment before he caught up to her, but he couldn't speed up without attracting unwanted attention. Besides, he recognized the direction Jess was heading, and it wasn't to Regent's place. She *was definitely* going to LaCave.

Short of running, he'd never catch her now, but it didn't matter. He'd find her in the club. He climbed down the stairwell and dropped onto the rough cement-covered path, just as a hand grabbed him from behind.

Before he could react, familiar lips covered his. Inhaling her vanilla scent, he groaned into her mouth.

"Are you following me, sailor?"

"God, woman, you're driving me to distraction tonight."

He felt her grin against his mouth and her teeth grazed his lower lip, sucking it in and releasing it in a seductively slow movement. "I noticed," she said in a sultry voice.

He cursed under his breath. "You had me fooled, gorgeous. I thought you hadn't noticed me."

"Your heart rate would have given you away, even if I hadn't spotted you the moment I stepped outside, lover."

He laughed and slid his hand inside the opening of her dress. Too bad the leather was a little too tight for his wandering fingers to get very far.

The sound of voices coming their way meant they were about to be distracted by club goers. "Dammit."

Jess kissed him quickly. "Did I tell you that Sampson arrived earlier? He's probably sleeping off his jetlag at Regent's place as we speak."

"Aha. You have a VNA kit with you, don't you?" he said.

"Of course."

"But that's not the only reason you're here, is it, my love?"

"No. I want to get Morana alone. Maybe I can convince her to open up and tell the truth."

Britt shrugged. He didn't think Morana was a sap for sentimentality. She had the shrewd eyes of a killer vamp, the type he usually wiped out without thought.

ONCE INSIDE THE club, Jess braced herself against the music that boomed so loud, she could feel it in her bones. People were dancing like fiends, bouncing up and down to the overwhelming bass sound.

Morana wasn't at the bar yet tonight, but her co-worker focused on Jess as she approached. His eyes narrowed and he bit his lower lip while he wiped down the bar, never quite taking his attention from her. His dyed black hair, heavy black-and-red makeup, and nose and lip rings probably helped hide the fact that he was a vampire. Especially since there were several humans in the club who had a similar look.

"Your name's Diesel, right?" Jess asked.

"You know it," he answered, feigning disinterest. "What can I get you?"

"Are you American?" Jess asked. His accent was a dead giveaway. An American vampire working in Paris? Holy hell, she'd never considered that vampires moved around in the world so easily. Or was Diesel an anomaly?

"You get a Kewpie Doll," he said. "I'm from Maine."

That told her one thing about him—he was old enough to remember Kewpie Dolls. "I didn't realize people like us moved around so much."

Diesel's expression turned cold. "Why the hell not?"

"Most can't control their baser instincts," she said, glancing over her shoulder and noting that Britt wasn't too far off.

"Shit, yeah. I know what you're saying. It's that way in Maine, too. There are a few of us who are more evolved, so to speak," he said leaning forward. "But not as evolved as you are. Word gets around the North American vampire grapevine."

Jess blinked. "You're kidding. I had no idea."

Diesel sniffed. "Of course you wouldn't. You're special, different from us. You have family, friends, and you're a cop. You don't need to scrounge to get food, do you? You don't need to listen for what's happening in your neighborhood in case someone stakes you when you sleep. Every vampire in North America has heard the stories about how you can walk in daylight. How do you do that, by the way?"

Jess ignored his question, instead asking, "Do you know where Morana is?" Had he told Morana what he knew about her abilities? She already hated Jess enough. If Morana knew, Jess would be lucky to get information out of her. Maybe that's why she seemed jealous of Jess. Regardless, Regent would be devastated if Morana dropped out of his life.

Diesel looked disappointed at her lack of response, but not particularly surprised. "She's got the night off. She's probably walking the streets. It's her way of taking a break."

Britt must've read her body language from across the room because he arrived behind her and touched the small of her back. "Everything okay, Jess?"

Diesel raised one eyebrow at Britt. "Him again?"

"We work together," she said. Diesel didn't need to know anything else.

Diesel made a clicking sound with his tongue before staring at Jess again. "It's really uncanny how much you look like Morana. If you had short hair, even I wouldn't be able to tell the difference."

Jess gritted her teeth. "Thanks for the info." She turned to walk away. "Britt, you coming?"

Britt followed her without looking back at the irritated vampire behind the bar. "Where are we going?"

"To find Morana."

"Sounds like a plan."

They walked for two hours. In that time, they saw plenty of lovers strolling around the city, but didn't catch a glimpse of Morana. Suddenly, her skin felt like it was crawling. Britt appeared to be just as uncomfortable. Something evil was coming their way.

"There's a shadow moving along the sidewalk over there," Britt said.

Jess stared hard at the darkness, in order to discern which shadows were real and which were not. "Wait! There's Morana and another shadow. It's following her," she said.

Morana strode the sidewalk as if she hadn't a care in the world. Tonight, she looked more like Jess. She'd dressed in jeans and a knitted shirt that showed her curves, but it wasn't her usual over-the-top haute couture design.

"The resemblance is uncanny," Britt said under his breath.

Jess didn't have time to react to Britt's comment. "Morana!" she shouted. "Look out behind you. You're being followed." She might not like Morana, but she didn't want to see her burned as badly as Britt had been.

They made for one of the many bridges crossing the Seine in order to meet up with her on the other side.

Morana stopped and looked behind her just as the shadow began gaining on her. She took several tentative steps away from the shadow, then yelled, "Get the hell away from me!"

The shadow slowed its approach, as if sentient. But then, suddenly it rose off the pavement and formed a globular shape in front of Morana.

"Get on the bridge," Jess shouted from the bridge.

But Morana didn't make it that far before the shadow grew tall enough to loom over her.

A sound emanated from it, as if it held a chemical charge. Tiny sparks built inside it until it thickened and took on a more demonic shape. With its blacker than black hollows for eyes and a gaping mouth that let out another ear-piercing sound, Morana seemed unable to get past it. Then it lashed out at her, sending her flying back against the brick wall. As if in slow motion, she slid down the wall in a heap.

Britt lurched forward, but Jess grabbed the back of his leather jacket. "No, stay here. Don't take a chance on being burned again unless you really have to. Another dose of their poison might kill you. Besides, this thing is more powerful than the other shadows we've encountered. Let me try this time."

"I don't like it," he said, but knew better than to deny her. "I'm not hanging back for long, babe. If you run into any trouble, I'll be there."

"Understood." She walked toward the end of the bridge, just as the demon attacked Morana again. Its long shadowy fingers made red welts across her face, while she continued to curse at it. But her words only seemed to give it more strength. Every move she made to fight against it only seemed to help it grow in size.

Jess crouched for moment, then sprang off the bridge. Somehow, she managed to get around the demon in order to stand side-by-side with Morana against it.

The demon seemed taken aback for a moment, maybe because she and Morana looked so much alike. Its surprise didn't last long, though. It lashed out again, slicing her arm open.

But something happened—something more than being attacked by a shadow. She caught a moment of understanding. All of a sudden, she *knew* what the shadow was thinking as it fought. Even though the wound burned like hell, probably because it came from the fires of hell, she was stunned by the fact that she'd gained information she'd never expected.

She now sensed there were millions of shadows building below the ground. And yes, this shadow had a mind. It and the others were going to take over Paris. They'd already possessed the necessary humans. Though, after they took power, the humans would no longer be necessary—they'd all die.

Gritting her teeth, Jess covered the wound on her arm with her hand. She wanted to shout to Britt to tell him what she knew, but the pain grew until it was almost unbearable.

She'd been burned by holy water more than once, but since she'd arrived in Paris, she'd taken to carrying a bottle of it, just in case. Tonight, she'd neatly hidden it in her pocket. She popped the cork stopper and held it aloft. "Try to avoid letting any of this hit you, Morana. It's holy water, and it burns."

"Jesus," Morana screamed, stepping back and letting Jess toss the contents at the looming beast. The water hit the shadow's center mass. At first, it didn't seem to have any effect, but two seconds later, it started to sizzle and steam. A keening moan echoed inside it making it waver, then diminish in size. That gave Jess the idea of reciting a prayer. A prayer of salvation.

The shadow instantly shrieked and flattened onto the sidewalk before slithering into the cracks of the wall so quickly, it was hard to follow its movements.

Suddenly, her head started spinning. She might have passed out for a second because suddenly Britt was crouching beside her, taking her arms and helping her up. She wondered why, until her legs gave out and she collapsed against him.

That was when he picked her up as if she were weightless. "Crap, Jess. I should have come with you."

"Where's Morana," she asked weakly.

"Your so-called twin? She took off," he said, acid dripping from his words.

A weird sensation rippled through her. "What's wrong with me?" she asked, noting that even her voice was weak and her body felt drained of most of its energy.

Britt gave her a serious once over. "You've been sliced open. You're actually bleeding, and your wound looks very bad."

Bleeding. Vampires didn't bleed. She glanced down to see her inner arm had been opened. "It must be poisonous. That kind of injury shouldn't even slow me down."

"We've got to get you to Regent and Sampson. The toxin is spreading way too fast."

"Don't worry, I'm a vampire. I can survive this little wound," she said. "I can probably walk by myself, too. I have something important to tell you . . . ." No sooner had she uttered those words than she felt the last vestiges of her energy draining away.

She fell into the void and then was gone.

Chapter Twelve

BRITT RACED DOWN the street on pure adrenaline, with Jess in his arms. He knew there were certain things that killed vampires instantly. So far, she was still alive, but he had no idea how she'd been affected by that demon. His heart raced at the thought. He couldn't lose her.

Her skin around the wound had turned black, with arterial lines spreading and moving up her arm toward her face. By the time he neared Regent's apartment, her neck had been compromised. Before they made it inside, the black lines had spread and moved along her jaw. What would happen when her face was completely covered?

The security door was always locked, so Britt slammed his elbow against the buzzer to Regent's place.

"Yes?" Regent said. "Who is it?"

"It's me," Britt shouted. "Open the door—Jess is hurt."

The buzzer rang like a friggin' firehouse siren in Britt's head, echoing his panic. He tore up the steps and kicked Regent's door open before the priest had a chance to open it. Jess had gone slack in his arms.

Was he too late? Dear God, it couldn't happen this way.

Both Regent and Sampson crowded around Jess who was still in Britt's arms. Sampson grabbed his doctor's case then asked, "What happened to her?"

Britt gave them an immediate account.

"Get her on the couch," Sampson said in a stern voice.

Britt shoved through and gently set her on the couch. Her head flopped sideways while her eyes stared unseeing at the wall behind him.

"Dear heaven! Look at her arm," Regent said, immediately putting a sash around his neck and starting to pray.

Sampson got out a syringe and injected some of his own blood along the slash line. He had healed her this way once before. Was it possible again?

Britt moved out of the way and waited at the end of the couch while Sampson worked on her.

He started his own private regime of silent prayers, intermittently broken by panic. How in hell were they going to fight off these demons? *If* Jess survived. Dear God! No, don't think like that. *And that bitch Morana ran off and left Jess to die.*

Anger welled up inside him until he got control in order to open his heart to recite a healing prayer for the woman he loved beyond life itself. He'd think about that coward Morana when the crisis was over.

Sampson had sweat glistening on his forehead. Regent's lips were moving, his eyes closed. Every now and then, he'd open them to look at Jess's injury, then close them again, and go right back to praying more fervently than before.

Finally, Britt couldn't wait any longer. "It's not working."

Sampson stopped injecting the blood and leaned back on his heels. Regent opened his eyes and tears slipped quietly down his face.

"It's not a vampire injury," Sampson said. "It's demonic. What works on a demon?"

"Holy water, for starters," Regent said. "But that would make things even worse. The prayers are having minimal effect."

Sampson dug in his bag for anything else he might use. When he came up empty, he shook his head slowly.

Britt's gut tightened so hard, it felt like a muscle spasm. "You're not giving up," he said, scanning Jess's features now that more of the black poison had worked through her system, patterning more of her face. "Regent, have you got any herbs left?"

Regent nodded quickly, but more tears spilled down his cheeks. "But she always says they don't work."

"Anything is worth a try right now, isn't it?"

"I think Britt's right, Regent," Sampson said. "Who knows? Maybe the herbs, in tandem with the blood injections, will heal her."

Regent rushed into the tiny room off the kitchen and opened a cupboard. The odor of dried herbs filled the small apartment instantly.

Regent pulled leaves from several bags and used a mortar and pestle to crush them before he added the tiniest bit of holy oil. He stirred them all together quickly with his hands, praying for salvation the whole time.

The scent of the mixture changed once the oil had been added. It was pleasant, and Britt couldn't stop from inhaling deeply. It seemed familiar to him, somehow. Was that the scent he remembered when he'd been brought back from death? After the bastard vampire named Constantine had killed him?

At least, everyone had thought he was dead . . . until he'd been stolen from his coffin and taken to where a secretive group of monks were holding out in New York City. For weeks, he'd suffered endlessly. He had no idea at the time that his body had died and that someone with great ability was in the process of reanimating his veins, tissues, and organs. The pain had been merciless, but the scent of the oil had helped to calm him. He had to pray it would do the same for Jess.

Regent sprinkled the small bits of herbs into her open wound, then placed both hands over it and prayed even louder.

Suddenly, Britt had the urge to touch Regent's hands, which were holding the bandage on Jess's arm. Britt placed both hands over Regent's, and pressed until a blue light erupted from his solar plexus and slid quickly down his arms. It hovered for a moment and then pushed itself through their hands and into Jess.

The process created a burst of air, forcing their hands away when the light impacted Jess's flesh and melted into her. Britt hoped to hell it didn't kill her. Uriel had told Britt he couldn't harm Jess with his light, but did that mean he could heal her?

Sitting back, he waited where he could better see the subcutaneous movement of the light as it moved through her. The black arterial lines were slowly receding, but Jess was still unconscious.

Finally, her incision began to heal, slowly at first and just at one end. But as the extensively branching black lines disappeared, the wound seemed more able to heal itself.

When her flesh was clear of all traces of the infection, the light erupted from Jess's flesh just above her heart and flew back into him. Britt felt nothing, could feel nothing, until he knew that she would make it.

Sampson bent over Jess and patted her hand gently in an attempt to revive her. "Jess. Jess. Wake up. You're going to be okay," he said.

"Jess," Regent urged. "Wake up, please!"

Britt's knees turned to jelly. He dropped to the floor beside her because his body had virtually become boneless. His world would end without her. He willed her back to him, but she remained unconscious. What had happened to his damned blue light? Why hadn't it worked?

He barely dared a glance at Regent. "Is she—gone?"

Regent's frown lines suddenly dissipated at the sight of the burgeoning morning sun through the living room window. "Maybe not—if she's gone into stasis."

Britt followed his gaze. "OMG! We have to get her into a room with no windows fast," he said, grabbing her and lifting her quickly.

"The hall closet is the only place that is completely sealed when the door is shut," Regent said. "Let me quickly clear out the shoes and coats." After he and Sampson emptied the closet, Regent grabbed cushions off the sofa and made a quick mattress for her.

Britt clung to the hope that Jess was merely in stasis—that they had actually healed her. Dawn was fast approaching and there was a chance that she'd merely moved into that undead state until nightfall. Unfortunately, they wouldn't know if she'd made it until later that evening.

Regent shut the door tight and they looked at each other. It was going to be the longest day of their lives.

DURING THE DEMON assault, Morana ran like a scared schoolgirl, leaving Jess at the mercy of that horrifying attacking shadow. After all, she'd put herself in that position. No one had asked for her help.

Still shaking from actual goddamned fear, she ran toward sanctuary—LaCave. The club had closed two hours ago, making it the perfect place to go. At one point, she'd halted and pressed her hands over her face, thinking about how Jess had been slashed open. It would have been her body cut like that, if not for that stupid woman's intervention.

Yeah, she'd seen the shadow slice Jess open, just as she'd torn away into the night. But at least Morana would live to fight another day. She looked out for number one. Her twin should have learned that lesson long ago. Too bad that Regent would be so broken up over the loss of his sister. Irritation spread through her body. Hopefully, he wouldn't think she'd fill in.

Since sunrise was imminent, she'd have to use her secret room in the catacombs for stasis.

Before she entered the tunnels, the reality of what had happened tonight fully hit her. She slammed a hand against the wall, making part of the brick crumble away.

She was a coward! She'd always believed herself to be the bitch who feared nothing, but now she had to face the real truth—she'd panicked and left Jess to die. She could pretend she didn't care about everyone else, but inside, she was the only one who knew that she ruined everything she touched. It was Sinclair's fault. He'd raised her that way.

An ugly sensation burned in her stomach. Britt had witnessed her cowardice and she was sure he wouldn't let her get away with what she'd done. Maybe she was more afraid of retribution from him than the fact that she'd abandoned her sister.

She gasped as her arm suddenly burned. Smoke wafted off her when a thin beam of sunlight reached her. Uttering a string of curses, she dove down the stairwell and landed at the bottom with a few more burns. *Shit! That smarted.* But the wounds would heal during her dead time.

But first, she needed to get to her secure location. It wouldn't be good to be caught down here by a cataphile or a cop while she was in such a vulnerable state.

She surged down the tunnels at a speed only a vampire could manage. The darkness and damp air soothed her burned flesh. If only she could gouge out the image of the shadow ripping Jess's arm open and seeing her fall to the ground, just as easily.

Relief flooded her when she made it to her safe room and quickly locked the metal door. She'd cut it close before, but never this close. She hadn't quite reached the bed when her world went dark.

She smiled. Morana looked out for herself—always.

No one else mattered.

Chapter Thirteen

BRITT SAT WAITING while Regent and Sampson had tea and toast. Personally, he couldn't eat a thing until he knew Jess was okay. If only he could check on her, make sure she hadn't turned to dust inside that closet.

"She's okay, Britt. She's going to be okay," Regent said, as if he could read Britt's mind. Hell, whatever he was thinking was probably written all over his face.

Britt lowered his head and gripped his hands tightly on his lap. "What if she's not?"

"She is! Think, man, you sent your healing light into her—the same light that saved Uriel from vampirism, the same light you used to save yourself a few nights ago. You have the power to save Jess. Your love will not fail her," Regent said.

Weight edged slightly off his shoulders. Regent had a way of making people believe him. "I couldn't have done it without the herbs," Britt said, releasing his hands from the grip that had made his fingers practically numb. "The more I think about it, the more I realize there was something about the odor of the herbs and oil that struck a chord in me. That scent forced the light out. Hopefully, it managed to heal Jess."

Sampson shook his head. "I wish I could test your blue light. Take a sample and see what it's made up of."

"Is that possible?" Britt asked.

"Probably not. It'd be like trying to bottle lightning."

"I will submit to tests whenever you like," Britt said. "But not until Jess is okay."

Sampson looked heavenward. "That's okay, Britt. There are some things we have to take on faith. Your light is one of those things. I believe in you and your light, and so does Regent. And Jess believes in you more than anyone."

Britt hated the pressure they'd put on him without meaning to. If Jess died, that would mean he'd failed her. His blue light wasn't a gift but a horrendous burden. And worse, how would Regent take it when Britt told him that Morana had run off and left Jess to die?

She'd taken off like a scared cat. Vampires didn't do that. They were usually fearless. His Jess was fearless. Britt had known from day one that Morana was trouble, yet even he was surprised by how much of a coward she was. If Jess died because of it—and because he'd waited too long on the bridge—he'd never forgive himself . . . or her.

Regent appeared to be using his skills as a priest to keep himself from falling apart. He couldn't properly concentrate though, often stopping mid-sentence and staring at the closet door. Then he'd get up and stalk around his apartment, looking at every knickknack, before lowering his head again in prayer.

All three of them were very aware when the sun finally lowered in the sky. It seemed to take forever, but the second it extinguished, no one moved. Instead, they sat at the kitchen table, staring at the closet, waiting for the door to open.

Britt listened for any sound, but all he could hear was the pounding of his own heart driving blood through his veins and into his brain.

When the closet door rattled and Jess opened it, the three of them jumped to their feet simultaneously. Her hair was a mess and her skin had pink marks everywhere the veins had been black. She had deep shadows under her eyes and was still sitting on the floor after she'd thrown the door open. She looked like hell, but she was alive.

"You shoved me into your closet, brother? Why?"

All three of them raced toward her, but she held up her hands to ward them off. "Back off. What's wrong with you three?"

"You don't remember?" Regent asked.

"Oh, I remember, all right," she said. "I remember that demon trying to dissect me. But wait! There's something important I have to tell you." She paused, and took a breath. "Weird as it seems, for a moment or two, I got inside its head. The demons have an agenda. They aren't just random devils roaming the streets; they're planning to take over Paris."

"Crap," Britt said. "We've got to find a way to stop them, and fast."

"Tomorrow, I'm supposed to visit the two priests who've been possessed," Regent said. "I think it's time we learn more about what these creatures are doing to people."

Still sitting on the floor in a lotus position, she ran her fingers through her hair. "I feel like my arm is stuffed with dry leaves," she said, rubbing her hand over the bandaged wound.

"It kind of is . . . my dear," Regent said. "It was my herbs."

"And they worked?" she asked in an astonished voice.

Regent grinned from ear to ear, and sat beside her on the floor. "They actually might have helped, you know."

Sampson patted Britt on the shoulder. "Those, in combination with Britt's blue light, healed you."

Jess looked at each of them in turn. "Is that right?"

"Maybe you're not a vampire any longer?" Sampson suggested. "After all, Britt did save James, Terry, and Sephina."

Jess's heart twisted. *Wishful thinking.* It wasn't Sampson's fault—he didn't know. She hated to see the hope cross Britt's face. *Don't do this to yourself, Britt*, she willed. But it was too late. Sampson had planted the seeds and she could tell Britt wanted to believe it could be true.

"Don't want to break your bubble, but I'm still a vampire," she said, poking the cold flesh of her arm and trying to sound tough so no one got too upset about her death-sentence. "But at least I'm still kicking," she said.

"How do you feel?" Sampson asked.

"A little rough around the edges," she said, thinking about Morana and wondering if Regent knew their so-called sister had abandoned her. She glanced at Britt. Had he told Regent? But all she saw was guilt and concern on his features.

"I'm okay, Britt. You saved me, again."

"I didn't do it alone, my love. Your brother somehow initiated my light with his herbs."

She made an impressed face then winked at Regent. "Really? Who would have guessed that those dried-up old leaves would actually work someday."

Regent clasped his hands and looked heavenward. "Glory be that you're back, my love, and with your sense of humor intact."

She rolled her eyes.

"Can you get up?" Sampson asked.

Everyone knew Jess didn't like being fussed over, especially moments after she woke. She'd cut them a break this time, given the circumstances. "Yeah, sure, I'm totally fine," she said, even though she noticed an unusual weakness in her limbs when she pushed off the floor. But she hid it from the men since they were worried enough.

"There is sustenance in the bottom of the fridge," Regent said. "I had it restocked yesterday."

Bless him! He probably knew she'd stretched the truth about her strength. She could have kissed him for being prepared enough to have a fresh supply of blood in the house. Kissing him—now that *would* shock him to death.

It probably didn't escape any of them that she'd barely made it to the fridge, all the while trying not to give away her weakness. While she drank, they turned away. They knew full well she didn't like anyone to witness her vile need for blood—and she needed more than usual this time. She drank like a ravenous beast who hadn't fed in days.

Finally satiated and feeling back to normal fairly quickly, she joined the men in the living room.

"Dear?" Regent said.

She nodded. "Much better, thanks," she said. She didn't have to say more. They discussed the demon attack and what Jess had learned. Regent would report it to the committee as soon as he could, without giving away all of the details.

Finally, when they resorted to small talk, Jess decided it was time to go. She couldn't abide mundane chatter any longer.

Regent jumped to his feet and followed her and Britt to the door. Fine wrinkles etched into his forehead reminded her of how different his physiology was now that he was a middle-aged man again.

"Don't worry, Regent. I'm fine—if you can call being a vampire fine. I'll be sure to avoid those beastly shadows from now on if I can help it."

"I'm so glad to hear you say that," he said. "I wanted to ask you to stay away from them, but I wasn't sure you'd be happy to hear me cosseting you."

"If you didn't look out for me once in a while, I'd think you'd lost your edge, brother." She patted his shoulder and let him squeeze her hand.

Britt had been fairly quiet since she'd exited the closet. He'd nearly lost her, and she knew he'd blame himself for letting her go after the shadow alone, even though she'd insisted.

Halfway down the block, Britt slowed his pace and pulled her into his arms. Since it wasn't unusual to see a couple necking on the sidewalks in the city of love, she returned his hot, sultry kisses with all of the emotion she could manage. She was still more fatigued than she let on.

His large, capable hands circled her waist and pulled her against him while he nuzzled along her neck and then moved back to her lips again. "I thought I'd lost you," he murmured into her ear.

She ran her hands slowly up his chest, then to the nape of his neck where she threaded her fingers into his hair. She gave a little tug, urging him toward her until his mouth crushed against hers and they kissed until she almost felt breathless. It took talent to make a vampire feel that way.

More than that, he'd been able to bring her to heights of emotion that vampires were incapable of experiencing, right down to her heart beating in her chest. He'd always been able to make her physically *feel*, if only for a few seconds before the pall of death wiped away the thrill of life again.

"I love you," he said.

She bit her lip. "And I love you." It seemed right that it happened on the street near a brick wall. They'd had their first kiss pressed against a wall very similar to this one. Was that why Britt had chosen this spot?

Jess leaned back against the brick and caressed the side of his face. "I never thought I'd ever say this to you, Britt, not because it isn't true, but because I didn't want to bind you to me—to an evil vampire. The thing is, I've come to realize, vampire or not, I can't live without you. Maybe I'm just being selfish to expect you to want to be with me forever."

He groaned. "You're anything but selfish," he said with that sexy smile that melted her bones just a little. "I have to admit, I didn't think you'd ever utter those words. You're always so concerned about our backgrounds."

"Backgrounds?" She actually laughed at that. "Is that what we're calling the fact that you're an angel and I'm a devil, now?"

"You are far from a devil," he said. "Well, maybe a little devilish in bed." He winked at her and let his hands slip down her sides, his thumbs caressing the sides of her breasts on the way. It was the best he could manage in public, she guessed.

"Shall we go home? If you feel up to it, that is."

She looked around. Tourists were wandering the streets alongside the riverbanks holding hands and kissing, too absorbed in each other to worry about onlookers.

"Race you," she said, and took off at a pace much faster than a normal human could muster. She had to prove to him she was fine.

When she reached the apartment and looked back, he wasn't even in her sights. Had she moved that fast? Feeling almost light-hearted at her regained strength, she mounted the steps to the third floor and opened the door. Britt was already there.

She hadn't even seen him pass her.

Eyes wide and mouth slightly ajar from shock, she shut the door behind her and locked it. "How'd you manage to get here before me? And without me seeing you?" Damn it, she shouldn't have asked. She knew the answer. She'd been weakened by the attack. How long would it take her to heal fully? But maybe his angelic self was growing in strength and speed, too. Racing him might be more of a challenge in future.

He pulled off his sneakers, tossed them in the closet, and shrugged out of his jacket and shirt right there in the foyer, exposing a muscled chest that any woman would drool over. His gaze devoured her whole while he bent his index finger and motioned for her to follow him. She instantly forgot about their race. Instead, she held her breath while he tugged her willingly down the hall to his bedroom.

After her near-death experience, nothing would feel better than making love with him tonight. After all the unknowns on the streets of Paris—the demons, the serial killer—nothing else mattered at this moment but the two of them.

"Is my room okay?" he whispered, taking a nip on her earlobe.

"It's perfect," she said, not the least bit worried that he could hear the breathlessness in her supposed tough vampire voice.

On their way down the hall, he stopped twice to kiss her—to ravage her, really.

By the time they entered his bedroom, she was desperate. She couldn't get enough of him—not tonight, not ever.

His gaze alone set her on fire, and his kisses spread those flames through her. He pressed her onto the bed, then turned her slightly in order to unzip her red leather dress that left little to the imagination, anyway.

"Did I tell you how sexy you look in this dress?"

Her breasts spilled out and he molded one into his hand. She pressed herself against his bare chest because she needed to feel his warm skin against hers.

"But much sexier without it," he added, his gaze practically raw.

She wanted him to take her slowly so they could enjoy every inch of each other. In their job, one never knew which night would be their last.

While he kissed her, she focused on that pleasure. They were taking the rest of the evening off and there was no need to rush through this.

Britt's deliberate attention to her body was torturous bliss. Even though she wanted him now, she didn't want to miss every erotic moment as he expertly brought her flesh to life, over and over again.

Every rush of his pulse forced vampiric desire to flood to her core. Even though her teeth lengthened, she managed to keep that lustful need under control—for now.

Oblivious to her growing teeth, he caressed every inch of her body, while she murmured little sounds of pleasure. He muttered endearments in her ear and let his tongue and lips travel over her, kissing her in places he'd never kissed before. She arched her back and lost herself in the monumental pleasures he elicited.

She smiled at him. "I swear you make my flesh come alive," she said, pressing her lips against his chest. "I feel every sensation when you make love to me, every pulse-pounding erotic moment." He was that good, and she let herself relax in order to experience everything he was willing to give her.

He kept up with her extreme abilities as a vampire, now, more than ever before. Friction built until she thought she might burst into flames. But his stamina didn't wane and he made her want to scream out his name.

She held back, waiting for him to reach the same heights with her. Suddenly, he shuddered against her and she followed, collapsing onto him with a sigh of delirious pleasure. Was she crazy, or had that been the best sex she'd ever experienced? Ever!

Each time they made love, it got better and better. But . . . wow. For a few minutes, she felt human again. Human and loved. "That was wonderful. So wonderful," she said breathlessly.

"You can say that again." His skin was slick with sweat while her flesh remained cold and dry, reminding her that her physiology rarely changed on the outside. But inside, her heart actually pulsed with love. Sadly, the effect wouldn't last long.

His arms wrapped around her nakedness and held her tight. "Can you wear that dress again tomorrow?"

"No." She gently shoved him away in mock irritation.

Even now, as they basked in afterglow, her thoughts couldn't stop from going back to last night's incident . . . and her supposed twin's actions.

She had to find Morana and demand why she'd turned tail and ran.

"Shower?" Britt asked, glancing at his watch on the bedside table. "You don't have much time before the sun comes up."

"Really?" They'd been making love for hours. Talk about a night to remember. "Yes, let's go."

She slid her soap-covered, slick body against his in the shower. He was more than ready for another romp, but time was too short. She stepped back and allowed him to finish his shower while she quickly did the same.

After drying off, she slipped into a new silky black nightgown and held his hand as they strolled toward her room. "I can't stand this place," she said.

"I know. What can we do to fix it?" he asked, sounding instantly concerned.

"I'm going to search for a bigger rooftop apartment. If we're going to be in Paris for months, I have to have something more comfortable than this. I thought I could handle it, but it's getting to me."

"Why do you think they gave Regent three months to come up with a way to defeat the shadows?" Britt asked suddenly. "It's not very long, when you consider we're talking about demons taking over the country."

Jess bit her lip. "Maybe they didn't expect the shadows to be as dangerous as they are. Now that we know what we're dealing with, there's no saying how long he might be here."

Britt let out a long breath. "I still think the three month thing is unusual. There's something else going on. But, as usual, I imagine we'll find out the hard way."

She laughed out loud. "I just love it when you sound as cynical as me. And as realistic."

"Can I help find another apartment?" He stopped beside her bed while she climbed onto it and positioned herself.

"Sure. It would be great if we could find something similar to the one we have in New York."

"I'll do my best." He kissed the tip of her nose.

That reminded her that he wasn't sleeping much these days. "You will rest, though, right? You need sleep at some point."

"I'll sleep," he said. "But I only need a few hours—three or four—and I'm good to go."

"I wonder why you don't need as much sleep now."

He shrugged. "Wish I knew. There are so many things about me now that are still unknown. I have no control and virtually no understanding. Considering I've met two others like me, you'd think I could have managed to get them to share more information."

"I guess they had their reasons. Don't worry. You'll get the hang of it eventually. In the meantime, it's fun experiencing new things with you. Who doesn't like a surprise?"

"Are we talking about in the bedroom now?"

"If only. Sorry," she said, and kissed him thoroughly, then let him pull the sheet up to her arms. She was already stiffening and her lips would no longer move when he left her room, locking her safely inside.

Chapter Fourteen

THE NEXT EVENING as she showered, her thoughts turned again to her shadow attacker and Morana's desertion. Even if she looked beyond the fact that Morana might be her sister and should have helped her, Jess found it odd that a vampire would run away without first trying to fight. Morana was different than other vampires, and Jess wanted to know what had made Morana that way. Was it a genetic thing in their family? When they were turned, did their vampirism take an unusual route?

Jess had plans for tonight, but she wasn't going alone. Britt would be with her. Tough vampire or not, she knew enough to have backup against the shadows from now on.

"Evening, gorgeous," he said the minute she stepped into the kitchen. They were obviously on the same wavelength—he was sitting at the dining room table dressed in his fighting leathers.

She eyed him up and down. "Great minds think alike."

"After you've had your sustenance, let's get to work. We can't just sit back and let the shadow creatures take over. Do you think Veronique and her team will object if we do some research of our own?"

Jess paused. She hadn't even thought about that. "If Veronique doesn't want our help, she shouldn't be the captain of her unit."

Britt opened a drawer in the kitchen, pulled out his silver stake and shoved it into his shoulder holster, then loaded three bottles of holy water onto his belt. Jess cringed, but since the holy water had worked on the shadows, she added a couple of bottles of her own.

"You keep your stakes in the kitchen drawer now?"

He shrugged and winked at her. "Since we don't have many dishes, I thought I might as well."

She winced at the thought. She was sure he didn't mean to make her feel bad, but it reinforced the fact that their relationship was anything but normal. They couldn't go out to dinner together, or go to a concert. And there wouldn't be any popcorn while watching a movie. Well, no popcorn for her, anyway—he loved the stuff.

"What are you thinking about?" Britt asked, pulling her hand up to his mouth and kissing it. "You look so serious."

"You know me. Vampires don't smile without a very good reason. It's my version of normal," she said, reluctantly extricating her hand from his and going to the front door.

It was hard not to stare at him while he pulled on his sneakers. The reality of what she was truly was blossomed in her gut whenever he looked at her and his features softened. How could he love her? He deserved better.

Okay, she was in a mood today. But sometimes, it was hard to face the fact that she'd never be able to give him what he needed, things any other normal human being would give the man she loved. Not a truly happy smile, or a bubbly conversation. . . . And she certainly wouldn't be able to give him a child. He should have children. Little versions of Britt would be so wonderful to have around.

Maybe being attacked by the shadows had affected her unholy side more than she'd realized. She needed the hunt to expel the anger and frustration of being undead. She had too much darkness in her to pretend to want to live like a human, even on vacation. She needed to get her anger out in a way that didn't compromise her. If she stayed in Paris, she'd have to find a way to work out her angst.

While hiking down the sidewalk with Britt, she said, "Even though there's a lot for us to deal with here, I suddenly feel like being a tourist tonight." She was testing him to see if he was feeling as pent-up as she was.

He nodded absently, already full cop mode. "Huh?"

She repeated what she'd said.

"Right. We are tourists," he said. "Tourists who are going to kick ass tonight."

Question answered, Jess inhaled and bit back a grin. "I think we should check out the scenery in that direction," she said, lifting her head and sniffing the air. Evil left a trail of pollution that was often easy for her to follow. It was an unusual talent, even for a vampire. Her ex-vampire partner, James, had always admired that ability.

They strode purposefully down a few back alleys and managed to scare off a cat or two, not to mention a street person or two, but nothing worthwhile. The deeper they got into old Paris, into the parts of the city that France would probably like to forget, excitement grew inside her. This was the place they'd likely find a battle worth fighting.

Another homeless person staggered past them. "Got money?" he asked in broken English. He must have heard them speaking earlier.

Britt reached into his pocket and handed the man ten euros.

"Don't be too generous," Jess whispered.

"I just want the guy to get a good meal," he said. "He looks like he's starving."

"But he could waste it on alcohol or something," she said.

Britt's hands tightened at his sides. "The guy's existence filled my mind, Jess. He's down and out, but not a product of self-destruction—just bad luck. An ache in my belly telegraphed the man's hunger. This man has known more of it than he should have. Honestly, Jess. You might think I'm crazy, but I knew the minute I saw him."

Her conscience twisted. Thankfully, Britt had enough humanity for both of them. "You're a good man, John Brittain," she said.

He gave her arm a gentle shove with his elbow. "Don't go all mushy on me, Vandermire," he said.

"Like that'll ever happen." Her footsteps faltered, then the air stilled. She held up a hand and listened. "Watch yourself, Britt. There's a vampire nearby."

"Where?" he asked.

"Behind us." She spun around to face the stranger moving in on them with obvious intent. If she had time to high-five Britt first, she would have. She needed this fight tonight. It seemed that not all vampires in Europe were civilized after all.

"Can we help you?" she asked, in case she'd read this guy wrong.

The vampire didn't speak. Maybe he didn't understand English. Either way, his teeth were out and so was his anger. He appeared to be as hungry as the street person they'd seen earlier, and he was obviously intending to satisfy that hunger with them.

By setting his sights on Jess, likely because she appeared to be the smaller of the two, he'd made a fatal mistake. She pulled her blade out of her pocket slowly and with emphasis, flashing it back and forth. Shaped like a cross with jewels in the hilt, it had been difficult to get into Paris, but she'd figured out a way because it was her favorite weapon.

The vampire slowed his forward momentum then stopped and frowned.

"What? Are you scared of a little thing like this?" She slashed the blade back and forth in the air.

His eyes were thin slits now and his teeth had extended. He licked his lips. "I'm hungry and I want to drink you, vampire. I want to absorb your abilities."

"Really? Even if that were possible—which it isn't—it would be hard to do when you're getting your ass kicked." She jumped into the air, twirling like an ice-skater, and coming down at him with the knife aimed and ready.

Teaching him a lesson, she leaned forward and sliced his face open, then waited for him to make the next move.

He held a hand to his face, then looked at his blood-covered palm in surprise. He seemed pretty thin and rangy, in worn black cotton pants and a T-shirt. His hair was short and his face deeply shadowed. He brought his fingers back and licked the blood off them. *Jesus, Mary, and Joseph!*

Britt leaned against the wall of the alley, his legs crossed in repose. Because she needed the battle, he'd wait.

When she dove sideways to avoid the vampire's lunging teeth, she spotted another vamp. "There's another one coming and he's all yours, Britt."

Britt had already noticed.

She returned her full attention to the vampire in front of her. Unfortunately, he wasn't much of a fighter, and she wasn't getting the adrenaline surge she'd craved. Maybe this vampire hadn't been around as long as the others. That would explain his lack of skills.

"Is that the best you got?" she shouted at him, crooking her finger at him to bring it on.

Angered by her taunt, he charged. When she stretched out a toe and tripped him, he bashed into the brick wall. *Idiot.* And when he jumped up again, snarling and hurling more curses at her in both languages, she bared her own elongated teeth.

He adjusted his belt and growled low in his throat while her gaze shot to his gold-studded, heavily decorated belt. The gold studs were fillings from teeth . . . which meant he'd killed a lot of humans in a city with a supposed peace pact. This unworldly, gaunt beast deserved to die.

The fact that she was eyeing his belt made him grin, baring lengthening teeth in which he'd also inserted gold from his victims. It seemed he had a penchant for victims with fillings. So why attack her?

Then she realized the real reason. That stuff about her abilities was just to throw her. She touched the gold-heart locket she wore tonight. It had been a gift from Regent, complete with pictures of their parents inside.

"You like gold, do you? Well, you're not getting my necklace, you bastard," she growled at him. From her peripheral vision, she saw Britt raise his stake to finish off the vamp he'd been fighting. She knew the moment he'd killed the vampire because she heard the explosion of molecules. Since Britt had taken the guy out so forcefully, she guessed he'd missed fighting, too.

After seeing the other vampire vaporize, her attacker seemed to have second thoughts, and he scrambled to get away. He crawled partway up the wall before she grabbed both of his arms and ripped him backward, then slammed him onto the pavement where she planted her foot on his chest and slowly, deliberately held her blade aloft. She wanted him to know what was coming. He should experience the fear he'd elicited in his victims.

He writhed under her foot, which was currently jammed into his jugular notch. His tongue extended when she pressed harder. It would hurt, but it wouldn't kill him. That part came next.

"Tonight you meet your evil maker and burn in hell," she said, just before she jammed the blade into his heart. She stepped back, waiting for him to vaporize.

He died all right, but his body remained. *No!* Her first instinct had been accurate. He was young. Very young, in vampire terms.

At home, she had a team to dispose of vampires who didn't burst into molecules at the moment of their death. What the hell would she do with the corpse of a vampire in Paris?

Britt approached and looked down at the body. "What're we going to do with this guy?" he asked, striding to the end of the alley and scanning the sidewalk in both directions. "We can't just leave him here." He returned and pushed back the vampire's lip to see that his lengthened teeth remained. "He's a dead giveaway to the fact that vampires exist."

"Funny," she quipped. "We have to figure this out. Even after the sun comes up, there'll still be a burned body that will require answers. We need to get him out of the public eye."

"Someone's coming," Britt said, grabbing the vamp by the heels and dragging him to the far side of a nearby Dumpster where he couldn't be seen.

They waited and listened until the footsteps stopped outside the alley opening.

"Are you going to hang around in there all night?" Veronique's voice called from the entrance. "Or do you want my team members to take care of that body for you?"

Jess and Britt stared at each other, before coming out to greet Veronique. "How'd you know we were there?" Britt asked.

"How'd we know?" she asked in a cynical voice. "You're hunting in our city. This is our territory, remember? We try to keep the peace." Her arms were folded over her chest and her fingers tapped angrily on one arm.

"Peace, my ass, Vee. We were attacked. If you were watching, you already know that." She strode back to the corpse and grabbed him by the heels, dragging his body closer to the opening of the alley. Seeing those gold fillings on the vamp's belt angered her all over again. "I guess this guy's been killing under your radar. You might want to pull up all of your cold cases with victims who had gold fillings. I have the feeling this bastard's been responsible for most of them."

Veronique looked instantly peeved. "I didn't say we were infallible. I said we *try* to keep the peace. I'm sure you still have human casualties in New York City, no matter how hard you try to keep people safe. No vampire-hunting team can be everywhere."

Jess gritted her teeth.

"Okay," Veronique said slowly. "So, why are you here tonight?" She stared at Jess and Britt with that stone-cold stare she'd perfected. "You were obviously looking for a fight tonight."

The fact that Britt had slipped his stake back into his shoulder holster hadn't gone unnoticed by Veronique.

"I admit it. We thought we'd blow off a little steam, but only if we were attacked first," Jess said, raising her hands in a questioning manner. "And we were."

"I know. I saw it from my location over there," she said, pointing to a Plexiglas booth on the highest rooftop in the area.

"Funny, I didn't sense you," Jess said.

"It's soundproof and completely sealed, so no odors can leak out," Veronique said, sharing a tip that Jess would take home to her team. She'd just imparted a little bit of free goodwill.

"This alley is also a particular hotspot for vampire attacks in Paris," she said. "We can pretty much monitor the vampires from up there."

That certainly explained why a lookout would work for them.

A van pulled up and two men dressed in black jumpsuits exited and approached the body without saying a word.

"Take this one for disposal," she said.

"Is that all you do?" Jess asked. "Dispose of them?"

Veronique turned a quizzical gaze on her. "What else would we do with them? Stuff them and keep them on our mantel?"

"No. Have their VNA extracted. Keep a record on file so you'll know if they come back."

"VNA?"

"It's like DNA, only for vampires." It shocked Jess that a country as old as France didn't have that kind of technology. But then, they didn't have Sampson Case, Forensic Vampirologist extraordinaire.

"I think you and I are going to have to talk," Veronique said. "I've never heard of such a thing. How does one extract this VNA with most bodies turning to dust and blowing away?"

"We capture some of the molecules in a vial. My specialist developed the technique, and we actually have quite a large database in New York City."

"And the purpose of doing this?"

Had she not been listening? "For one thing, we like to make sure they stay dead." Jess frowned. "And, if they've recently killed someone, that person's DNA is extractable from the vampire's VNA too."

"Mon Dieu."

Jess watched Veronique's men efficiently stow the body, then drive away.

Britt tightened his jacket over his stake before he pulled out the vial of ash he'd extracted from the vamp he'd just killed. "I managed to get a sample of the vampire I staked. I'm pretty sure you'll find he recently killed a homeless person."

"You're not talking about the man we met earlier, are you?" Jess asked, feeling bad for Britt.

He nodded, his mouth in a thin line. "I guess it's not safe for humans around here."

"No, it's not," Veronique said. "But I can't very well go on the news and warn transients to stay away from here, now can I?"

"I'm not blaming you," Britt said. "It's just that we'd met the man moments before the vampire killed him. He seemed nice, if down on his luck."

Veronique looked serious. "My team found his body already."

"So everything's not as peachy between humans and vampires as we've been led to believe," Jess said.

"I'm sorry I couldn't tell you the full scope of our problems. I was sworn to secrecy." She shrugged her shoulders. "Now that you know the truth, I'll be able to disclose a little more." She glanced at her watch.

"I see." Jess shoved her hands into her pockets. She could tell Vee would disclose only what she had to. Sharing information was going to be like pulling teeth.

"I'm sorry we got off on the wrong foot, Jess. I shouldn't have arrested Britt, I know. But I was desperate. There's something I haven't told you about the victims."

Jess glanced at Britt, who looked like his spine had locked. "What is it?"

"Those two victims found in the tunnels . . ."

"Yes?" Britt said, an urgent tone in his voice. "What about them?"

"They were numbers nine and ten."

"Crap," Britt growled. "You damned well knew it wasn't me, then. I wasn't even in the country for the others."

"I know. I'm sorry. But I wanted to give the killer a little leeway to make a mistake. If he thought we blamed you for the murders, he might get sloppy."

Jess planted her hands on her hips. "We're police officers, as well. You damn well should've told us that," she said.

"I couldn't." She glanced over her shoulder. "I think I might have a leak in my unit. There've been a few too many stings that have gone wrong lately."

"Seems as if you're in a helluva mess," Britt said.

"And you were at the right place at the right time, John. I had to take the opportunity when it presented itself."

"His friends call him Britt, but you can call him Lieuten—" Jess said, but Britt placed a hand on her shoulder.

"Britt is fine."

Veronique flushed, obviously effectively chastised. "Again, I apologize. I hope we can get past this and work together."

"Especially now that you've seen what efficient fighters we are," Britt stated.

"What I don't understand is this," Jess said. "If you have some sort of pact with vampires, why are they still out here killing humans? And why does everyone pretend it isn't happening?" She paused a moment, then said in a lower voice, "I'd also like to know what hit squads are."

"Hit squads? Where'd you hear that?" Veronique asked, instantly on alert again.

Jess told her about her encounter with the vampires who wanted Veronique to know they weren't involved with the serial killings.

"Why did they tell you and not me? It doesn't make sense . . . unless they know about the leak, too." She stared up at the tops of the buildings, as if searching for more vampires. "I think it's time we really talked. We should go get a drink," Veronique said, suddenly looking pale and tired.

Jess nodded. "Okay, but I doubt they'll have my brand."

"You might be surprised," Veronique said. She contacted her team on her cell phone. Once she'd verified they didn't need her, she led Jess and Britt a few blocks deeper into the old city and down an alley into a secluded bar, jam-packed with patrons.

Some of them were vampires, Jess noted.

Britt leaned down to Jess's ear. "Do you see what I see?"

Her eyes narrowed while she looked around the dark interior of the bar. "I do. And I don't care what they serve here. I'm not risking that the drink came from an unwilling donor."

"Claude, have you a table for me and my guests?" Veronique asked.

"Absolutely. Your usual is ready," he said.

They were led to a table in the corner where he removed a reserved sign.

"I'm surprised you think this is a place where we can speak openly," Britt said, eyeing the many vampires in the room.

Jess didn't blame him; vampires had acute hearing, after all.

"Actually, we can speak freely here. You said you've met a vampire who claimed to have a pact with the police?" She indicated the individuals in the room with a sweep of her hand. "Well, the vampires in this room are all members of that pact. We often share intel. And whether you believe it or not, there are some individuals in this room I'd trust more than my own officers."

BRITT SLID AN understanding glance at Jess. "I understand that kind of trust." But only with one person, not a roomful of unknowns.

Veronique leaned over and pressed a button at the end of the table. A low resonant hum blocked out all sounds around them. "We're perfectly safe to speak now. No one else in the room can hear us now."

"That's quite the technology," Britt said.

Jess remained silent.

"First off, I want to tell you that we do, in fact, have a treaty with vampires. The pact was made with some of the oldest vampires in the city, but a few of the younger ones are causing trouble," Veronique said.

"Is trouble a common occurrence?" Jess asked.

"Not usually. But this year, we've had a few incidents. The general consensus is that these issues are stemming from a recent influx of immigrants."

Britt thought about Morana's friend, Diesel. "Vampire immigrants?"

"Yes, believe it or not," she said.

"Now that you mention it, we've had a few unwanted immigrants in New York, ourselves. Mostly master vampires who come in and try to control vampire populations, bending them to their will. It's like the Mafia moving in and taking over. So far, we've been able to eradicate them, but it's never an easy feat. Maybe that's what's happening here?"

"I hope not," Veronique said. "Who was the vampire who told you he and his kind weren't involved in the killings?"

"Morana called him Vin," Jess said, then described him.

Veronique seemed to know who he was. If she was disturbed by the information, she didn't give anything away.

A lanky, well-dressed vampire approached their table with a ceramic chalice in his hand. "Good evening, Captain LaFontaine." His cold, black eyes settled on Jess and stayed there for way too long before he sat beside Veronique.

"Hello, Vlad," Veronique said.

Britt's muscles tightened to the point of nearly cramping. "Vlad?"

The vampire turned his attention to Britt. "Calm yourself, human. It's just a nickname. I'm no relation to Vlad the Impaler, of course."

"Of course," Veronique said quickly, as if trying to assuage the vampire.

"Tell me, have you caught the serial killer we've been hearing about?" he asked.

"No. Not yet," Veronique said. "Have you heard anything, Vlad?"

The vampire took a long drink from his chalice, the whole while monitoring Jess. That made Britt's green-eyed monster get twitchy. Jess must've sensed his mood, because she took hold of his hand under the table.

"No, but I have feelers out. If I hear anything, I'll let you know," Vlad said, rising from the table.

"Thank you very much," she said, more formally than Britt expected.

Vlad bowed slightly toward Veronique then let his gaze scrape across Jess once more before he left them.

"He couldn't take his eyes off you, Jess," Britt said. "Are you sure you trust him, Veronique?"

"He *is* a bit of a Lothario," Veronique said.

Britt watched him across the room. Vlad was now flanked by two beautiful ladies and wasn't paying any attention to Jess anymore. "That vamp had better not make any wrong moves," Britt said, unable to keep the suspicion out of his words.

Veronique looked instantly alarmed. "Nothing can happen to Vlad, do you understand me? He is the linchpin in our peace treaty. He is a very important vampire around here."

"He certainly seemed sure of himself," Jess said. "Arrogant and rich."

A server approached, a human one. The second the man placed the mugs in front of Britt and Veronique, Britt grabbed his and guzzled half of it before coming up for air.

"Whoa," Veronique said. "You're even thirstier than I am." She took a long drink and set her mug down.

Britt didn't trust Vlad or any other of these so-called members of the peace treaty between vampires and humans. He'd seen some of the older vampires in New York. Hell! He'd helped a sketchy member of the Fallen partially cure three master vampires. Those vamps were not the peacekeeping sort, no matter how hard they tried to project that image. They honored one person, and one person only—themselves. Hopefully, Veronique wasn't easily fooled.

"I'd like to hear more about this peace treaty," Jess said. "If you can share the information without breaking any rules, that is."

Veronique looked appreciative at Jess's patience. Britt had always admired the way Jess could instill confidence in the person she was working for information. Veronique was no different than anyone else.

"I'll make inquiries," she said.

"Thank you." Jess turned her gaze back to the other side of the room where Vlad was watching them again. "Hasn't our friend over there ever met a female cop?"

"I'm sure you're quite a unique individual to him and to the hierarchy. They'd probably like to know more about you."

Britt didn't like the sound of that. Nor the reference to the hierarchy.

"Why'd you bring us to this pub?" He noted that Jess's head had snapped around at his comment. Vampire or not, she was usually much more diplomatic than he'd ever be.

Veronique glanced quickly over both shoulders before she spoke. Maybe she didn't exactly trust the resonant hum, or she worried about lip readers. It wasn't as if she'd told them anything ground-breaking yet.

"I'm sure you know there are worse things than vampires threatening the city right now."

"Such as?" he asked.

She took another sip of beer, likely to give herself a moment to think about her answer. Didn't most French people drink wine? Wine was being served pretty liberally here. He glanced around at all the vampires in the room. Maybe it wasn't wine. He shuddered.

"Don't play games with me, Brittain. You both know what I'm talking about. I have it on good authority that you've both been attacked by shadows while in Paris. What I'm wondering now is, why you haven't come to me with that information?"

Jess suddenly looked more ticked than diplomatic.

Veronique missed Jess's expression. Her mistake.

"So why haven't you reported the incidents?" she continued. "You're cops. You know how important it is to keep your own city safe. Why haven't you at least afforded me the same courtesy?"

Her last words sounded rather desperate. But hell, given what they'd seen of the shadows, he didn't blame her.

"We haven't reported them because we don't know what they are. We were trying to figure it out first," Jess said.

"There have been several attacks on citizens. Even the vampires seem to be spooked by these things," Veronique said, her features suddenly looking haunted.

"You say humans have been attacked?" he said. Odd. He remembered that human walking right through them, coming out the other end unaffected.

"Yes, we've had a rash of people exhibiting psychotic behavior. Most have been admitted to the hospital, but even in their state, they seem to have lucid moments when they rant about the shadows."

Britt's hands went numb from fisting them so tightly. "I don't like the sound of that," he said. "Have any of the affected people been helped by doctors? I mean, have any of them been released from the hospital?"

Veronique lowered her head and studied her hands folded in front of her. "None. They're getting worse, in fact. Most of them are in padded rooms."

"Jesus!"

"I agree," Veronique said. "And you? You're being very quiet, Jess. You know something, don't you? This is why your brother is here, isn't it? There have been rumors that the church is involved in all of this, somehow."

Jess remained silent in a way only a beautiful vampire cop could be. Britt's neck muscles tightened and he closed his eyes. Images of possessed and psychotic Parisians flooding the streets struck fear in his heart, especially since he'd been on the receiving end of what those creatures could do.

How the hell were they going to stop shadows?

Chapter Fifteen

THE AIR IN THE bar seemed to have thickened. It was getting hard to breathe. "I need some air," Jess said, pushing out of her seat and leaving Veronique and Britt staring after her.

Imagine Veronique actually expecting her to explain Regent's reasons for being here. In New York, she and Veronique had become friendly, but Veronique's attempt to gain information about Regent had reinforced Jess's reasons for not trusting most humans. And she was deeply disappointed in Veronique.

They were on the same goddamn side. Didn't she realize that? Or did she see Jess as another freaking vampire to squeeze information out of? Is that what Vlad was to her?

Jess waited outside for Britt. The air was sultry tonight with a sliver of the moon hanging in the sky. Sometimes sultry wasn't a good thing, since odors here on the streets were far from enticing.

It had been bad enough that several vampires inside had been staring at her. But Veronique pushed her too far. She'd had enough of the French police and their nonsense.

One thing she knew—there was more to that vampire named Vlad than met the eye. Maybe Veronique wasn't who Jess thought she was, either?

Britt stepped outside seconds behind her. "Hey babe. What's up?"

"I just got tired of the bullshit," she said, then started walking. Britt followed.

"I know. Sometimes it's the game we play as a cop, though."

"I don't like it. If Veronique wants to find out what we know, she's chosen the wrong way to go about it. Bringing us to a bar where vampires and humans intermingle was a thinly veiled attempt to warn us not to get heavy-handed with their pact members."

Britt stopped near the street corner. "Have you considered she might be stuck between us and the vamps, and maybe even their so-called hierarchy?"

Jess stared at the cobblestones. "I hope you're right. I thought she and I had an understanding. But her actions tonight disproved that."

"I have the feeling she wasn't supposed to tell us about the treaty. Did you see the vampires' expressions when we entered the bar? There was definitely some animosity and distrust there. When I left, Vlad had her in the corner and it looked like he was reaming her out."

"Good," Jess said.

"Good?"

She rammed her hands into her pockets. "I hate this."

"Me too. But I've learned one thing—I think we need to find out more about this pact before we fight any more Parisian vampires."

"I'm more concerned with her questions about the church's involvement," Jess said. "I think we should warn Regent that the police are digging for information. He said their work was top secret."

Britt snagged her hand and held it while they crossed the street. It wasn't something she'd allow in New York—she had a reputation to uphold—but here, she could be a little less bad ass once in a while. She needed his touch right now.

"Regent's not going to like hearing that Veronique knows about the church's involvement," he said.

"We'll have to give him a heads-up."

As if Britt understood that she needed to let off some steam, he allowed her to set the pace as they meandered toward their apartment and to Jess's detested bedroom. It seemed they could saunter the streets of Paris every night and still find new sections they hadn't seen before. Not everything was dark in Paris. It was a city of lights, and its beauty sometimes astounded even Jess.

As they neared the more popular tourist area of the city, Jess wriggled her fingers out of his. "I'm worried about something else," she said, walking a few steps ahead of him now and pretending to be interested in the window displays.

"Morana?"

"That's right."

"Why don't we go back to LaCave to see her? Maybe she feels guilty for running off, though I doubt it," Britt said.

"That's better than returning to that horrible apartment," Jess said. "I wish I'd seen it before we moved in." But then Jess's gut squirmed at the thought of coming face-to-face with Morana again, too. Still, she might as well get it over with.

Pebbles rattled on the cobblestone behind them, along with a soft footfall. Britt's body language told her he was well aware of their tail, so

Jess didn't bother saying anything. Instead, she managed a surreptitious glance back.

"It's one of Veronique's officers," she said in a whisper. "I saw him at the precinct."

"Why would she put a tail on us?" Britt's shoulders were taut, and for a moment, she was afraid he'd stop and confront the man.

"Ignore him. We have nothing to hide from the French police."

They entered the tunnel and made their way to the club, which was in full swing, as usual. Music boomed and people's voices echoed inside the underground chamber to the point that it was nearly unbearable for Jess's ultra-fine hearing. She spotted Morana and Diesel working the bar with only three other humans tonight.

It was clear that Morana had spotted Jess the minute she stepped inside the cavern. And if her expression said anything, it was that she didn't care that she'd left Jess to die at the hands of the shadows.

Jess reached into her pocket and touched the VNA kit Sampson had given her. There was one thing she *would* do tonight—she'd get the material for Sampson to ascertain once and forever if she and this vamp were related. That way, she could appease Regent and forget about Morana Longina.

Deep down, that uncomfortable sensation in her stomach hit again. If she and Morana were of the same flesh and blood, Jess would have to come to terms with it, and try to accept her for Regent's sake. But she didn't have to like her.

Morana quickly whispered something to Diesel when they approached the bar. Diesel searched out Jess, then shook his head at Morana. When Morana started to leave the bar, he grabbed her arm, but she yanked herself free away and spat something angry at him. Jess would have been able to hear what she'd said, if the music hadn't been so damn loud.

Morana stared at Jess, then tipped her head toward a tunnel leading away from the din.

"Want to go alone?" Britt asked.

Jess could have kissed him for that. In fact, she did. He turned the kiss into a deep, telling one. By the time she pulled herself away from him, Morana was glaring at her from the tunnel opening with her fingers drumming on the cave wall.

Jess hadn't considered until now that Morana might be jealous of her relationship with a man who honestly loved her.

"Thanks Britt, I'll be right back," she said.

Britt winked at her before he made his way toward Diesel. He'd seen the argument with Morana, and he'd undoubtedly want to question him about it while Morana was out of the way.

Morana stepped deeper into the tunnel. Whatever her motives tonight, Jess knew she wasn't likely to apologize. Judging by her expression, she was pissed that Jess had shown up here tonight, instead of being relieved she was alive.

Moving a few feet down the dark tunnel to a point where only vampires could see each other clearly, Morana waited with her feet positioned in a fighting stance. Her eyes were angry slits and her eyeteeth jutted over her lower lip.

Jess stopped advancing and held up her hands to slow down the unwarranted situation. She wasn't going to kick Morana's ass for running, nor call her a coward—because she didn't care. Morana was a vampire and a stranger who meant nothing to her.

"What's going on?" Jess asked, suddenly feeling as if she'd dressed down for the occasion.

"Why are you here?" Morana asked, not making eye contact. Her multi-layered blue-tipped hair matched the powder-blue mini-dress and 60s-styled go-go boots she wore. Her hoop earrings were as big as dinner plates. And her lipstick was nearly white, as was her eye shadow, which topped triple thick false eyelashes.

"It's not the end of the world that you ran away," Jess said.

Morana's expression turned caustic. "Is that so? Who gives you the right to judge me, one way or another? I don't care what you think!"

She'd try another approach. "Okay, why'd you run, then?"

"Not everyone has someone they can trust in a difficult situation. If I don't protect myself, no one else is going to help me," she said in a way that made Jess feel almost guilty about having backup, while Morana had no one.

Jess had the baby brother who loved her, and that love had been strong enough to have saved her partial soul. She also had the handsome cop-slash-man-of-her-dreams. In contrast, Morana hadn't fared quite as well. And she most likely resented Jess because of it.

"Like I said, what happened with that shadow was serious. You were right to get the hell out of there. If you'd stayed, you might not have made it."

Morana's eyes narrowed even more, as if Jess had just insulted her. "How *did* you survive the attack?"

"By the skin of my fangs," she said. "It was touch and go for a while. Those damned creatures are deadly to everyone, vampires included. Do you have any idea where they're coming from?"

"No idea at all."

"Britt and I have seen more of them recently. They seem to be growing in numbers."

"What are they?"

"Wish I knew," Jess said. "But, for now, we should probably avoid them whenever possible."

"That's one thing we can agree on," Morana said cynically.

Jess nodded. "Changing the subject, I would still like you to do the VNA check, if you're still willing."

Morana's shoulders actually slumped, and she let out an exasperated sigh as she leaned against the cave wall. A low-grade creaking sound echoed through the chamber as a truck moved on the street overhead.

"It doesn't matter to me, one way or another," she said. "If you feel you must, go ahead and do it."

"Great." Not waiting for Morana to change her mind, Jess whipped out the kit and took a saliva sample then shoved it into her pocket. "Thanks for this," she said.

Morana grunted. "Now go away, and leave me alone."

Jess left her without another word and returned to the bar where Britt was still questioning Diesel, who didn't look happy about it. Diesel's gaze kept flicking to the tunnel opening, no doubt hoping Morana would come back and rescue him.

Jess approached and sat on the stool next to Britt while Diesel wiped the area in front of her. "Get you something?"

"Do you have O positive?" Jess asked, thinking she was making a sick joke. This was a human bar after all. Diesel turned away from her, grabbed a glass and went to the cave wall where he poured her a glass and returned with it.

"Twenty euros," he said.

She gaped at the glass. She was actually thirsty. "Has anyone died in the making of this beverage?" she asked.

"Who are you, frigging Mother Theresa with fangs?"

"No need to be sarcastic to customers," Morana said, stepping behind the bar and extending a quick, meaningless smile to Jess. "No one has been hurt. As distasteful as it is, we buy our product from blood banks."

Britt leaned over and peered into her glass. "How do you get away with this? Doesn't anyone notice? I mean the human patrons?"

"We don't get that many vampires in here, so it's not an issue,"

Morana said, flicking a nervous glance at someone over Jess's shoulder.

Jess looked around for what Morana had seen.

Vlad, the vampire from the pub, was speaking with a patron on the far side of the room. Jess nudged Britt and he glanced back too.

"Who's he, then?" Jess asked Morana, feigning ignorance.

"Just some guy who comes in now and then," Morana said, but her expression wasn't so disinterested. "He seems to be staring at you, Jess. He must have the hots for you, too," she said irritably, then glared at Britt.

"Since you and I look almost exactly alike, maybe it's you he's interested in," Jess said.

"*Merde*. That'd be the last thing I'd want. He's a powerful individual in Paris, and it's best to stay off his radar. He's not the kind of . . . person you'd want to make friends with." Morana stole a glance at Vlad again. "Don't say I never do anything for you. That was one important tidbit of information that you can take or leave. I suggest you take it."

Diesel gasped and yanked Morana aside. "What are you doing? Do you want to get yourself in more trouble?"

Maybe Vlad was far enough away in this raucous room that he hadn't heard the conversation. Maybe.

Jess and Britt shared a glance. Vlad had just become person of interest number one. What was it about him that made the French police and vampires alike react so obviously around him?

Jess checked her watch. "Let's go."

Britt nodded and downed the last of his Scotch. They made their way home, avoiding Pont Neuf, as well as the other places they'd seen the shadows. It had been a long enough evening. They didn't need any more drama.

They didn't talk much before Jess went into stasis, because the dawn was almost upon them when they arrived. She crawled into her nightgown, blew him a kiss, and shut her door.

She heard him lock it after she crawled onto the bed.

AS USUAL, SHE HAD no sense of time passing when she woke the next evening. For all intents and purposes, it felt as if she'd closed her eyes and opened them again. Expecting to find herself alone in the apartment, she didn't bother dressing right away after her shower. Wearing nothing but her filmy black bra and panties, she wandered into the kitchen and went straight to her special refrigerator.

She must have been concentrating awfully hard because she hadn't sensed Britt in the room until she heard keys clicking on the computer.

At least he had been working on the computer . . . until she strode into the room nearly naked. Now his eyes were glued to her form, making her feel very sensual and desired.

"I thought you'd still be out," she said glancing down at her lack of attire. Lately, he only arrived home an hour after she rose.

Hell, her own libido ramped up in reaction to the way his gaze raked over her. She glanced at her watch again, wondering if they'd have time. Britt was not a fast lover—he took his time. She closed her eyes for a moment, contemplating the possibilities.

"Well, if this is the way you dress when I'm out, I'm never going to tell you when I'll be home again, just in case I get another lingerie show."

"Funny, Britt. It's not like you haven't seen me naked." She turned from him to drink her blood and felt his gaze staring at her ass.

"Like what you see?" she asked after she downed her sustenance and safely discarded the refuse.

"You're damned right I do. Holy hell, you need to either come over here right now, or throw some cold water on me and get dressed."

She laughed out loud. "You'd better grab a cold shower then. Because, as much as I'd like to go over there, I need to talk to Regent tonight. We need to find out what happened when he went to see the two priests who'd been demonically possessed."

"I was afraid you were going to say that," he grumbled, as he got to his feet.

Now it was her turn to ogle him, in his tight jeans and T-shirt that clung to his muscles in all the right places. The worst part was, he had no idea how appealing he was. His actions weren't a play to get her to change her mind about having a romp in the sack, though it almost worked anyway.

"Let's get this show on the road, shall we?" she said reluctantly, turning away from him.

"Wait, what about my cold shower? I thought you might join me."

"Funny man. Let's go."

Britt's eyeballs were still glued to her, she could feel them. "Ahem," he said.

"What?" She frowned.

"You really must want this information very badly," he said.

"Why are you saying that?"

"Because you're about to leave the apartment in your most desirable little black outfit."

She glanced down at herself and mouthed a very nasty curse word that made Britt grin from ear to ear. That didn't happen very often.

"I'll be right back."

"NEED ANY HELP?" Britt asked, while trying to wipe that lascivious smile off his face and before she caught him still staring at her frilly panties and curvaceous rear.

He should have known better. She retaliated by bending over slowly, removing her shoes and setting them back down, the whole time arching her back and extending her posterior in a centerfold kind of way that made him instantly sorry for his smartass comment. She'd very effectively shut him up . . . mainly because his mouth was so dry right now, he could barely swallow.

He watched her the whole time she walked toward her bedroom. Then she blew him a kiss and shut the door.

When she returned a few minutes later, she was all business.

"Want me to drive?" he asked.

"No. Let's walk."

Once outside, he knew why she'd decided to walk. She was monitoring for demons, checking the crevices in the walls, looking for shadows. But all was quiet on their way to Regent's place.

Jess rapped twice on Regent's apartment door before they walked in, only to find her brother looking deeply distraught.

"What's wrong?" she asked.

"I'm fine." His eyes lacked the sparkle of mischief often evident in their depths. Obviously, whatever he'd seen had been traumatic.

Britt touched the small of Jess's back. He knew nothing devastated her more quickly than her brother's pain.

Sampson was busy working in the corner on his laptop, his glasses on top of his head, seeming oblivious to Regent's state of mind, but more likely trying to do something to help him.

Regent picked up the remote and shut off the TV that no one had been watching. "Jess, you won't believe what I saw," he said. "Those poor priests are completely possessed. And they have powers that are unholy!"

"What do you mean by 'powers'?"

"The demons have completely taken over their minds. Somehow, they have telekinetic abilities that allow them to send inanimate objects shooting across the room. They are scarred with horrible wounds that seem impossible for their bodies to handle." His hand was shaking when he rubbed his chin. "It's horrific." His eyes appeared haunted.

"Can't they do something to help them?" Jess asked. "After all, exorcism is one of the church's specialties."

Regent let out a breath. "Considering the afflicted men are the best exorcists within the church, it's not looking good. It's as if the demons sought out the exorcists first to get them out of the way. One priest's mind has been warped to the point that he may never be the same again. Apparently, he can't sleep unless he's been heavily drugged and even then, he screams."

"What is the church going to do?" she asked.

"They're calling in anybody who's ever been involved with demonic possession, specialist or not, in case someone might have some idea what to do for these men. It's not looking good for their salvation." Regent eyed Britt, and a flicker of hope crossed his features. "Maybe we're *all* here for a reason. It's looking like the only way we're going to get to the bottom of this is by using the special abilities we each possess."

"It's looking as if we're involved, whether we want to be or not," Jess said, moving closer to Sampson and glancing at his computer screen. "What are you working on?"

Sampson glanced up quickly, almost as if he hadn't realized she and Britt had arrived. "Before I left New York, I scanned all of the ancient vampire scrolls and saved a copy on my hard drive. Since the words influence vampires, I'm hoping they might have some effect on demons. I'm looking through them for any reference to shadows."

"It's worth a try," Jess said, then placed a hand on Regent's shoulder. "Why don't you rest, brother? You look exhausted. And you can't do anything if you're ill."

"I know. It's just that I didn't sleep very well last night." He turned away and stared out the window, his expression haunted. "We have to find some way to stop those shadows before they move on to possessing ordinary citizens. But how will we be able to help them, if we can't even help our own priests?"

"I have bad news on that front. Apparently there have already been other possessions in Paris."

"Where did you hear that?' Regent asked, carefully grabbing Jess's arm.

"From the French police," she said in a low voice.

"Saints protect us!" Regent stared right through her. "It's truly started."

Chapter Sixteen

NO DOUBT EVERYONE thought she'd gone mad when Jess marched into the kitchen and hauled the kitchen table into the center of the living room.

"We haven't lost yet," she said. "We *are* going to stop those demons. From now on, this is our war room. We'll plan our strategy here."

Everyone talked at once, discussing what they knew . . . and what they didn't, until a rapping on the door broke up the conversations.

"Who could that be?" Regent said, starting toward the door.

"Wait." Jess slipped past him. "I'll go. From this point on, you need to be careful. So far, the demon shadows have been targeting anyone who has the ability to wipe them out. I hate to say it, but that puts you in even greater danger than the rest of us."

Regent quickly stepped out of the way, allowing Britt to flank Jess as she opened the door.

Just about to knock again, Morana stood there, dressed casually in jeans and a T-shirt.

Jess gritted her teeth. Morana looked more like her than ever before. If her hair hadn't been short and blue-tipped, it'd be hard for anyone to tell the difference.

Rather than invite the vampire in, she simply said, "Yes?"

"Can I come in?" Morana asked in a peevish voice, while peering into the room. Spotting Regent inside, she called, "Hey, brother. How's it going?"

"Morana. So nice to see you," Regent said, pushing forward and smiling for the first time tonight.

"Why are you here?" Jess asked, still holding the door from opening fully.

"I've come to help."

Jess frowned. "Help with what?"

"Don't play coy, Jess. We both know the shadows are building. Soon, they'll be strong enough to take over. And I can't let that happen any more than you can."

"And how do you intend to stop them?" Jess asked, thinking that, if faced with the shadows again, Morana would likely run away the minute things got tough. It seemed to be her M.O.

"I know you think I'm a coward. But you're wrong. Those bastards aren't going to get the better of me again," she said.

That speech sounded a little bit too rehearsed. What was she up to?

Regent gently shoved past Jess and took Morana's hand. "Come in, dear."

Jess's gut twisted. *Not a good idea, brother.* But it was too late, he'd already let her in.

Regent wanted to help this vampire he thought to be his sister . . . even if doing so meant letting her put him in danger.

"Actually it's getting worse out there," Morana said. "The shadows have switched from attacking the occasional person, to attacking anything that stands in their way. They're taking vampires out as fast as humans. I had a couple of close calls myself on the way here."

Regent gasped and crossed himself.

"Someone had better turn on the news. Maybe we can find out more about what's going on," Sampson said from his position on the far side of the kitchen table.

"This is Sampson Case, Jess's Forensic Vampirologist. He's the one who's going to prove you and Jess are twins," Regent told Morana.

Jess's teeth scraped over her bottom lip and she fought back the urge to spew a few curse words.

Meanwhile, Sampson looked back and forth between them, then whistled between his teeth. "I've never seen twins so identical before."

"But you haven't done the tests yet, Sampson. You can't say we're twins, not yet," Jess argued a little too strenuously.

Sampson instantly looked contrite. It wasn't like him to make a statement with no science to back it up.

"You're right, of course," he said. 'I'll hold off on observations like that until we have a definitive answer."

With her hands fisted at her sides, she wanted to punch something. At least she was being the consistently inconsiderate, unfeeling vampire bitch that she was.

Regent's disappointment in her was clearly evident, too. Given everything she'd put him through, he deserved better.

"Time to get this show on the road," Britt said in a loud voice, drawing everyone's attention away from her.

Morana moved around the living room, until she could see the screen on Sampson's computer. Jess noted the way she frowned as she tried to read over Sampson's shoulder. Did she recognize any of the ancient vampire text?

"What's this?" Morana asked.

Sampson snapped the computer closed and ran a hand over his smooth head. "Just something I'm working on."

Jess's insides relaxed just a little. Her faithful scientist didn't trust Morana either.

"What about holy water as a deterrent?" Regent asked, seemingly unaware of the undercurrents of tension.

Jess nodded. "Maybe, but it didn't seem to do anything to help the priests," she said. Regent had told her that holy water had been the first thing the church had tried.

"That's true," Regent said with a sigh.

"Who is inflicted?" Morana asked, looking suspiciously at Jess.

Hell! Did her supposed twin really expect them to spill everything they knew, just because she wanted to join their little group? Jess ignored the question and planted her hands on the table. "Maybe the first thing we should do is set up a street watch. Let's get people scanning the streets, watching the shadows from a safe distance. If we understand where they're coming from and where they're going, it might give us an idea about what they're up to."

"That's a fantastic idea," Britt said, while the others nodded in agreement.

"Morana, is there any chance you can organize the vampires? I mean, could you get them to pass along that type of information to you?" Regent said.

"I think I can," she said. "I'm sure some of them will help me."

"And we'll provide information from our end," Jess said.

Morana frowned at that, making Jess wish she knew more about this peace treaty.

She turned to Britt. "You and I will work together in the field. Together, we should come up with something. And if Morana does the same, we should have enough to get Regent and Sampson started. If we can find a pattern, maybe we'll be able to figure out what they're planning."

"I wouldn't have it any other way, doll," he said.

"And as much as I'd like to be out there in the field, I think data gathering is a good place to start," Regent said, disappointment evident in his voice. "And that way, you won't be worrying about me, Jess. You can concentrate on what you have to do," he said.

She nodded, then glanced at her watch. "I'm also going to call Veronique into this meeting," Jess said. "Does anyone have a problem with that?"

Jess watched Morana's irritated expression, but the vampire didn't comment. Nor did she ask who Veronique was. *Interesting, and not in a good way.*

Jess quickly dialed Veronique's number. "Hi Vee. Britt and I have put together a team to work against the shadows," she said. 'We'd like you to be part of this."

"When?"

"How does right now sound? We're at my brother's apartment." She gave the address.

"I'll be right there," Veronique said, hanging up instantly.

Jess shut off her phone. "She's on her way."

When Britt rose and stretched, making his muscles ripple, Jess noticed that Morana seemed to enjoy the show a little too much.

How much more of this new sister could she take?

Jess hated petty jealousy. It wasn't her style. So she dug deep and did her best to ignore Morana's obvious interest in Britt. Besides, he didn't even notice.

In the meantime, Regent had pulled out a tourist map of Paris and taped the edges to the table. As a group, they used a red marker to pinpoint the sections of the city where the shadows had been spotted so far.

There were several red circles in the Champs-Élysée area, and a few seemed to be branching off toward the Arc de Triomphe.

Jess wasn't surprised that the shadows had been drawn to the memorial. The Arc was a stunning piece of architecture, constructed to honor those who died in the French Revolutionary and Napoleonic wars. It was the perfect place for the demons to gather their troops, and stomp on everything good in this city.

"Maybe we can make the Arc de Triomphe our point of eradication?" Regent said.

"How?" Sampson asked.

"I think it's a bit too early for us to say that that's their target for sure. Who knows where they'll end up?" Britt said.

Jess frowned. "More importantly, we need to find out what caused them to rise up in the first place," she said.

"Wait, I hadn't thought of that," Regent said. "What caused these shadows to escape from hell? Demons need a release ... or at least, that's what is written in our philosophies."

Britt slammed his fist into his open hand. "Yes! If we can find out who let them loose, or how they escaped, it might give us a better way to—"

The doorbell rang. Regent broke away from the group to answer it, then ushered Veronique inside.

"Does everyone know Captain Veronique LaFontaine?" Jess asked.

"I don't," Sampson said.

"Veronique, this is my good friend, Sampson Case," Regent said, introducing him. Sampson beamed at Regent's description as he stood and shook the captain's hand. His reaction to Morana hadn't been even close to warm.

Jess could have hugged him.

When it became obvious Veronique didn't need an introduction to Morana, Jess's stomach burned. Why had Veronique lied about knowing Morana before, that evening they'd asked her to do a search on the fingerprints they'd found?

"What's she doing here," Veronique asked, looking back and forth between her and Jess. *"Mon Dieu, c'est incroyable!"*

It was Morana's turn to roll her eyes. "There's a slight resemblance," she said dryly.

Regent clicked his tongue and gave her a forget-denying-it-honey look. Morana simply ignored him.

Come to think of it, how did Morana know where Regent lived? Had he told her? Or had she been following them, too?

"From the observations we've made so far, we believe the entities are moving toward the Arc de Triomphe," Jess told Veronique

"But why?" Veronique said in a distraught voice. "Why a place as important as that?"

"We have no idea. But I think we need to gather all the data we can, from every possible source. Then we should all meet back here again tomorrow night and share what we've found," Jess said, glancing at her watch again. She couldn't wait to get out and do some intel tonight.

An hour later, the discussion had finally wound down, and she and Britt were getting ready to hit the streets. But first, she hauled Veronique aside. "I think I have some news about your serial killer," she said.

Veronique looked shocked. "What?"

Jess held up her arm and showed what was left of the pink scars. "One of the shadows did this to me. It slit my arm open, looking much like the bodies in the tunnel. Your serial killer might be a demon. Or demons."

Veronique exhaled and squeezed her eyes shut for a second. "I was afraid it might be something like that. The lack of evidence at the scenes, no DNA.... It wasn't adding up."

"It'll be damned hard to prosecute a demon," Britt added.

"Then we'd better figure out a way to send them back to hell," Veronique said, though her voice wasn't as firm as her words. "It's something the police department has been trying to figure out for the last two weeks." Veronique stared directly at Regent, as if she knew his role in this whole thing. "With little result so far, I'm afraid."

Jess's jaw tightened. It seemed everyone knew about his secret committee.

Regent flicked a knowing glance at Jess, and she nodded in agreement. They often shared moments of realization like this.

"Tomorrow night at ten o'clock, then," Jess said.

"Tomorrow night." Veronique made her way to the door without a backward glance.

The second the door closed behind her, Morana said, "Bitch."

Jess leaned forward, her hands planted on the table. "You have a problem with Captain LaFontaine?"

"You might say that," she said, crossing her arms over her chest in the same way that Jess always did. "She's been harassing me for two years. I couldn't believe it when she walked in here. I'm not sure I can work with her."

Jess's attention arrowed in on Morana. Again, she wondered why Veronique hadn't told the truth, earlier. She'd find out, one way or another.

"That's fine, Morana," Jess said. "You don't have to continue with us. We appreciate that you considered it, if only for a time." *Bye-bye!*

Morana's eyes turned black and she glared at Jess. "I intend to do what I said I'd do, whether you like it or not."

"Don't worry," Regent said, putting himself between them. "We'll get things worked out."

"But not tonight," Jess said. "Britt and I have things to do."

"I have to leave too," Morana said, ignoring the rest of them. "Until tomorrow night." She got up and left the apartment, slamming the door behind her.

"Guess that means she's going to work with Veronique after all," Britt said with a wicked grin.

"Don't hold her temperament against her," Regent said, locking his hands in front of him. "She hasn't had the benefit of a loving family to help her mediate her anger. She's done pretty well, given that fact."

God! Morana has Regent wrapped around her little finger.

In a way, Jess couldn't fault her younger brother. She knew he'd wanted to accept Morana as their sister, right from the start.

Jess looked at her rough-edged fingernails. "Even if she turns out to be our sister, she's still a vampire. And vampires do whatever they have to do to survive."

"But Jess, you've proven that statement wrong, over and over again," her brother said.

"Oh, Regent, let's not go there. Besides, Morana is not me."

"But you've found other vampires who are instinctively able to maintain a partial sense of self. They can control their darker needs without the benefit of . . ." He stopped talking, instantly.

She knew why.

Because the truth of matter stunned her instantly—why hadn't she thought of it before? There were a few vampires who *could* partially control their own darkness—and they didn't need constant prayers to maintain it.

Oh hell! He was right.

That meant she was darker than any of them, only managing to maintain herself with prayers. Her gut swooped, making her reach out and press her hand against the table for support.

Regent instantly looked distraught. "No, Jess. *Do not* take what I said that way!"

"When Regent was in Rome and I was unable to pray for you, you maintained your*self*," Britt reminded her.

Barely. She knew it and they knew it. Damnation. She chewed on her upper lip and turned away to hide the sudden moisture behind her eyes. There was every possibility that Morana was a better person-slash-vampire, than she'd ever be.

Regent walked over and wrapped his arms around her in a bear hug. "Please, Jess, that's *not* what I meant."

Whether he meant to say it or not, there was a whole helluva lot of truth in it. Somehow, she'd begun to believe the hype about herself, that she was some kind of special vampire. Crap! Deep down, did she actually think she was better than Morana because she could walk in daylight under special conditions? Namely, a lot of extra prayers?

She took a ragged breath. She didn't want to upset Regent right now, so she pulled herself together, hiding behind the cool persona that was her trademark. "I'm not upset." She forced a bright smile and gently extricated herself from his arms before he sensed the truth in her tense muscles.

"You have an army of people who put their lives on the line for you every night," Sampson added. "People don't do that unless their leader is worthy of that kind of loyalty."

She nodded, but was still caught up in her own devastation. The reality of being a vampire always on the edge of losing herself, hit home. She couldn't begin to compare herself to the vampires in Europe, who seemed more civilized than she'd ever imagined.

She must've managed to fool her brother, though, since he'd started to relax.

"Let's not get too maudlin, boys. I'm not a girly-girl, I'm a tough vampire, remember."

Regent nodded and hope seeped into his expression. He wanted it to be true.

Hell, so did she. Because right now, she felt like a fractured child whose reality had been changed forever. But at least she'd managed to make everyone believe her.

She glanced at Britt who'd been fairly silent. *Well, not everyone.*

She clapped her hands together. "Let's get back to the business at hand—all those demons running rampant in Paris," Jess said. "Britt and I are going to find something to use against them tonight if it kills us."

Regent groaned.

"I haven't had a chance to check the results of the VNA sample you got from Morana, but it should be ready soon," Sampson said.

"I think it's great Sampson has a lab here. I have the feeling we're going to need him working at full capacity, especially if things keep going the way they have been," Britt said.

"That's what makes me get out of bed every day," Sampson said, shoving his glasses back on top of his head. "You coming to check out the new lab with me, Regent?"

Regent searched Jess's eyes. Apparently, she hadn't completely fooled him, after all.

"You go, Reej, but stay off the side streets. It's too risky at night."

If he had feathers, they'd be ruffling right now. "If it's risky for me, it's risky for you, too, Jess."

"Yes, but I'm harder to kill."

"Need I remind you again, you can be killed?"

She sought Britt's help in mollifying her brother. "Once upon a time, I believed I was at risk every night when I was hunting. But now that I have Britt by my side, I think my odds are a lot better than they used to be. Don't you agree, Regent?"

"I have to admit that is true," he said.

"You know I'll do everything in my power to keep her safe," Britt said. "And she'll do the same for me."

Good thing he added the second part.

MORANA CALLED HER father on the phone right after she left the apartment. It rang and rang, but he didn't answer. Funny. She'd tried to contact him other times, and he hadn't been there, either. Where did he go? If he had Watcher meetings at night, he'd certainly kept them a secret from her.

She adjusted her shirt over her blue jeans and strode purposefully to her destination, an exclusive place called Club Noire, where only vampires gathered, along with the humans who lusted for the bliss they got from being bitten. Some of them were worse than addicts. Not that anyone she knew minded.

She stepped inside. They kept the place so dark, only vampires could see well. The humans were already out of their element, but in the dark, they were less likely to be terrified at the sight of vampires feeding on those who'd offered themselves.

Diesel had just finished feeding on a rotund woman in his booth. Her eyes held that haze of climatic enjoyment. He wiped his mouth when he saw her and stood. "Morana, I'm surprised to see you here. You haven't been around for weeks."

"I come here all the time, but lately only after work," she said. It was still two hours before LaCave opened.

"Why are you here early tonight, then?" he asked.

She glanced around the room. "How many vampires are here that we can trust?" she asked.

He shrugged and looked around the room. "That depends on what kind of trust you need," he said.

"I need help tracking the shadows. They're taking out vampires as well as humans now. I've joined a taskforce that is trying to track them. We need vampires willing to notify the group about the shadow's activities."

He shook his head and ran his teeth over his bottom lip. "You might be asking a lot from our kind. But there might be some here who fit the bill." He touched her shoulder.

It took strength not to wrench away from him, especially after she'd seen where he'd been biting that human.

"Are you helping the cops now, too?" he asked.

"Not really, I'm helping us. Vampires."

"But the cops are involved, aren't they?"

"Yes, but we won't have anything to do with them. I'll be giving the information to Jess Vandermire, and she'll pass it along."

"Damnation," he said.

"We will be damned if we don't at least try to help. The shadows are actually demons, and they're not discriminating between humans and us. They take whatever they want. As far as I can tell, there's not much we can do to combat them. Not alone. We're going to need help to survive this onslaught." She paused for a moment, thinking. "I know. We can get the vampires to leave their findings at LaCave each evening. That'll protect their anonymity."

Diesel shook his head. "Okay. It's your funeral." He jumped onto the table nearest him and shouted. "Turn off the music! There's something important you all need to hear."

Someone shut off the sound and except for those still feeding, all glowing eyes turned on Morana who'd jumped up on the table next to Diesel. She told them what she needed and asked for volunteers. No one agreed right away, but she'd expected that.

Before she left, though, she had a handful of vampires who'd discreetly agreed to help her. And once word got around about the importance of this job, she was sure she'd have more. It wasn't only her sister, the famous Captain Vandermire, who could get things done.

BRITT OFTEN TOOK Jess's hand in his while they walked down the sidewalk, saying it made them look like human lovers strolling the streets. She liked believing it could someday be true.

But the discussion tonight had left her feeling sorry for herself. So she wasn't the amazing vampire who every other vampire in North America wanted to be. She'd been too full of herself, and maybe she'd needed that wake-up call.

When something rustled to her right, Britt squeezed her hand. He'd heard it too.

The streetlight illuminated the sidewalk ahead, clearly highlighting two shadows slithering toward an alley. Seconds later, they heard a scream.

She and Britt broke their handhold and raced toward the screams.

A street person stood before them. He was in rags and standing beside a cardboard box, not far from a Dumpster. The box probably held all his worldly goods.

His eyes were frantic and he reached out a hand for help just before a black shadow demon slithered completely into his mouth. The man's eyes were wide, and filled with terror while the demon crawled inside him.

"What can we do?" Britt grabbed his cross and held it up, shouting a few prayers at the man.

But the demon had obviously taken over and was safely holed up inside the human, making it impervious to the cross. It merely laughed at Britt.

"Holy water?" Jess shouted. It had worked before. She grabbed a bottle off her belt and splashed water at the man housing the beast.

It merely soaked him. The demon laughed at them. "You can't harm me now. Not while I'm wearing a skin suit," the croaking, vile voice taunted them. The man's tongue extended farther than she'd believed possible, and he licked his chin and his cheeks, while his eyes rolled back in his head. A gurgling sound erupted from the man—or the beast, she wasn't sure which.

"Damn it, we could have used you-know-who as backup out here tonight," she said to Britt.

"Who? The priest?" the demon said in a horrendous, cutting voice, as if the mere act of speaking was shredding the man on the inside.

Jess panicked instantly. As feared, the shadows knew about Regent. He *was* in danger.

Grabbing her blade, she dove at the street man and held it at his filthy throat. Blood now oozed out of the corners of the man's mouth.

"If you kill him, I'll take another body," the demon warned. "But first, I'll make him bite off his own tongue."

The demon must've let the man's consciousness surface for a moment, because he screamed and his eyes begged pitifully for help. If this was an example of what Regent had seen happening to the exorcists, she understood his fear. And worse, it seemed that she couldn't kill the man in order to end the demon. Or could she?

She backed away and leaned toward Britt. "We can't fight this thing unless we kill the host. I'm not prepared to do that, unless we have no other option."

"What will we do with this guy, then?"

"It depends on what the demon is going to do in that body. If he's going to harm someone, we can't just leave him there," Jess said.

"There's something else we should consider," Britt said not taking his eyes off the man. "Even as shadows, they have powers they can use against us. What abilities will they have, housed inside a human?"

"There's only one way to find out," Jess said, again approaching the homeless man with long stringy hair, wearing dirty clothing and hosting a pair of red demon eyes.

The demon spat out a string of vile curses until suddenly, its demeanor changed. It smiled at Jess, showing a row of rotten teeth and a tongue that flicked in and out like a lizard's. "Come closer, vampire. I could make you very happy. You can join me in hell and we can create a new realm of devils."

"Gross," she said, looking back at Britt. "Did this thing just come on to me?"

Britt grimaced and moved in on the man. The vagabond's head twisted at an impossible angle, following Britt's movements. "Angels aren't invited," he said in a terrifying rasping voice. "You have no place here, evil one."

"I'm the evil one?" Britt mocked. "I think you'd better look in the mirror. What is your name, demon?" he asked.

The demon's flicking tongue stopped and his brows drew over his red-glowing eyes. "You will not have my name."

"We just want to help you," Jess lied. "What do you want here? What are you trying to achieve?"

The demon slavered and drooled, and maybe the street man peed himself, because suddenly the odor coming from him was rank. "I want you to die," the demon said.

"Well, join the club. There are plenty of others who want the same thing for me," she said. "And do you know how I answer them when they tell me to die?"

The man continued twitching, his arms shooting around as if he'd been jacked up on electricity. "I don't care, vampire." He rubbed his crotch. "I could make you beg to be mine."

Jess's stomach nearly heaved, and it took a lot to turn the stomach of a vampire. She instinctively held up a hand, warning Britt to back down. When she looked at him, his blue light had escaped his solar plexus and was hovering in front of him.

The demon shielded his eyes from the light.

What do you know? It doesn't like the light.

"You can't win with angel fire either, son of Jibril. You aren't strong enough against the army that is coming. We will take everything back. This is our place, and you will be in Hades, where you should have always been."

Britt got closer to the demon, and as fearless as he seemed to be, the thing shrieked when the light nearly touched him. "Don't come any closer. If you do, this old man will die a horrible death," it said, then keened and slavered.

Jess considered that, but she didn't stop Britt. "It's lying," she said. "Demons always lie."

"Lies are truth," the demon chanted about a dozen times. But it slowly backed away from Britt's light until it was pinned between the wall and the Dumpster as Britt moved closer.

"You will pay, servant of the Lord. Yours will be a crime against humanity. I do not kill this human, you do!"

Britt looked quickly at Jess and she nodded, urging him to continue. Unexpectedly, the street person straightened and screamed. There was a knee-buckling cracking sound while his head spun completely around. His eyes bulged, his tongue protruded, and he dropped to the ground. Dead.

The shadow slithered out of him quickly and disappeared into the cracks of the brick.

"I didn't expect that," Britt said, obviously feeling the weight of the man's death.

"It's proof that we can't force demons out without risking the host," she said softly, hoping Britt could see the truth in that.

"But I just caused that man's death," Britt said, desperation weighing his words. "I killed him, as surely as if I'd done it with my own hands."

She sniffed the air. "He was dying anyway, Britt. I can smell it. He had terminal cancer that was burning through him. It might have been a mercy for him to go quickly."

"I'm not sure that makes me feel any better. But at least now we know if we threaten the possessed, the demons will kill the person they occupy. That'll make it even harder to fight them."

"Did you hear what he called your blue light, Britt? It's angel fire. I've heard of that before," she said. "Oh right, in the good book."

He nodded. "But why should we believe him? Why didn't Uriel tell me the light was called angel fire? It might have helped me understand it better. And the demon called me son of Jibril. I've never heard that, but it feels right. I don't think the demon was lying about that."

"Maybe."

"Putting a name to your blue light might help you to learn to control it. If it is angel fire, Regent might know a lot more about it than we first thought. After all, he studied theology for years. We'll ask him tonight . . . and warn everyone not to try to extricate the demons from the priests or they'll die, too."

Britt's attention had shifted back to the dead man in the alley. "What will we do with him?"

She considered their options. "You don't want to just leave him?"

"No. What if he's not really dead but still possessed?"

"I hadn't thought of that." She yanked her cell phone out of her pocket. "Sampson, how big is your rental car? Is it big enough to take a body back to your lab for testing?"

"Yes, where are you?" he asked.

Jess told him what had happened and gave him the address. "We need to make sure he's not still susceptible to demon possession after he dies."

"Demon? That's not really my field of expertise, but I can try."

"Thanks, Sampson," she said, then put her phone away. They couldn't leave victims lying around the city waiting to reanimate and wreak havoc.

When Sampson and Regent arrived twenty minutes later, Jess noted that Regent had taken the time to lay a plastic tarp on the floor of the trunk. They maneuvered the man into the rented sedan and quickly closed the trunk.

Jess didn't mention angel fire to Regent yet because she could tell Britt was still disturbed by what had happened. Since he'd learned he had angelic DNA, he'd been reading the Bible for any references to angels. Even though he'd found several mentions of angel fire, she'd never once equated those references to the blue light that emitted from Britt's solar plexus. But it had done some amazing things. He'd actually healed three vampires. On the other hand, he'd also wiped out a cavern full of vampires descended from the Mayans. The fact that his blue light might indeed be angel fire was probably scaring the hell out of Britt. Theological references touted angel fire as being a weapon unlike any on Earth. He couldn't help but be worried that he barely had control of this weapon that most often seemed to act of its own volition.

She bit her lip. That part concerned her, too.

Chapter Seventeen

MORANA WAS THE last one to arrive at Regent's apartment the following night. She and Veronique eyed each other suspiciously over the war-room table, before she moved to stand next to Regent, who took her hand in his and squeezed.

Jess watched them from the other side of the table.

Even though she tried to hide it, Morana didn't look thrilled by Regent's affection but then, she was a vampire. She didn't need constant reassurances of love . . . and most likely didn't want it, either.

Before anyone got started on their findings, Veronique stepped up. "I have bad news, I'm afraid. We can't kill the demons once they've invaded our people, or the demons will kill them. In fact, last night we threatened a possessed person and the demon walked him off the side of a building." She swallowed. "It was horrible."

"Unfortunately, we had a similar experience with a homeless man in an alley," Britt said. "We were going to report the same thing."

Regent cleared his throat, and all eyes turned toward him.

"What is it, Regent?" Jess asked.

"I found something in the archives. As Jess and Britt know, I believe this happened before, during the French Revolution. A group of demon worshippers attempted to awaken demons by calling them through the bones under the city. They used an incantation that lured them up from hell . . . but it backfired when the demons became vampires. Luckily, the church moved in and somehow stopped the insurrection."

Jess's heart skipped a beat and she pressed against Britt for moral support. "We can't wait for the demons to turn into vampires in order to stake them. We have to stop this now. Do you have any idea how the church stopped them?"

"Unfortunately, no. That wasn't in the document I found. But I'll keep looking," Regent said.

"It doesn't look like it's happening that way this time, anyway," Britt said. "The shadows haven't shown any sign of becoming vampires.

Besides, they're killing vampires, as well as humans."

"And if we kill vampires, it will break the tenuous pact we currently have with Parisian vampires," Veronique said.

Morana snorted and Veronique ignored her.

"I'll discuss this with some of my colleagues," Regent said. "If there is a way to stop them, we will find it." He drew in a deep breath.

While Britt stared down at the map, she could see the tension wafting off him. "How many have been possessed so far?" he asked.

Veronique bit her lip. "It's hard to say. Last night, we spotted dozens of shadow demons. Tonight, it could be hundreds. We're being overtaken, and there's not a damn thing we can do about it."

Jess turned to Regent. His face was pale but determined. "Reej? Maybe I can start going through the archives with you? We need that information."

"No, I'm sorry. That's not possible. I'm working in a closed section of files. You'd have to have a pass to get inside, and that's not going to happen."

Since when did a pass stop her?

He gave a quick shake of his head, telegraphing a message—it wasn't safe for her. "Okay. Britt and I will continue using our own methods," she said.

"Good luck with that," Veronique said. "We've tried everything, and nothing has worked. All we've managed to do is get good citizens of Paris killed. I urge you not to harm anyone else."

"Sampson, did you learn anything when you autopsied the homeless man?" Jess asked.

"Hold on, what are you talking about?" Veronique asked angrily. "You can't just take people off our streets and autopsy them."

"He was a homeless man killed by a demon," she said. "We intend to return him to your own forensic pathologist as soon as we can," Jess said. "If you recall from your visit to New York, Sampson is a well-respected pathologist working with the NYPD. Our first objective is to make sure the man is truly dead and can't come back at the demon's will."

"That is *not* acceptable. You must return him now."

Jess frowned at Veronique. "Do you have specialists who can verify that he won't come back as demon spawn?"

Veronique dropped into a chair, looking as if she'd been punched in the gut. "No. Nor had we considered such a thing. Is it really possible?" she asked.

Sampson chewed his lip. "Maybe. I'll keep the corpse for a few more nights, just to make sure it doesn't happen."

"I'm sorry, Jess," she said. "I shouldn't have second-guessed you."

Morana rolled her eyes.

"Morana?" Jess asked. "Do you have anything to report?"

Morana's eyes narrowed slightly at Jess before she masked her irritation. "Only that the vampires are not happy that the streets are being overtaken by the possessed. Overall, it won't change their nocturnal habits that much. Even though most of them don't really care—as long as demons don't kill people, they can still be a food source—I've found a few who are willing to help."

Regent gasped at her cold-blooded comment and let go of her hand.

Morana noticed. "But I'm sure more of them will see that we need to help, once word gets around. We can't just sit by and watch our city be overrun by hell's vermin."

Jess hadn't expected to get much help from the vamps. Especially since she had a feeling that Morana was feeding the vampires information she shouldn't. Still, there was no way she'd convince Regent that Morana shouldn't be at these meetings.

Veronique hung back at the end of the night's session and pulled Jess aside. "I wanted to ask about the demon's attack on you," she said. "About your arms being slashed in the same manner as our murder victims."

She nodded. "Yes?"

"Do you honestly believe the murderer might be a demon?"

Jess shrugged her shoulders. "I don't know. Didn't you say the murders started some time ago?"

She nodded.

"Were the demons spotted in the city at that time?"

"No. But that doesn't mean they weren't here," Veronique said. "Maybe one demon was sent ahead of the others to scout the territory. If so, that might explain why the perp is a particularly sadistic killer."

"I guess it's a possibility. But, if that's true, we'd have demons overtaking the city, as well as one serial killer demon who has a thing for slashing open women who'd visited LaCave." Jess inhaled. "I wonder. . . . Why only women, and why LaCave?"

"If that's true, and we do manage to catch the serial killer. . . . How do we incarcerate a demon?"

"If you ever do catch it, I believe Regent will be able to contact the right people with the resources you need." Though, thinking about the possessed priests.... Maybe the church wasn't as powerful as she'd hoped.

"Oh, right," Veronique said.

"What kind of resources does the church have against demons, other than their usual attempts at exorcism, which I hear aren't working?" Morana asked.

Her first instinct was to be impressed by Morana's intel, until.... *Hold on! How'd she know about the exorcists?*

Regent chose that moment to cut in. "As I said earlier, according to my research, this has happened before. From what I've gathered, a missing script from the church archives was instrumental in fighting the demons off. We have to find it. If we do, we might be able to defeat the demons again."

"I hope you're right, Regent. Because right now, we're in very deep trouble. We can't stop them, or we'll kill their innocent hosts," Jess agreed.

Regent grabbed his hat and strode to the door. "I'm going back to the archives. Will you and Jess see me there, safely, Britt?"

"Certainly," Britt said.

Jess nodded to him and said her good-byes to Veronique and Morana, who immediately left the apartment, going in opposite directions.

When she and Britt got outside with her brother, Jess said, "Regent, I know you believe Morana is our sister, but I don't think she should be at our nightly sessions. She's not like me. I don't think she cares whether the demons take over the city or not."

"You can't really believe that," Regent said. "I don't think you're being fair to her. Can't you at least give her a chance?"

Jess rolled her eyes and caught Britt's tight-lipped expression. He obviously agreed with her, but didn't want to upset Regent. "Yes, I do believe it. But for you, brother, I will give her a chance."

"When will Sampson have the VNA results?" Britt asked as they strode down the sidewalk.

Jess didn't have a chance to answer when a shadow crossed the street a distance ahead of them, going straight at a young couple. It slid into the man so fast, they couldn't help him.

"Jess, grab the girl and get her out of harm's way," Britt shouted, then dove at the man whose eyes were already glowing. The takeover had been fast and complete.

"What's happening?" the woman wailed, trying to fight Jess off.

"Let me go. Randolph? Are you all right?"

But Randolph was far from all right. He was drooling and cursing and trying to attack Britt.

"Sir, I'm hoping you're in there and you can still hear me. We're going to try to help you. We can't extricate the demon or it will kill you," he said. "Have faith and we'll find a way."

The demon laughed while Britt let Randolph go. He had no other option. "You're all going to join us in hell!"

"Randolph," the woman screamed. "Don't leave me. What's happening to him?"

Jess tried to calm her, but the woman fought her, attempting to run back to her lover. Jess and Regent held her as gently as they could. Finally, the fact that one of them was a priest seemed to make the woman less combative.

"Father, why are you letting him leave? He might hurt himself. Why are his eyes so red?" Her voice hitched.

Regent took her hand. "We have to believe that as long as we leave him alone for now, we'll be able to get him back. He's been possessed by a demon. If we attempt to help, the demon will kill him."

"Oh no!" She turned and threw herself into Jess's arms. Jess felt so out of her element, Britt looked sorry for her. She awkwardly tried to pat the woman's back.

Suddenly, the woman shoved herself away. "Why are you so cold?" She furtively glanced at the rest of them, as if they might be the same creatures that attacked Randolph. She obviously thought they were all demons, or at least dangerous to her.

A taxi turned the corner and Britt stepped out and hailed it for her. "Go home and stay there until the city is safe," he said. "Don't let anyone in unless you're sure they haven't been compromised."

She dove into the vehicle and didn't look back.

Jess called Veronique to have someone come and round up Randolph before he hurt someone.

"I'll send an officer right away, though where we're going to put the man is another thing. Our cells are full of the afflicted."

"Hang in there, Vee, we'll find something."

"I hope to God you're right, Jess." She hung up.

Regent and Britt tried to keep Randolph semi-calm. Thankfully, the van arrived within minutes, and he was taken away.

"Quick," Regent said. "Get me to the archives. I'll be meeting my committee there tonight. We have to hope someone has found something. We have a veritable army of priests looking for a solution."

"Fingers crossed," Jess said. "Let's go."

"Follow the river," Britt said. "They dislike the water."

By the time they dropped Regent off, she and Britt had spotted at least twenty citizens roaming the streets, snarling and swearing.

Now, as they stood in the middle of Pont Neuf, they watched more and more people joining the ranks of the demonic. What the hell were they going to do?

"The newspapers will be full of this tomorrow. It can't be kept secret any longer," Britt said.

"No. And it shouldn't be. People need to stay inside."

Britt leaned on a parapet and cast a worried look her way. "Do you really think anyone is safe? Even in their homes?"

Jess's shoulders drooped. "No. I don't imagine they are, especially if the demons enter as shadows. What about the churches? Notre Dame?"

"Of course! Get out your cell phone," he said. "We can tell the media that people should go to the churches, hunker down there until it is safe to come out."

Jess dialed directory assistance and, with stilted French, she managed to contact the city's most prominent TV channel. Without giving her name, she switched to English. "You have to tell people they'll be safe in the churches of every denomination. Instruct them to go directly there until the insurgence is over." She hung up while the person at the other end was still asking how it would be stopped.

"Can you get Sampson to Notre Dame? He can wait in my office, and I'll meet him there later tonight after I do my search at the archives."

"Will do. Stay safe, brother," Jess said, dropping him off at the archive building.

"Phone us when you're ready to leave the archives, and we'll escort you back to Notre Dame," Britt said.

THIRTY MINUTES LATER, they escorted Samson to Notre Dame, then went back out again. It was getting worse on the streets—much worse.

Even the rooftops were becoming infested now, so they made their way back to the bridge. Shadows swelled under every streetlight on the both sides of the bridge.

"I don't think we can make it back to Regent through that mess. We'll have to find another route," he said.

She gritted her teeth. "We *have* to find another way, Britt. I won't desert Regent. These shadows are everywhere!"

Britt looked around, trying to figure out a way to get back to the archives. He stared down at the water. Slowly, a long rowboat glided out from under the bridge. *Holy hell! Our salvation just arrived.*

"We can go up river on that boat, until we're closer to the archives. Then we just have to figure out a way to get to Regent over land. Hopefully, there won't be as many shadows there," Britt said, grabbing her hand and climbing up onto the cement bridge rail. "Jump."

She didn't hesitate. They both jumped. He prayed they'd make the deck of the boat before it slipped off down the river.

The man steering the craft nearly had a heart attack, judging by the way he was clutching his chest.

"Friends," Britt shouted quickly.

The man nodded at them several times, but his hand gripped the motor handle tightly. The cigarette hanging off his lower lip had gone out long ago.

"Parlez-vous anglais?" Jess asked.

"Oui, yes," he said in a strong French accent.

"The shadows, the demons up there." She pointed at the street above and he nodded vigorously, fear evident behind his wide eyes. "They're afraid of water. We're safe in the boat," she said. "We need to get to my brother at the archives. Can you take us as close as you can?"

"Oui, oui. Asseyez-vous."

"Did he really understand what we said?" Britt asked.

"I think so, if his English is like my French. I can understand more than I can speak." As they floated along the river, the tiny trolling motor making not much more than a whirring sound, they heard heart-wrenching screams coming from the streets above.

"We're in trouble, aren't we?" Jess said.

"Don't give up, doll. You, more than any of us, know we can fight evil and win. This is no different than facing a vampire horde."

"Really?" She sounded unusually panicked. "How do you figure that? We've both been nearly killed by these things. We can't possibly win."

Britt thought hard about that, as another scream rent the air, with diabolical laughter following. His instinct was to rush to save the person, but he couldn't without killing the host. He bit his lip. "We have to pray that Regent has found something we can use. We're here for a reason, Jess. We're here to help save Paris. I know it."

"Oui, oui," the boat driver said vigorously, pointing at the street.

When the old man slowed the motor, Britt motioned for him not to get too close to the edge of the river. "It's safer for you here," he said. "We can jump."

The man looked skeptical.

They stood, and the boat rocked for a few seconds before they easily jumped to the nearby bank. From there, they waved a thank you to the man. He tipped his hat and responded in French, then revved up his little motor and disappeared into the dark.

Quickly climbing the bank, they noted the streetlights had been knocked out here, even though there were still lights on inside the buildings on this block. Maybe the residents were still safe—for now.

"Uh oh!" Jess said. "Without the streetlights, we won't be able to see the shadows. How do we handle that?"

"I have an idea," Britt said, concentrating for a second before angel fire erupted from his solar plexus. This ball of light was larger than normal and hovered in front of them like a brilliant blue lantern. They both saw shadows scurrying to get out of its illumination. "Get in the light, Jess, and stay there. I think we might be safe to travel to Regent."

"The demons are afraid of it now, but they're sly. I hope they don't find a way to get through," she said, stepping carefully into the light. Funny—that light had wiped out a hundred vampires at once, yet it didn't harm her.

He inhaled her fragrance and felt her soul. Once she came into his light, he could see her true self. Not that she'd want him to know her that well.

They walked as fast as possible toward the archives. Inside, the building was fully lit but the front steps crawled with shadows. Moaning, wailing, and unworldly sounds filled the Paris night, making the fine hairs on Britt's arms stand on end.

Jess faltered before they mounted the steps. "Those sounds," she said. "They're awful."

"They're meant to scare us," he said. "But we're safe in the light." He hoped. Who knew if that many shadows could be kept at bay? *There is only one way to find out.*

They ascended the stairs. Shadows thronged around them just barely outside his blue light. *So far so good.* But how long would his energy last?

They made it to the front doors and stepped inside.

Three people were sprawled on the floor at the reception desk. Two were dead, and one was badly injured—but not possessed. Jess reacted instinctively by grabbing her cell phone in order to phone for an ambulance.

"Don't bother, Jess. It'll just put the EMTs in danger."

"Right," she said and shoved the cell phone back into her pocket. They wrapped the woman's wounds as best they could with bits of her own clothing and stepped away. She'd passed out. Hopefully, she'd make it. She looked around.

"Regent? Oh God, Britt, where's Regent?"

Chapter Eighteen

THE FARTHER THEY got into the archives, the more damage they saw. The building was trashed. There were holes in the walls, lights hung from the ceiling with wires nearly gnawed through, and sparks shot out randomly as they passed under them. Shadows crawled on the floors and up the walls outside the protection of Britt's angel fire. Shrieks and moans came from every direction.

"Regent!" Jess shouted. "Where are you?"

No answer.

Britt touched her arm and she jerked her head around to see him put his finger over his mouth. She rolled her eyes. *Of course.* He knew where Regent was. But if Regent answered her, he'd give his position away. Where would be the safest place in this building?

She racked her panicked brain. Odds were, they had a hermetically sealed secure room for the most valuable books. If so, Regent could be inside. Maybe all of the priests were inside, as well. But where would that be? In the basement, maybe?

She pointed downward, and Britt nodded. They made for the back of the building and worked their way down the stairs to a sub-basement where they found a biometrically coded door.

"What are we going to do now? There's no way inside without the code," she said, looking around. Safety lighting still gave a little illumination in the hall, and a fire hose and axe remained intact behind a glass case nearby. "Hold on, I'm going to break the door down," she said.

She broke the glass with her elbow, grabbed the axe, and slammed it into the metal door. The coding machine blew apart and flew in all directions, but the door didn't budge.

"Stand back," she said. "I'm going to get this door open one way or another."

"Wait, doll. You're almost out of range of my light. Maybe there's something else we can do."

The keening amped up around them, reminding them that the

demons knew what he'd said and most likely couldn't wait to get their claws into her again.

"I don't care. I need to find Regent before it's too late," she said.

"You can't help him if *you're* dead," he said, clamping his hand gently on her shoulder. "Think about this, Jess. I'm not willing to risk your life. Not now. Not ever."

Her fear drained away. Damn it, she knew exactly how he felt. She'd be saying the same thing if it had been him taking the risk. "Okay, but if we don't find a way quickly, I'm going to take my chances."

Britt nodded, and she could tell he was frantically trying to come up with a plan.

"I've got it," he said almost immediately. "Let me get the door open. You stick close to my back so you'll still be protected."

She frowned at him. "You're not serious. My brother might be dying in there. I'm not taking a back seat on this one—demon attack or not."

"Okay, second scenario, I'll stand beside you, so you'll still be protected by my light while you pound on that door, hopefully without cracking my head open with the axe," he said.

She could have kissed him for not demanding to take over. He knew she had to do this, especially since she had the strength of ten men.

She slammed the axe as hard as she could into the door. By the third swing, it was beginning to crack near the lock. One more strategic hit and she'd have had it . . . except that the axe split and landed on the floor outside Britt's light. The demons swarmed it, making it corrode before their eyes. *Crap!*

"What if . . ." Britt said, " . . . we kick the door in together."

She grinned at him. "Hurry!"

He joined her, and they kicked about a dozen times before the door finally gave way. Demons spilled into the opening before either of them could get inside. The room instantly filled with shadows, as if a hole had opened up and black ocean water gushed inside.

There was one place the demons seemed unable to touch. In the center of the room, there was a glass-paneled structure filled with shelves and books. Inside it, three men were seated at a table. She nearly broke contact from Britt in her hurry to make sure Regent was safe. Luckily, Britt held tight.

When they waded through the black undulating mass, it spread like the Red Sea for them, but only because of Britt's angel fire. Only when they reached the glass-encased room and Jess spotted water bubbles between the layers of the glass in the walls, did she realize why the demons couldn't get any closer—the water must be blessed for stronger protection against evil entities. Was this a common precaution, or did the church expect this kind of uprising? No time for postulating, she spotted a glass door with another biometric code.

Unable to see clearly through the water, she got a little panicky, but the moment Regent spotted her, he ran to the wall and pressed his hands against it.

"We think we know how to stop them," he shouted. "Only we can't come out. If we do, they'll kill us."

Jess nodded. Regent's voice was muffled but with her acute hearing, she caught every word. "Wait a minute," she shouted and turned to Britt.

It was then she noticed Britt's pallor, and the sweat beading his forehead. He'd been using his angel fire for too long. Worse, she'd seen what had happened to evangelist Malcolm Fisk last year when he'd exhausted himself with the use of his light—he'd actually gone blind. That meant Britt could be in deep trouble if they didn't get out of here soon.

"Can you hold on a few minutes longer?" she asked Britt.

He blinked a couple of times and swiped the moisture from his face. "Of course!"

Britt was lying and she knew it. She glanced at Regent—he knew it too. Regent shook his head while his face contorted weirdly behind the shifting water that moved inside the walls.

She glanced at a table in the background and a small glowing light caught her eye. "You've got a computer in there!"

Regent nodded.

"Is it connected to Wi-Fi?"

"Yes, it is." Excitement lit his eyes when he saw where she was going with her question.

"Can you send us the information we need to take the demons down?"

She heard whispers around her, as if she were in a cave of thousands, all muttering at the same time. "Do it fast, brother, or I fear your Wi-Fi connection will be lost."

The priests tore back to the desk and went to work. One of them typed, the rest looked as if they were reading off information from texts they had on the desk.

"Let's get out of here, my love. Regent is safe for now, and I can't hold this illumination much longer," Britt said.

"Hurry then, let's go." The ocean of demons looked like bloodsuckers crawling over each other, trying to stay ahead of them as they climbed the steps back to the main level. Even though she was within his protective circle, the intense blackness threatened to suck all hope from her world.

Worse, Britt was obviously weakening. Could they make it to the outside?

Since the hallway no longer had visible floors, doors or windows, they had to hope they could make their way back to safety before Britt's energy depleted completely.

"Wait a minute. Are we going the right way?" Britt asked, still gripping Jess's hand.

She reached out, feeling along the wall for the railing. "Just keep feeling your way. Hurry."

It seemed to take forever to make it to the hallway leading to the foyer. At least, she was pretty sure that's where they were.

Only Britt's angel fire kept them insulated from the pressing void. His light was losing its strength—their protective barrier was getting smaller and closing in on them. Britt grunted and didn't respond while she finally found the reception desk with her hand and led him to the front door of the building.

If she hadn't been so scared, she'd have made a joke about having echolocation, but this really wasn't the time.

Suddenly, they were outside, with hopeful stars twinkling above them. That said, the ground still writhed with shadow demons, and Britt's waning light still somehow managed to part the sea of shadows to show pavement.

"Hurry. We've got to make it to the bridge before your energy collapses."

"Lead on, babe," he said in a voice that expressed everything—his love, his devotion, and his exhaustion.

"Two more blocks," Jess shouted, sensing his energy waning. "Can you run?"

They darted forward, his hand clinging to hers. Had his grip lessened? She squeezed his hand and urged him forward. The second they made the bridge, his light disappeared, and he dropped to his knees.

"You okay?" she asked. He was dripping in sweat, but he managed to nod.

She pulled her cell phone out of her pocket to see if she'd still had a connection. So far, so good. Now she prayed the Wi-Fi towers were still working.

They weren't alone on the bridge, either. Citizens who hadn't made it to the churches crowded here for safety. Every bridge in Paris was probably occupied.

"As soon as Regent's message comes through, save it to your mini SD card, just in case. We don't want to lose it," Britt said.

Jess continued to monitor their surroundings. "Dammit, we could use a boat again," she said.

"Madame?" a voice called from the river below them. "Do you need me?"

She leaned over the bridge and looked down. "It's him," she shouted to Britt, trying to be heard over the voices of the many fearful and crying people around them. She leaned over the side again and smiled. *"Merci, monsieur. Merci!"*

He nodded, his dead cigarette still hanging from his lower lip, then motioned for them to hurry. Even the banks of the rivers were undulating with demons now. They desperately wanted to get at those people protected by the water. Somehow the magic of the Seine, or the water itself, saved them.

Jess leaned over to whisper to Britt, who was still on his knees. "Britt, did you hear me? We're going to get a boat ride back to Notre Dame. Then we can find a computer and figure out how to stop these things."

"I'm with you all the way, babe," he grunted in exhaustion, shoving himself to his feet. It seemed that he'd used every ounce of energy he had.

"Can you climb up onto the side of the bridge to jump into the boat?" she asked, grabbing his elbow to help him.

"I'm not that tired," he said, smiling at her. "I can do it. You go first, and I'll come next.

"No frigging way. What if you have trouble?" She scowled at him. "Get your ass over the side of that bridge, or I'll throw you over."

He laughed. "I love it when you go all Rambo on me." He scrambled up onto the bridge with less effort than she expected, then grabbed her hand to help her, to prove his capability.

She could have ignored his hand, and normally she would have, but not this time. She let him help her. His outward strength was almost as impressive as his inner strength.

He jumped first and waited below to catch her. She dropped lithely into his arms, and they both found a seat with minimal rocking of the boat.

The boatman grinned at them.

"Notre Dame, please?" Jess said. He couldn't take her directly to Notre Dame, but close. Surely they could make it that far over land, blue light or not.

The man's trolling motor started up, and this time they whizzed along the river fairly quickly, until they'd gone as far as they could go. He stopped the boat close to the shoreline. Again, the riverbank was crawling with demons.

"How do we get up there?" Britt asked, eyeing the distance from the boat to the bridge itself. "I'm not sure I can jump that far, and I have no light to protect us on the riverbank."

"I can," Jess said, glancing around the boat and spotting a rope near the bow. "May I borrow your rope, *monsieur*?"

He nodded quickly, motioning for her to take it. He didn't seem the least bit surprised that she was going to jump from the boat to the bridge. Odd. But she didn't have time to think about that right now. She took the rope and jumped. Once on the bridge, she tied the rope to a post on the bridge, then dropped it down for Britt to climb up.

He managed to make it up the rope and over the side onto the bridge again. A stranger reached out and grabbed his hand, helping to pull him the rest of the way.

His strength hadn't been totally diminished, but they still needed him to have every ounce he could muster.

"I'm glad to see your energy is coming back," she said.

"Me too," he said. "We're going to need my light to get us into Notre Dame. Suddenly, his strength seemed to flood back. "Actually, I'm pretty sure I can get us there. I should be exhausted, but I feel like I've been replenished somehow. Maybe it's the water."

She thought that Britt had more strength than he knew, but this time, it felt like he'd gotten some outside help. "Thank God!"

Britt nodded.

She leaned over the side of the bridge and called to the boatman. "Come with us, *monsieur*. We can get you into the church safely."

He shook his head and tipped his hat, then started up his trolling motor and sputtered away under the bridge.

"That was a bit odd," she said to Britt. "Shouldn't he want to come with us?"

Britt shrugged his shoulders. "Maybe he's a good Samaritan, hoping to help other fellow Parisians?"

Jess frowned. "A good Samaritan who didn't even flinch when I jumped from his boat to the bridge? Shouldn't he have been shocked by that?"

They both rushed to the other side of the bridge to look for the man. Strangely, his boat was no longer anywhere to be seen. Who was the mysterious boatman who'd helped them twice, then disappeared? Could he have been another angel sent to help them?

"What just happened?" Jess asked.

"I'm not sure," he said. "But, I think somehow, we're getting help from a higher power. Let's go, doll. We have a city to save."

"If we can," she said, then frowned again and glanced back at the silent river, hearing not even the slightest sound of a trolling motor in the distance. A sound she should have been able to hear.

She blew out a breath. "I think you're right, Britt. We're getting help. And we're going to need every bit of it."

When he reached out and took her hand, light erupted from his solar plexus, bright blue and powerful, encompassing both of them as if he'd used it for the first time tonight. "Then let's make a run for it, just in case my energy doesn't last as long as I hope it will."

REGENT SAT AT THE desk inside the water-protected room. Air recirculated inside, and so far, it hadn't given out. If it did, they'd be finished. That said, he'd noted that someone had put an emergency oxygen supply in the corner with masks. Three of them. Odd.

"If we can find it, we can get the information to my sister via cellphone. There's no way we can leave this protected place. We'll have to be quick though because once the demons realize what we're doing, it will easy for them to shut down all the power. I have the feeling that Jess and Britt will have to be a lot more creative in order to stop them."

"That's why we brought you here, Father. After all you accomplished in New York, we knew you'd be able to help us here," one of the priests admitted.

"You knew this was going to happen?" Regent asked, frowning at the man.

"Not exactly. But we'd seen signs of demonic possession increasing. We fought it, but they always seemed to have the upper hand. We needed someone who could fight against evil like a soldier, instead of a priest. When your name was put forward by Cardinal Vasilli, we grasped at it with both hands." He nodded at Regent, his hands folded penitently on the solid oak table. "You are our warrior, Father. Word of your abilities has spread throughout the church."

"I'm nothing without my sister," he said. "She's the power behind my abilities." His skin crawled at hearing Vasilli's name.

One of the priests looked shocked by his admission. They knew she was a vampire. So let them be shocked. It was true, after all. If they wanted help, they needed to know exactly where that help was coming from. His sister—his strength, and the most amazing woman he knew.

Strangely, Morana crossed his mind and guilt flashed through him. He needed to know if she was his sister, as well. Hopefully, Sampson was still safe at Notre Dame and working on the answer.

But Morana was another matter he'd take care of later. She hadn't been willing to stick her neck out too far. That might change when the results of her VNA test came back, though. If she experienced sibling love, it might change everything for her. Right now, though, he had more important things to look after, and he continued searching through the texts in front of him. And strangely enough, what he was looking for was suddenly in front of him.

"Here it is," Regent shouted. "The final part of the passage. This is what we've been looking for all along. It's a special prayer—one that can send the demons back to hell." He read it aloud and one of the priests started typing it frantically into Regent's phone. Regent nodded and the priest hit send. Regent could only pray the message got to Jess and Britt in time.

He crossed himself. There were millions of demons teeming in the city. How could a single prayer help them? There had to be more to it. He prayed there was another solution, one they'd find before it was too late.

Chapter Nineteen

BRITT RACED ALONG the sidewalk with Jess. His strength had to have come from a panicked need, because his light was dimming. He knew it, and Jess did too. But they still had a block to go.

Notre Dame loomed ahead of them like a huge Gothic harbinger of death. Rather than looking like their salvation, the Gothic lines of the building reminded him of darkness and fear. Why was he thinking this way? Was he being affected by the millions of demon shadows? If so, that meant they were they starting to break through his defenses.

"Hang on, Britt. We're nearly there," Jess shouted. As if sensing his weakening state, she pulled him along now.

His heart pounded in his chest and his lungs burned like fire with every exhalation.

As they crossed the last few feet to the main doors of the church, weakness made his feet move as if they were mired in devouring mud. Each sucking, tearing step wrenched at the muscles of his legs. With his light waning, the demons were grasping, clawing at his boots. There was no time to check and see if they were getting through the leather again.

"Hurry," Jess shouted, turning back and looking at him with something akin to panic on her face.

She'd never have that kind of expression for herself, only for him. That made his heart swell and his light encompassed them again, just long enough for them to burst through the huge doors of the church. The demon shadows stopped a foot from the door. They couldn't get any closer.

He fell to the floor, and Jess dropped beside him.

His light blinked out. Had he lost it forever? Not even a spark lingered inside him, or at least it seemed that way.

It didn't matter. They'd made it inside the church.

He took a quick glance at Jess and realized this church didn't hold the same fuzzy feeling for her. She looked pained when she finally pushed to her feet.

He crawled over and grabbed onto a wall to pull himself up. His legs felt so weak, they barely supported him.

"You going to be okay in here?" he asked.

"I'll manage," she said through her teeth. "Better odds than the streets."

Britt scanned the weary and terrified people in the church behind them. This was the most holy, and probably safest, part of the church, but it was also the most deadly for Jess.

"Let's find Regent's office. It's in one of the distant sectors of the building." The farther they got from the center of the church, the less devastating the effect on her. He hoped.

He hobbled down a hallway toward Regent's office. He'd only been here once before, but it was fairly easy to find. "Sampson must be in there, since I didn't see him in the church itself," Britt said.

Jess clutched Britt's arm and gritted her teeth against the pain of this blessed building. Britt wanted to wrap her in his arms and carry her, but he could barely keep himself upright now. They were both in a damnable fix.

Suddenly, Jess sighed and stood straighter. She was less affected here. But as good as that was for her, it might also mean the shadows could creep in. Britt looked around the area. There wasn't a flicker of movement on the walls or ceilings. So far, at least.

"That's his door," Jess said.

"How did you know?" Britt asked, considering that she'd obviously never been inside.

"I can smell his things. He's even got some of those damnable herbs in there."

Britt grinned and knocked before opening the door slowly. "It's just Britt and Jess," he called out, in case someone thought demons were breaking in. He wouldn't want to be shot by a terrified person inside.

"Get in here, you two," Sampson shouted. "I just received the email from Regent. I've been working on the logistics of distributing the rites they found in a previously lost book of the Bible."

"What? A lost book of the Bible?"

"Yeah. Lost." Britt rolled his eyes. "At least they knew enough to pull it out when we needed it."

They gathered around the computer and read the script. It was in Latin. Even though Britt had never spoken the language before, he could speak it now. It flowed off his tongue with an energetic resonance. And once he'd recited the words, they were stuck in his memory—all of them. Weird. Maybe his angelic DNA could maintain such things?

"We have to test it first," Sampson said.

Jess tried to say the words, but they obviously pained her even more. "Guess it's not going to be me who sends the devils back to hell."

Britt already knew exactly how it had to be done. "Someone has to step outside and try it."

"That's not a good idea," Jess said, sounding panicked. "There has to be a better way. You have no light left. Britt, you're not going to . . ."

He leaned in and kissed the top of her head. "I am. I'm the only one who can."

"But you're weak. Maybe you should wait until your energy returns?"

He shook his head. "We can't wait. Too many people's lives are at stake. We heard the screams out there on the streets. There's not a moment to waste."

She lowered her head and her silky hair fell forward. "I know. I just don't want to lose you," she said.

"You won't." He straightened then tested his wobbly knees. This has to be done. "Let's go," he said.

Jess and Sampson followed closely behind him. He reached the main doors, grabbed the oversized handles, and ripped them open. "Stay inside, no matter what happens," he said to Jess. "You too, Sampson. If this doesn't work, someone else needs to figure out a way to utilize the words."

Sampson nodded, his expression one of deep concern. "Good luck, Britt."

As Britt stepped outside, he heard the monumental wail of a million shadows encompassing the city. They were growing exponentially. How could one man shouting a prayer stop that, angelic DNA or not?

He tried to activate his light. Nothing happened.

Not more than a foot away from the door, the shadows gathered—waiting for him. They seemed unable to come any closer, and that gave him a tiny advantage. He could shout the prayer from here without being attacked, hopefully.

He looked back at Jess, watching through the open doorway, and saw her smile. He knew she was in excruciating pain, but she pushed herself past it. She always did.

He could do the same. He turned and began reciting the Latin in the loudest voice he could muster, and the words took on a magic of their own. At first, he heard a low moan from the nearest shadows, as if they were gathering strength for attack.

It felt as if the words projected an energy he didn't understand, but that didn't matter. That energy was strong.

He repeated the Latin verse over and over again until he was chanting in a deep, methodical cadence that he could feel in his bones.

That's when it started.

The demons began screaming and bursting into flames. One by one, and then dozens by dozens, they disappeared, but only within a fifty-foot perimeter of him. He couldn't shout loud enough to be heard by all of them.

No sooner had he banished the thousands around him than new shadows bled back in, ready to rip him to shreds given the tiniest break in his protection.

He repeated the procedure three times, and each time, the demons were banished, then more of them filled the space where the others had been.

Finally, he stopped. The prayer worked, but only as far as he could shout. He went back into the church and Sampson pulled the door closed behind him.

"It works, up to a point. But I can only affect those within the vicinity of my voice," he said, trying not to let his lack of hope show. "We'll never stop them this way. There are too many of them, and they just move in the second the banished are sent back to hell."

"That means we have to come up with a way to reach all of them at once," Sampson said.

The second he said that, the power went out in the church. Britt peered onto the streets. The city was in complete darkness, other than the occasional fires burning in the distance. Fires that firemen could never reach, not with demons roaming the streets. "It already looks like hell out there," he said squinting against the darkness. "Any ideas, Sampson?"

"Not without power. We could have used television, Internet, and radio, but now that's impossible."

"Can we find a way to turn the power back on?" Britt asked.

Sampson looked frustrated. "Even if you could, it wouldn't last long. Not long enough to send out a signal everywhere. We need a source that is strong enough, and high over the city so your voice, through sound waves, will hit everywhere." He shrugged. "Looks like we're back to square one," he said in a haggard voice.

Jess bent over and grabbed her midriff. For a second, she thought she might scream from the pain.

Britt grasped her on one side and Sampson on the other. They half carried her, half dragged her away from the front doors.

By the time she got back to Regent's office, she couldn't bear the pain caused by being too close to the main part of this powerful church. Most vampires couldn't enter a church at all, since it burned them as quickly as holy water. Her partial soul gave her the ability to enter this holy place, but it didn't stop the terrible pain that came with it, reminding her that she was a soulless vampire who could never gain salvation. She slumped onto a chair in Regent's office. They needed a plan and quickly. Britt and Regent had been too busy with demons to pray for her as often as she needed, and the pain was an indication that she was closer than ever to becoming a monster.

Britt paced back and forth in front of her. "The good news is that the words work," he said. "Maybe we need to find the highest place in the city where we can blast sound out for miles."

Jess's cell phone beeped, and she extricated it from her pocket. "How am I getting a message with the power out in the city? Is there a chance the cell phone towers are still working?"

"I doubt it," Sampson said. "The blackout seemed pretty pervasive." He checked his phone. It was dead.

She read the message and jumped out of her seat. "Eiffel Tower! It says Eiffel Tower!"

She paced back and forth, and Britt moved aside for her. The only light in the room came from the fire burning in the fireplace. "A message that can't be sent. A boatman who disappears." She looked at Britt and watched the smile of acknowledgement spread across his handsome face.

"We *are* getting help."

"Help?" Sampson said anxiously. "From where?"

"That's a good question," Britt said. "But we're going to accept it, with the grace it was given. The Eiffel Tower is a radio transmitter, is it not?"

"I think so," Jess said, excitement bursting inside her. "And it's tall enough to be able to send radio waves over the city. Theoretically, we could send out a blast of prayers that everyone would hear . . . if we had the technical expertise to do such a thing."

She slowly turned to look at Sampson. "Weren't you in the military as a radio technician before you became a doctor?"

He nodded, though his expression looked pained. "I wasn't very good at it, Jess. That's why I changed professions."

"You're better than Britt or I could ever be. We've got to get you and Britt to the Eiffel Tower. Now."

"And how do you propose we do that? My inner light is exhausted. Even if I use the words to protect us along the way, I can only shout for so long before I lose my voice. I'll need to save it for the tower if we hope to have any chance at all," Britt said.

She blew out a breath. The thought that came to her might be crazy, but there was the tiniest of hope. "What if there's a blessed vehicle here that the church uses for dignitaries?"

"Dignitaries? Like who?" Sampson asked.

"A person who might visit the French Papal Palace when he's in the neighborhood."

"How likely is that?" Britt said.

"There's only one way to find out," Jess replied, grabbing his hand. They raced down the long corridor toward the church itself. Jess's pain grew with each step, but she forced it out of her mind.

The church brimmed with citizens and priests and a cardinal or two, she noted.

"I'll get someone to come down here," Britt said and genuflected before striding down the aisle toward the massive altar. Jess would never manage to get that close.

She inched backward to press against the main doors. She could step outside and still be protected for a short distance, but if she did that, she'd let the demons know something was up. They'd be suspicious.

Sampson stayed close, providing moral support without touching her. He was such a good man. He was going to make his way through the demons to try and save a foreign city and people he didn't even know. That's how wonderful a man he was.

Then came Britt, all broad shoulders and masculinity striding toward her, a set of keys dangling from his hand. She wanted to run to him and wrap her arms around him and never let go. Were they getting help again? What were the odds of having a blessed vehicle here? She had no idea, but it meant they might actually make it to the Eiffel Tower, a short distance from here.

"Let's go," he said. "We don't have time to spare."

"And the power problem when we get there?" Sampson asked.

"I spoke to one of the priests," Britt said. "He said the tower has its own backup generator power source in the bunker. All we need to do is get it up and running. That's your job, Sampson."

"Geez, this is going to be a stretch. I hope I remember how to use the equipment."

Since the vehicle was outside the building, Britt managed to blast away the shadows with the powerful Latin words while they made their way to the security of the vehicle.

It seemed the demons had learned from their earlier encounter. Knowing they'd be vaporized by Britt's voice, they slithered away quickly before bursting into flames.

"They're too smart. They'll be hard to beat," she said, snapping her seatbelt in the front passenger seat.

"We can't think that way. Don't forget, we're not doing this alone. We have help," Britt said.

Sampson asked. "What are you talking about?"

"I couldn't explain it, even if I knew," Britt said. "I'll fill you in later."

"If there is a later," Sampson muttered from the backseat, his hands nervously clutching the seat ahead of him.

The vehicle started with one turn of the key. "Here we go," Britt said, rolling down the street toward the Louvre, then on to the Eiffel Tower. Again, it was like being in a black void. Shadows covered everything around them, no doubt to disorient them. Even so, the blessed vehicle had the ability to clear a very small path ahead of them so they could see they were still on the road. And the river was visible as well, which meant they wouldn't end up in there. Even though the moon was full tonight, its rays seemed to be absorbed by the hellish shadows that were trying to send them off course.

After hitting about a dozen too many curbs, they arrived at the Eiffel Tower and parked directly underneath it, near a side-entrance.

Even before Britt opened the vehicle's door, he shouted the powerful Latin prayer, as they prepared to break into the tower.

Shadows wormed their way up the parapets ahead of them, completely covering the steel girders, as high as they could see.

"We have to be organized once we get inside. Jess, you protect Sampson and get him to the bunker to work on the power. I'm going to have to make my way to the top of the tower so I can spread the prayers across the city once everything is ready."

"But how can I protect him? The words don't work for me."

Britt held his cell phone out to her. "When I was on the steps of the church, I recorded the prayers onto my voice memo while I shouted it out. It's turned up as high as it'll go. It should help but, Jess, the cell phone's charge is down to half. I'm not sure how long it'll last, so you'll have to be fast. You and Sampson do your thing and get back to me so I can keep you safe."

He'd found a way to give them a fighting chance.

"Sampson, you know what to do," Britt said.

"I hope so," he said.

"Since it's a radio tower—" Britt said "—we should be able to hook into it somehow with a loudspeaker. And then with your radio expertise, we'll make it as loud as we can." He thought about it. "If we're lucky, the radio waves will carry the prayers even farther. Maybe they won't have to be physically heard for the radio waves to work."

Sampson looked slightly panicked.

"And where will you find that kind of equipment? A loudspeaker might not be just lying around in the Eiffel Tower?" Jess said. And she didn't even know if radio waves worked that way.

"I'm hoping against hope that there's a way. If we are getting outside help, there will be something."

WHEN HE PUT it that way, Jess instinctively knew he was right. "Okay. But how will I keep Sampson safe? I'm not immune to the shadows and neither is he. Even if I recite the Latin if we lose battery power, it doesn't have the same effect as when you speak the words."

"You'll find a way," Britt said. "Will you do the honors?"

It was easy to break in via a side-access door. Jess just kicked it in. Again, the shadows poured inside ahead of them. They squealed and faded back at Britt's chanting, then filled in again behind them.

Britt used a crowbar to jam the door shut behind them. It didn't help. Shadows oozed through the cracks and followed them. They'd attack the first chance they got.

Before Britt started to climb, Jess grabbed him by the collar and planted a quick kiss on his lower lip. His mouth quirked into a smile, but he kept chanting.

"We'll see you at the top, my love. Good luck," she said, then turned on his cell phone. The chanting began, protecting them quite well as she and Sampson made their way down to the bunker.

AFTER OVER SEVEN hundred steps, Britt stood near the apex of the Eiffel Tower, where he took one quick rest from chanting. Just a second, that's all he dared. He'd been followed by the smoky black things from the underworld, just waiting for him to slip up. At least there was a small platform up here for him to stand on.

He began chanting again. As luck would have it, he'd found something better than a loudspeaker on his way to the very top of the tower. He'd come across a microphone. Hopefully, that meant there'd be a place he could plug it into, to create the best loudspeaker ever. He knew it hadn't been left there by accident, though. And he had the feeling that under normal circumstances, this wouldn't work in a million years.

When he stepped onto the platform, the wind blew hard enough to steal his voice away for a second. Added to that, his prayers had lessened in volume, allowing the shadows to expand to the edges of the tower, slithering and sliding toward him before he found an audio jack in a black box connected to the mainframe of the structure. He plugged in and prayed Sampson had hooked up the proper elements. He needed sound now, before the demons drowned him out permanently.

He started reciting the prayer into the mic. Nothing. It didn't work. He continued chanting, praying, keeping the shadow demons at bay. They were flowing up the stairs and up the sides of the girders, building up on the platform all around him.

Suddenly it happened. His voice rang out with such strength and amplitude, it was hard on his own ears. He continued chanting the prayer as clearly as possible, until the words took on a strength and cadence of their own.

The wind grew, whipping at him as if claws were trying to drag him off the tower.

He clung to the metal structure with all of his strength. From up here, the city looked like a war zone. Fires burned randomly below. At least the citizens who weren't already possessed were safe in the churches. That gave him the impetus to keep going, to keep shouting out the prayers for their salvation.

LUCKILY, SAMPSON had found a panel where he'd managed to jerry-rig something so that Britt would have temporary power to the mike. But now he needed more juice to give Britt the amount of amplification necessary to blast the demons out of the city. He still needed to get into the equipment room to make some modifications—the sooner the better. Jess wondered how Sampson was handling the spirit-draining consequences of the demons trailing them. So far, he seemed okay.

"First, we've got to find the generator room," he said.

Meanwhile, Britt's voice chanted the words through the phone as they found another locked door in the bunker, again easily opened by Jess's vampire strength. "This is it," she said, holding the door open for Sampson to enter.

Sampson noticed something in the corner and went for it. Unfortunately, he forgot about staying within range of the words.

Jess dived after him, grabbing his sleeve. "Hold on," she said, "We have to maintain a fairly close distance to the phone. Don't wander too far, or you'll be toast."

Sampson picked up some sort of prying tool and smiled at Jess. "We might need this, though."

She shook her head. "Stick with me from now on."

They entered the room that was marked electrical. It hummed with energy, but from the demons, not from any power source.

"Even if we get the generator going, what's going to stop the demons from shutting it down?"

Jess hiked the cell phone volume to full. "We have to make this work. At least long enough for Britt to do what he has to do."

"I'll do my best, Jess. I'm glad to see this old generator is similar to some of the ones I worked on in my youth. How lucky is that?"

Yeah, lucky. . . .

Sampson found a large gas can and filled up the generator then turned it on, choked it, and pulled a cord until it rumbled to life. "Open the door, Jess. We need some cross-ventilation since the air system isn't working," he said, then shut the choke off and crossed himself. She'd never known Sampson to be overtly religious, so his motions surprised her.

"And look, the old radio system is right there," he said, pointing. "It won't take me long to get that hooked up, as long as there's no break in the old wires on the way to the top." He worked for a few minutes more, following wires from one place to the next.

"We have to hurry. Do you think you can do this, Sampson?" Jess asked.

"It's been a long time since I worked on radios," he said. "But, the basics are still with me. It's a long distance from here to the top, though. I'm not sure we can we do this without the demons shutting it down."

"We have to."

Jess had an idea. She quickly sent Britt's voice memo to her own cell phone. She turned it on and set it on the generator. Her cell phone was fully charged, so it might keep the demons away for a while longer.

"Right now, I'm linking an amplifier, I hope," he said.

Jess checked her cell phone. "Hurry. I'm not sure how long the cell phone will last, running non-stop."

He clicked on several switches and ran a hand over his glistening forehead. "I think I've done something, but who knows for sure? If someone is helping us . . ." Sampson said, looking skyward ". . . now's the time to make this thing work."

Jess closed her eyes. It had to work. They couldn't end this way. Humanity needed help.

Suddenly, they heard Britt's voice booming from above. The amplifier was on, in full force, and Britt's words were spreading out to the farthest reaches of the city.

"You've done it!"

Sampson shook his head. "I've made at attempt that seemed highly unlikely. The fact that it did work is a miracle."

"Don't forget, Britt is one of the Fallen. He might not realize his abilities, but he's able to do amazing things all by himself. If someone else is helping, even better."

Sampson nodded and glanced at the cell phone. "We have to leave that here if we want the generator to keep going."

"I know."

"Are we staying here?" he asked.

"You are. Britt is going to need some help on the tower. If nothing else, I'll give him moral support."

Sampson looked panicked for a second, before regaining his composure. He never questioned Jess. Maybe it was because she was his employer or because he was her friend and trusted her judgment enough to let her go.

She touched his hand. "Thank you for everything, Sampson. You've always been my rock. If I don't make it, keep going with your good work. Help the NYPD, and keep up your research on vampires."

"Jess, you will make it."

"I'm going to try."

She took a deep breath, even though she didn't theoretically need to. She started reciting the prayer and headed for the stairs. She'd been listening to it long enough to at least remember the words, even though she couldn't give them the same impact Britt could.

Shadows clawed at her feet, but with the prayers, they couldn't quite damage her. She climbed the tower at top vampire speed, and when she neared the highest point, she reveled at the sight of John Brittain standing there, all muscle and light, calling out across the city. Suddenly the demons around her started screaming, experiencing spontaneous combustion in reaction to his voice.

"It's working, Britt," she shouted. "Keep going."

Their eyes met and his voice grew stronger while her fingers linked with his. Sporadic gusts of wind blew at them, but they held onto each other.

Shadows tried to fill in around them, but they burst into flames and blew off in the wind.

Chapter Twenty

SEEING JESS WAS all he needed to replenish his dwindling energy. She always boosted him. With her by his side, how could they lose? Even from way up here, he could see the shadows disappearing from the streets. Their vile screams and moans had all but faded from his consciousness. It was as if they'd been in his head and now they were nearly gone.

Jess smiled at him. Wind whipped her hair around her face and she looked as if she belonged at the top of the nine hundred and eighty foot tower. Her beauty always stunned him.

"Keep going. They're nearly gone," she shouted. "We're winning."

From the corner of his eye, he saw a bird. No, it was larger than a regular bird. It had to be an eagle or a hawk swooping down on them. And it was aiming for Jess. It wasn't until he realized the thing was a new breed of shadow demon—one that could fly—that Britt feared for her safety.

The thing swooped, its wings making a terrible flapping sound while it dove straight at her. Was this the last vestige of the shadows? Had they formed together to make a stronger beast in a desperate attempt to win the battle?

It hit her with such impact, the whole tower swayed.

He held her hand tight and tried to pull her closer to him, while shouting the prayer at the flying beast.

Only, suddenly, her hand became slippery. He could no longer maintain his grip. Either that, or Jess had deliberately let go, afraid the next hit would take them both out.

The flying creature attacked again, knocking Jess to the far side of the platform and out of his reach.

"Stop, you fucking bastard!" he shouted, instantly forgetting to chant.

The newly formed beast swooped around the tower, empowered by Britt's break in his prayer. Its evil eyes and wicked mouth smiled at him. "Then you'd better stop right now. If you continue to kill us, I *will* knock her off. She's an evil bitch anyway. Why do you care about her? You, who murder vampires, but think you're good enough to be one of the Fallen."

"Who are you?" Britt demanded. He'd have power over a demon if he knew its name. His instincts told him that. His angelic DNA burned to control the demon and send him back to hell.

"We are many. Our names cannot be used against us."

Britt started shouting the prayer again, while, at the same time, reaching for Jess with one hand while holding onto the center spire of the tower with the other. But as if the beast could control the wind, it suddenly blew so hard, he could barely see.

One thing he did know. Jess was too far away, and he couldn't get his feet to move.

Jess turned to face the edge and leaned precariously over to look at the ground far below. One quick burst of air and she'd be gone forever. What could he do? Had she been possessed?

He looked down through the girders of the tower. As far as he could tell, there were no other shadows below. He'd killed the majority of them through the radio waves, maybe almost all of them. But this flying beast had some sort of immunity against the prayer.

He now sensed the absence of the other shadows in the city. They were all gone except for this last flying group of shadows. Could it stop him from succeeding?

Britt choked up. This big bastard was the last demon standing. Instinctively, Britt knew if this one survived, it would resurrect the others again. All of their efforts would be lost and Jess would be possessed, or worse. What could he do?

The demon took hold of Jess, twisting her features until she looked as if she'd become someone else.

"If I make her jump, I'll be sure her head is cut off on the way down. She won't be able to come back, and I'll live. You'll have failed her, and you won't be able to kill me." The demon laughed and landed on the platform next to her, then slid a razor-sharp talon up Jess's thigh, right through her leather pants. Her flesh opened up, and he could see the veins and tissue inside. The demon mimicked Jess crying for help.

Britt's gut twisted. What the thing didn't know was that Jess would never beg for mercy. Not for a second.

But Jess's life *was* hanging in the balance. A few months ago, she'd actually died and was revived when they'd saved Uriel from a fate worse than death. Thanks to Jess, he was now safe.

Britt focused on Jess again. How many lives did a vampire have? He couldn't risk this beast taking over her body fully. He started to pray as loud as he could. He had to kill this thing.

"You lose!" the demon shrieked, turning into a bird-shaped black dust cloud and diving fully into Jess, disappearing into her just seconds before she dove off the tower.

Britt didn't have to think. If Jess died, he'd go with her. His feet let go and he stretched out his arms as if diving into water, hoping that he would cut more quickly through the air and catch up. He did.

He wrapped his arms around her and they tumbled and flipped midair. While his body and mind spun out of control, he fought to think. He had to find a way to kill the demon before it was too late, even if it killed Jess in the process. She'd want that. He grabbed her close and pressed his mouth close to her ear. It felt like they were moving in slow motion, even though they were hurtling to the ground.

The demon inside her clawed and pushed and tried to get away, but Britt had his arms and legs tightly wrapped around her as he continued to pray. Suddenly, the shadows left Jess and the giant bird formed again, clutching them in his talons. It stopped their downward spiral and pulled them higher.

That didn't stop Britt; he recited the prayer over and over until the demons began to scream and curse. The shadows dropped them again, and they began a freefall more like skydiving, only now Jess was facing him. Her green eyes widened as the rest of the demons flew out of her mouth and burst into flames on the air, then blew away in the wind.

He'd forced the demons out, but it was too late. They were both going to die.

"Jess," he said in her ear. "I love you." He wondered why they hadn't hit the ground yet.

"I know," she said. "I knew what was happening all the time the demon was inside me. You did the right thing."

Britt's head began to buzz. He felt as if his body had just burst into flames. The heat inside him became so overpowering, so excruciating, he lost himself to it. Maybe it was a blessing that he didn't see the ground coming at them, faster than either of them could survive.

He heard Jess's voice from far away. "Britt. What's happening?" Then her voice faded away and his mind clouded. He didn't feel the impact of the ground. Did instant death mean no pain?

Seconds dragged on like minutes while his eyes remained focused on the beautiful face of Jess, the woman who meant everything to him.

Had her body been smashed beyond belief and he was still seeing her the way he always had? Were they both dead and he was seeing her soul?

"Britt, yank yourself out of it," Jess said suddenly, snapping her fingers in front of his face. He blinked.

"What the . . . ?"

"You saved us," she said. "We're both okay." He couldn't ignore the way she kept looking over his shoulder, as if there was someone behind him.

"Are they all dead?" he asked. "Did we kill the demons?"

"We squashed them like bugs," she said smiling.

"Why aren't we squashed like bugs?" he asked vaguely, still unable to remember how he got here, sitting on the ground in front of Jess.

"I'd say you've learned a new trick," she said. "Your angelic DNA kicked in and saved us. Saved me. Don't you remember?"

He shook his head. "I only remember my body burning. Maybe the demon slashed my back on the way down."

"No. That's not it," she said.

"How do you know?" he asked, finally unable to stop himself from turning to see what she kept looking at. His mouth dropped open. "Holy hell, I've got wings."

"You do. And they worked very well. We made a five-point landing."

"I don't remember that."

"Must've been the trauma of sprouting wings at such a critical time," she said, unable to take her eyes off the impressive, large silvery wings extending out behind him.

Sampson ran out of the building. "The demons are gone. . . . Wait a minute! What the—Britt, you've got wings!"

"I know. I have no idea how it happened, but I'm certainly glad it did."

Sampson stepped up beside Jess, who'd moved around Britt to stare at his back. She touched a wing, but to him, it was as if she'd caressed his shoulder blade.

"Can you feel that?" she asked.

"Yes."

"Neat."

"How does anyone expect me to live a normal life, walking around with these huge things waving behind me? I can't even fit in a car."

JESS WAS IN AWE. This cemented the fact that the man she loved was an angel. He had frigging wings that had sprouted halfway down the tower! She pushed at his wing again, testing to see if she could tuck it down under his arm. It wasn't going to cooperate.

"Ouch," he said.

Jess's cell phone rang somewhere and she turned to see it in Sampson's hand.

"It didn't die. I thought you'd want it back," he said.

"Thanks, Sampson," she said, taking the phone and pressing *talk*.

"Jess dear, are you okay? Were you successful? The power just came back on here. We'd like to leave the archives, but I wanted to make sure first," Regent said.

Jess looked around. "We got them all, didn't we, Britt?"

He nodded. "They're gone."

"I heard him," Regent said in her ear. "I can't wait to hear how you two did it."

Jess snickered, then looked repentant when Britt frowned at her. "Oh Regent, you're going to be so surprised. Britt single-handedly saved us and the city."

"I'm on my way. Tell me the rest when I get there," Regent said.

She could tell he'd put the phone on his shoulder while he spoke to the others. "It's safe to leave. Let's get out of here."

"We'll wait for you at the Eiffel Tower, then?" Jess said.

"See you in a couple of minutes." Regent hung up.

She shrugged her shoulders. "He's on his way. I didn't have time to warn . . . er . . . tell him your good news."

Britt stood and twisted so hard, he nearly turned in a circle trying to get a look at his wings. They flapped a couple of times. "Hey! I did that. I thought about moving them and they moved," he said.

Sampson was quiet, but Jess saw the excitement in his eyes. Her scientist wanted to figure out how those huge feathered things had sprouted from Britt's back—she'd bet her non-life on it.

"Face it, Britt. You've evolved."

He frowned. "I'm not sure I want this."

"It's not like you have a choice," she said. "It's kinda like being a vampire. We make the best with what we have. By my thinking, you got the better end of the stick."

He looked repentant. "Yes, you're right, Jess. Thank you."

She frowned at him. "Thank you? For what?"

"For making me realize I'm lucky, and I have to accept everything that being a Fallen one entails, especially things that saved us from a fall from that height." He tried to swallow. "I need to sit down again."

Jess held his hand while he sat, then she plunked down beside him on the curb. "You okay?"

"Yes, I'm just a little tired. All that chanting must've worn me out."

"Flying might have done it, too."

"I flew?" He shook his head. "Really flew? I didn't just slow down our descent?"

"Nope. You carried me like a superhero. It was cool." She grinned at him. "You might want to buy a pair of glasses. You know, for when you're undercover."

"Not funny."

"Uh, Britt," Sampson said from behind him. He'd been behind Britt ever since he first noticed the wings.

"Yes?" Britt turned around to see what he wanted. The wings were gone. "Hey, where'd they go?"

Sampson cleaned his glasses with the edge of his T-shirt. "They just started to shrink and finally disappeared. I can't even see a line where they came out." He adjusted his glasses and Britt could practically feel Sampson's breath on his back. Talk about a getting a check-up.

Too late, Regent pulled up in his vehicle. He got out and approached them, a huge smile on his face. "You did it. You sent the demons back to hell." He narrowed his eyes on them. "Wait, what's going on? You all look shell-shocked."

"Britt has wings," Jess said.

"What?"

"Angelic wings," she said. "The final few demons joined together into one massive flying demon. It possessed me, then made me jump off the Eiffel Tower. Britt dove after me." She turned to him. "Why did you do that, by the way? I'm assuming you didn't know you'd sprout wings?"

Britt looked troubled. "I'll be brutally honest, my love. If you were going to die, I didn't want to live without you. So I followed you down."

She inhaled sharply and pulled his hand and held it to her heart. "Please, don't ever do that again. I want you to live, no matter what happens to me. Promise me that you'll never do anything like that again, John Brittain."

Regent rubbed his chin with one hand. "I think I know how you sprouted wings," he said.

Everyone looked at him. "How?" they said, in unison.

"It was a selfless act. You were willing to give up your life in order to save Jess's. That's how you acquired your wings. You earned them, in essence."

"You know, that actually feels right," Britt said.

"I don't know," Jess said, shaking her head. "It's one thing, having a relationship with a man who has angelic DNA, but now that you have actual angel wings, you're pretty much fully fledged, pardon the pun. How can a vampire and an angel be together?"

Britt looked stunned by her statement. His mouth opened and closed, but before he could comment, Regent spoke up. "The same way you always have. You two are the same people you've always been. Don't ever second-guess that."

A tear slid down Jess's cheek. "I'm sorry, Britt. My insecurities make me afraid I'm going to taint you, but instead, I always hurt you."

He wiped the tear away with a gentle swipe of his thumb. "Never, Jess. I adore you beyond words. And after what happened tonight on the tower, you can't possibly doubt my feelings for you."

"You don't have to prove anything to me. You've shown me in so many ways." She smiled at him, unable to voice her true ragged feelings at that moment. If she didn't change the subject, she'd have a meltdown. She glanced over at Sampson, who was still poking at Britt's fully healed back through his shredded T-shirt.

"It's as if he never had wings," Sampson said, awe still in his voice.

"I wish I'd seen them," Regent said with a sigh. He looked around them as streetlights began popping on again, and people started poking their heads out of their apartment buildings. "Tomorrow, the city can start rebuilding," he said.

Jess's cell phone rang. "It's Veronique," she said, then read aloud the captain's text. *"Did you do this?"*

Jess texted back. *"We had a hand in it."*

"I don't know how to thank you," Veronique texted.

"No need."

"Can you and Britt meet me tomorrow to brief me on how you did it? Just in case it ever happens again?"

Jess made a face and looked at the men.

"Sorry. It's not a transferrable ability. Just be happy the city is safe for now."

No text came back and she figured Veronique was fuming. She'd probably hear from her later. She shoved her cell back into her pocket. "Has anyone heard from Morana since this whole thing started?"

Regent looked instantly pained. "No. Do you think the demons got her?"

"I doubt it. She's resilient and knows how to look out for number one. She probably went to ground when things got dicey. She'll turn up,

Regent, never fear," Jess said.

Jess's dawn alert started vibrating on her cell phone. "Time for me to go home," she said.

Britt stood and Regent hugged both of them.

"Isn't Paris exciting?" Britt said unexpectedly, a lopsided grin on his face.

Jess couldn't help but understand his unusual statement. "We nearly died, but I agree, it was a life-affirming experience."

Strains of purple began to filter into the dark sky.

Regent's cell phone rang. "Hello? Morana? Thank God you're okay," he said.

"Morana made it," he shouted to everyone. He listened to her speaking, nodding every now and then he said, "Okay then. See you tomorrow?"

Jess's eyebrows lifted. She'd hear about the conversation tomorrow night when she spoke to Regent. She could have listened in, but didn't have the energy right now. Her head was too full of the spectacular things that had happened tonight. She didn't even know how she could possibly come to terms with Britt having wings.

"Wait a minute," Britt said. "Isn't that . . . ?"

"Randolph?" Jess said. The man wandered past them on the sidewalk, looking confused and dazed. But he wasn't possessed anymore, nor did he recognize them.

"Guess that answers the question about the possessed. They should all be okay," Regent said.

"Oh wow, that's such good news," Sampson said.

Jess yawned, then stood and slapped one hand on her leg. "Bedtime for me, boys," she said. "We'll have a lot to discuss tomorrow night."

Britt took her hand and they strolled down the sidewalk. "I'm glad it's over," he said.

Jess tipped her head in his direction. "Me, too. So why do you sound like you don't think it's over?"

"Regent is in Paris for the next two months. And we haven't figured out how to decipher the ancient book he found. He was led to it deliberately. Which means . . . his work here isn't done yet. And neither is ours . . ."

The End

Britt's right! His and Jess's work in France is just getting started. Don't miss the next book in Lina Gardner's *City of Bones* trilogy, *Silenced by the Grave*!

About the Author

LINA GARDINER, author of the award-winning Jess Vandermire Vampire Hunter Series, has writing in her blood. Living in New Brunswick, Canada, a hotspot for legendary ghosts and tall tales of odd happenings, has probably added to her love of a good mystery. That, and the stories her grandfather told in the "parlor" when their grandmother wasn't paying attention, added to her love of storytelling, and the wonders of imagination.

CPSIA information can be obtained
at www.ICGtesting.com
Printed in the USA
LVOW11s1058210418
574055LV00003B/39/P